William M. Thackeray

The memoirs of Mr. Charles J. Yellowplush and The Diary of C.

Jeames de la Pluche

William M. Thackeray

The memoirs of Mr. Charles J. Yellowplush and The Diary of C. Jeames de la Pluche

ISBN/EAN: 9783337123994

Printed in Europe, USA, Canada, Australia, Japan

Cover: Foto ©Andreas Hilbeck / pixelio.de

More available books at **www.hansebooks.com**

THE MEMOIRS

OF

MR. CHARLES J. YELLOWPLUSH,

AND

THE DIARY OF

C. JEAMES DE LA PLUCHE, ESQ.

BY

W. M. THACKERAY,

Author of " Vanity Fair," " The Newcomes," &c.

LONDON:

SMITH, ELDER AND CO., 65, CORNHILL.

1866.

CONTENTS.

—◆◇◆—

THE MEMOIRS OF MR. CHARLES J. YELLOWPLUSH.

CONTENTS.

THE DIARY OF C. JEAMES DE LA PLUCHE, ESQ.

THE MEMOIRS

OF

MR. CHARLES J. YELLOWPLUSH,

SOMETIME

FOOTMAN IN MANY GENTEEL FAMILIES.

―――― ――――

I.

MISS SHUM'S HUSBAND.

CHAPTER I.

I WAS born in the year one, of the present or Christian hera, and am, in consquints, seven-and-thirty years old. My mamma called me Charles James Harrington Fitzroy Yellowplush, in compliment to several noble families, and to a sellybrated coach-min whom she knew, who wore a yellow livry, and drove the Lord Mayor of London.

Why she gev me this genlmn's name is a diffiklty, or rayther the name of a part of his dress; however, it's stuck to me through life, in which I was, as it were, a footman by buth.

Praps he was my father—though on this subjict I can't speak suttinly, for my ma wrapped up my buth in a mistry. I may be illygitmit, I may have been changed at nuss; but I've always had genlmnly tastes through life, and have no doubt that I come of a genlmnly origum.

The less I say about my parint the better, for the dear old creature was very good to me, and, I fear, had very little other goodness in her. Why, I can't say; but I always passed as her

B

nevyou. We led a strange life; sometimes ma was dressed in
sattn and rooge, and sometimes in rags and dutt; sometimes
I got kisses, and sometimes kix; sometimes gin, and sometimes
shampang; law bless us! how she used to swear at me, and cuddle
me; there we were, quarrelling and making up, sober and tipsy,
starving and guttling by turns, just as ma got money or spent it.
But let me draw a vail over the seen, and speak of her no more—
its 'sfishant for the public to know, that her name was Miss
Montmorency, and we lived in the New Cut.

My poor mother died one morning, Hev'n bless her! and I was
left alone in this wide wicked wuld, without so much money as
would buy me a penny roal for my brexfast. But there was
some amongst our naybours (and let me tell you there's more
kindness among them poor disrepettable creaturs than in half-a-
dozen lords or barrynets) who took pity upon poor Sal's orfin
(for they bust out laffin when I called her Miss Montmorency),
and gev me bred and shelter. I'm afraid, in spite of their kindness, that my *morrils* wouldn't have improved if I'd stayed long
among 'em. But a benny-violent genlmn saw me, and put me to
school. The academy which I went to was called the Free
School of Saint Bartholomew's the Less—the young genlmn wore
green baize coats, yellow leather whatsisnames, a tin plate on the
left harm, and a cap about the size of a muffing. I stayed there
sicks years, from sicks, that is to say, till my twelth year, during
three years of witch, I distinguished myself not a little in the
musicle way, for I bloo the bellus of the church horgin, and very
fine tunes we played too.

Well, it's not worth recounting my jewvenile follies (what trix
we used to play the applewoman! and how we put snuff in the
old clark's Prayer-book—my eye!); but one day, a genlmn entered
the school-room—it was on the very day when I went to sub-
traxion—and asked the master for a young lad for a servant.
They pitched upon me glad enough; and nex day found me
sleeping in the skullery, close under the sink, at Mr. Bago's
country-house at Pentonwille.

Bago kep a shop in Smithfield market, and drov a taring good
trade, in the hoil and Italian way. I've heard him say, that he
cleared no less than fifty pounds every year, by letting his front

room at hanging time. His winders looked right opsit Newgit, and many and many dozen chaps has he seen hanging there. Laws was laws in the year ten, and they screwed chaps' nex for nex to nothink. But my bisniss was at his country-house, where I made my first *ontray* into fashnabl life. I was knife, errint, and stable-boy then, and an't ashamed to own it; for my merrits have raised me to what I am—two livries, forty pound a year, malt-licker, washin, silk-stocking, and wax candles—not countin wails, which is somethink pretty considerable at *our* house, I can tell you.

I didn't stay long here, for a suckmstance happened which got me a very different situation. A handsome young genlmn, who kep a tilbry, and a ridin hoss at livry, wanted a tiger. I bid at once for the place; and, being a neat tidy-looking lad, he took me. Bago gave me a character, and he my first livry; proud enough I was of it, as you may fancy.

My new master had some business in the city, for he went in every morning at ten, got out of his tilbry at the Citty Road, and had it waiting for him at six; when, if it was summer, he spanked round into the Park, and drove one of the neatest turnouts there. Wery proud I was in a gold laced hat, a drab coat and a red weskit, to sit by his side, when he drove. I already began to ogle the gals in the carriages, and to feel that longing for fashionabl life which I've had ever since. When he was at the oppera, or the play, down I went to skittles, or to White Condick Gardens; and Mr. Frederick Altamont's young man was some-body, I warrant; to be sure there is very few man-servants at Pentonwille, the poppylation being mostly gals of all work: and so, though only fourteen, I was as much a man down there, as if I had been as old as Jerusalem.

But the most singular thing was, that my master, who was such a gay chap, should live in such a hole. He had only a ground-floor in John Street—a parlor and a bed-room. I slep over the way, and only came in with his boots and brexfast of a morning.

The house he lodged in belonged to Mr. and Mrs. Shum. They were a poor but proliffic couple, who had rented the place for many years; and they and their family were squeezed in it pretty tight, I can tell you.

Shum said he had been a hofficer, and so he had. He had been a sub-deputy, assistant, vice-commissary, or some such think; and, as I heerd afterwards, had been obliged to leave on account of his *nervousness*. He was such a coward, the fact is, that he was considered dangerous to the harmy, and sent home.

He had married a widow Buckmaster, who had been a Miss Slamcoe. She was a Bristol gal; and her father being a bankrup in the tallow-chandlering way, left, in course, a pretty little sum of money. A thousand pound was settled on her; and she was as high and mighty as if it had been a millium.

Buckmaster died, leaving nothink; nothink except four ugly daughters by Miss Slamcoe: and her forty found a year was rayther a narrow income for one of her appytite and pretensions. In an unlucky hour for Shum she met him. He was a widower with a little daughter of three years old, a little house at Penton-wille, and a little income about as big as her own. I believe she bullyd the poor creature into marriage; and it was agreed that he should let his ground-floor at John Street, and so add something to their means.

They married; and the widow Buckmaster was the gray mare, I can tell you. She was always talking and blustering about her famly, the celebrity of the Buckmasters, and the antickety of the Slamcoes. They had a six-roomed house (not counting kitching and sculry), and now twelve daughters in all; whizz.—4 Miss Buckmasters: Miss Betsy, Miss Dosy, Miss Biddy, and Miss Winny; 1 Miss Shum, Mary by name, Shum's daughter, and seven others, who shall be nameless. Mrs. Shum was a fat, red-haired woman, at least a foot taller than S., who was but a yard and a half high, pale-faced, red-nosed, knock-kneed, bald-headed, his nose and shut-frill all brown with snuff.

Before the house was a little garden, where the washin of the famly was all ways hanging. There was so many of 'em that it was obliged to be done by relays. There was six rails and a stocking on each, and four small goosbry bushes, always covered with some bit of lining or other. The hall was a regular puddle; wet dabs of dishclouts flapped in your face; soapy smoking bits of flanning went nigh to choke you; and while you were looking up to prevent hanging yourself with the ropes which were strung across and about, slap came the hedge of a pail against your shins, till one was like to be drove mad with hagony. The great slattnly doddling girls was always on the stairs, poking about with nasty flower-pots, a-cooking something, or sprawling in the window-seats with greasy curl-papers, reading greasy novls. An infernal pianna was jingling from morning till night—two eldest Miss Buckmasters "Battle of Prag"—six youngest Miss Shums, "In my cottage," till I knew every note in the "Battle of Prag," and cussed the day when "In my cottage" was rote. The younger girls, too, were always bouncing and thumping about the house, with torn pinnyfores, and dogs-eard grammars, and large pieces of bread and treacle. I never see such a house.

As for Mrs. Shum, she was such a fine lady, that she did nothink but lay on the drawing-room sophy, read novels, drink, scold, scream, and go into hystarrix. Little Shum kep reading an old newspaper from weeks' end to weeks' end, when he was not engaged in teachin the children, or goin for the beer, or cleanin the shoes, for they kep no servant. This house in John Street was in short a regular Pandymony.

What could have brought Mr. Frederic Altamont to dwell in such a place? The reason is hobvius: he adoared the fust Miss Shum.

And suttnly he did not show a bad taste, for though the other daughters were as ugly as their hideous ma, Mary Shum was a pretty, little, pink, modest creatur, with glossy black hair and tender blue eyes, and a neck as white as plaster of Parish. She wore a dismal old black gownd, which had grown too short for her, and too tight; but it only served to show her pretty angles and feet, and bewchus figger. Master, though he had looked rather low for the gal of his art, had certainly looked in the right place. Never was one more pretty or more hamiable. I gav her always the buttered toast left from our brexfast, and a cup of tea or chocklate as Altamont might fancy; and the poor thing was glad enough of it, I can vouch; for they had precious short commons up stairs, and she the least of all.

For it seemed as if which of the Shum family should try to snub the poor thing most. There was the four Buckmaster girls always at her. It was, Mary, git the coal-skittle; Mary, run down to the public-house for the beer: Mary, I intend to wear your clean stockens out walking, or your new bonnet to church. Only her poor father was kind to her; and he, poor old muff! his kindness was of no use. Mary bore all the scolding like an angel, as she was; no, not if she had a pair of wings and a goold trumpet, could she have been a greater angel.

I never shall forgit one seen that took place. It was when Master was in the city; and so, having nothink earthly to do, I happened to be listening on the stairs. The old scolding was a-going on, and the old tune of that hojus "Battle of Prag." Old Shum made some remark; and Miss Buckmaster cried out, "Law pa! what a fool you are!" All the gals began laffin, and so did Mrs. Shum; all, that is, excep Mary, who turned as red as flams, and going up to Miss Betsy Buckmaster, give her two such wax on her great red ears as made them tingle again.

Old Mrs. Shum screamed, and ran at her like a Bengal tiger. Her great arms went weeling about like a vinmill, as she cuffed and thumped poor Mary for taking her pa's part. Mary Shum, who was always a-crying before, didn't shed a tear now. I will do it again, she said, if Betsy insults my father. New thumps, new shreex! and the old horridan went on beatin the poor girl, till she was quite exosted, and fell down on the sophy, puffin like a poppus.

"For shame, Mary," began old Shum: "for shame, you naughty gal, you! for hurting the feelings of your dear mamma, and beating kind sister."

"Why, it was because she called you a—"

"If she did, you pert Miss," said Shum, looking mighty dig-nitified, "I could correct her, and not you."

"You correct me, indeed!" said Miss Betsy, turning up her nose, if possible, higher than before; "I should like to see you crect me! Imperence!" and they all began laffin again.

By this time Mrs. S. had recovered from the effex of her exsize, and she began to pour in *her* wolly. Fust she called Mary names, then Shum.

"O why," screeched she, "why did I ever leave a genteel famly, where I ad every ellygance and lucksry, to marry a creature like this? He is unfit to be called a man, he is unworthy to

marry a gentlewoman; and as for that hussy, I disown her.
Thank Heaven she ant a Slamcoe; she is only fit to be a Shum!"
"That's true, mamma," said all the gals, for their mother
had taught them this pretty piece of manners, and they despised
their father heartily; indeed, I have always remarked that, in
families where the wife is internally talking about the merits of
her branch, the husband is invariably a spooney.

Well, when she was exosted again, down she fell on the sofy,
at her old trix—more skreeching—more convulshuns—and she
wouldn't stop, this time, till Shum had got her half a pint of
her old remedy, from the Blue Lion over the way. She grew
more easy as she finished the gin; but Mary was sent out of
the room, and told not to come back agin all day.

"Miss Mary," says I,—for my heart yurned to the poor gal,
as she came sobbing and miserable down stairs; "Miss Mary,"
says I, "If I might make so bold, here's master's room empty,
and I know where the cold bif and pickles is." "O Charles!"
said she, nodding her head sadly, "I'm too retched to have any
happytite;" and she flung herself on a chair, and began to cry
fit to bust.

At this moment, who should come in but my master. I had
taken hold of Miss Mary's hand, somehow, and do believe, I
should have kist it, when, as I said, Haltamont made his appearance. "What's this?" cries he, lookin at me as black as thunder,
or as Mr. Phillips as Hickit, in the new tragedy of Mac Buff.

"It's only Miss Mary, sir," answered I.

"Get out, sir," says he, as fierce as posbil, and I felt somethink (I think it was the tip of his to) touching me behind, and
found myself, nex minit, sprawling among the wet flannings, and
buckets and things.

The people from up-stairs came to see what was the matter,
as I was cussin and crying out. "It's only Charles, ma,"
screamed out Miss Betsy.

"Where's Mary?" says Mrs. Shum, from the sofy.

"She's in master's room, miss," said I.

"She's in the lodger's room, ma," cries Miss Shum, heckoing
me.

"Very good; tell her to stay there till he comes back." And

then, Miss Shum went bouncing up the stairs again, little knowing of Haltamont's return.

  *   *   *   *   *   *   *

I'd long before observed that my master had an anchoring after
Mary Shum; indeed, as I have said, it was purely for her sake
that he took and kep his lodgings at Pentonwille. Excep for the
sake of love which is above being mersnary, fourteen shillings a
wick was a *little* too strong for two such rat-holes as he lived in.
I do blieve the family had nothing else but their lodger to live
on: they brekfisted off his tea-leaves, they cut away pounds and
pounds of meat from his jints (he always dined at home), and
his baker's bill was at least enough for six. But that wasn't my
business. I saw him grin, sometimes, when I laid down the
cold bif of a morning, to see how little was left of yesterday's
sirline; but he never said a syllabuh; for true love don't mind a
pound of meat or so hextra.

At first, he was very kind an attentive to all the gals; Miss
Betsy, in partickler, grew mighty fond of him; they sate, for
whole evenings, playing cribbitch, he taking his pipe and glas, she
her tea and muffing; but as it was improper for her to come
alone, she brought one of her sisters, and this was genrally
Mary,—for he made a pint of asking her, too,—and one day,
when one of the others came instead, he told her, very quitely,
that he hadn't invited her; and Miss Buckmaster was too fond
of muffings to try this game on again; besides, she was jealous
of her three grown sisters, and considered Mary as only a child.
Law bless us! how she used to ogle him, and quot bits of pottry,
and play "Meet me by moonlike," on an old gitter: she reglar
flung herself at his head, but he wouldn't have it, bein better
ockypied elsewhere.

One night, as genteel as possible, he brought home tickets for
Ashley's, and proposed to take the two young ladies—Miss Betsy
and Miss Mary, in course. I recklect he called me aside that
afternoon, assuming a solamon and misterus hare, "Charles,"
said he, "*are you up to snuff?*"

"Why sir," said I, "I'm genrally considered tolelably downy."

"Well," says he, "I'll give you half a suffering if you can
manage this bisniss for me; I've chose a rainy night on purpus,

When the theatre is over, you must be waitin with two umbrel-
lows; give me one, and hold the other over Miss Shum; and,
hark ye, sir, *turn to the right* when you leave the theatre, and say
the coach is ordered to stand a little way up the street, in order
to get rid of the crowd."

We went (in a fly hired by Mr. H.), and never shall I forgit
Cartliche's hacting on that memrable night. Talk of Kimble!
talk of Magreedy! Ashley's for my money, with Cartlitch in
the principal part. But this is nothink to the porpus. When
the play was over, I was at the door with the umbrellos. It was
raining cats and dogs, sure enough.

Mr. Altamont came out presently, Miss Mary under his arm,
and Miss Betsy followin behind, rayther sulky. " This way, sir,"
cries I, pushin forward; and I threw a great cloak over Miss
Betsy, fit to smother her. Mr. A. and Miss Mary skipped on
and was out of sight when Miss Betsy's cloak was settled, you
may be sure.

" They're only gone to the fly, miss. It's a little way up the
street, away from the crowd of carriages." And off we turned *to
the right*, and no mistake.

After marchin a little through the plash and mud, " Has anybody seen Coxy's fly ? " cries I, with the most innocent haxent
in the world.

" Cox's fly ! " hollows out one chap. " Is it the vaggin you
want ? " says another. " I see the blackin wan pass," giggles
out another genlmn; and there was such an interchange of
compliments as you never heerd. I pass them over though,
because some of 'em were not wery genteel.

" Law, miss," said I, " what shall I do ? My master will never
forgive me; and I haven't a single sixpence to pay a coach."
Miss Betsy was just going to call one when I said that, but the
coachman wouldn't have it at that price, he said, and I knew very
well that *she* hadn't four or five shillings to pay for a wehicle.
So, in the midst of that tarin rain, at midnight, we had to walk
four miles, from Westminster Bridge to Pentonwille; and what
was wuss, *I didn't happen to know the way*. A very nice walk it
was, and no mistake.

At about half-past two, we got safe to John Street. My master was at the garden gate. Miss Mary flew into Miss Betsy's arms, whil master began cussin and swearing at me for disobeying his orders, and *turning to the right instead of to the left!* Law bless me! his acting of anger was very near as natral and as terrybl as Mr. Cartlich's in the play.

They had waited half an hour, he said, in the fly, in the little street at the left of the theatre; they had drove up and down in the greatest fright possible; and at last came home, thinking it was in vain to wait any more. They gave her 'ot rum and water and roast oysters for supper, and this consoled her a little.

I hope nobody will cast an imputation on Miss Mary for *her* share in this adventer, for she was as honest a gal as ever lived, and I do believe is hignorant to this day of our little strattygim. Besides, all's fair in love; and, as my master could never get to see her alone, on account of her infernal eleven sisters and ma, he took this opportunity of expressin his attachment to her.

If he was in love with her before, you may be sure she paid it him back again now. Ever after the night at Ashley's, they were as tender as two tuttle-doves—which fully accounts for the axdent what happened to me, in being kicked out of the room; and in course I bore no mallis.

I don't know whether Miss Betsy still fancied that my master was in love with her, but she loved 'muffings and tea, and kem down to his parlor as much as ever.

Now comes the sing'lar part of my history.

CHAPTER II.

BUT who was this genlmn with a fine name—Mr. Frederic Altamont? or what was he? The most mysterus genlmn that ever I knew. Once I said to him, on a wery rainy day, " Sir, shall I bring the gig down to your office?" and he gave me one of his black looks and one of his loudest hoaths, and told me to mind my own bizziness, and attend to my orders. Another day,—it was on the day when Miss Mary slapped Miss Betsy's face,—Miss M., who adoared him, as I have said already, kep on asking him what was his buth, parentidg, and ediccation. " Dear Frederic," says she, "why this mistry about yourself and your hactions? why hide from your little Mary "—they were as tender as this, I can tell you—" your buth and your professin ? "

I spose Mr. Frederic looked black, for I was *only* listening, and he said, in a voice agitated by amotion, " Mary," said he, " if you love me, ask me this no more : let it be sfishnt for you to know that I am a houest man, and that a secret, what it would be misery for you to larn, must hang over all my actions—that is, from ten o'clock till six."

They went on chaffin and talking in this melumcolly and mysterus way, and I didn't lose a word of what they said, for them houses in Pentonwille have only walls made of pasteboard, and you hear rayther better outside the room than in. But, though he kep up his secret, he swore to her his affektion this day pint blank. Nothing should prevent him, he said, from leading her to the halter, from makin her his adoarable wife. After this was a slight silence. " Dearest Frederic," mummered out miss, speakin as if she was chokin, " I am yours—yours for ever." And then silence agen, and one or two smax, as if there was kissin going on. Here I thought it best to give a rattle at the door-lock ; for, as I live, there was old Mrs. Shum a-walkin down the stairs !

It appears that one of the younger gals, a looking out of the bed-rum window, had seen my master come in, and coming down to tea half an hour afterwards, said so in a cussary way. Old Mrs. Shum, who was a dragon of vertyou, cam bustling down the stairs, panting and frowning, as fat and as fierce as a old sow at feedin time.

" Where's the lodger, fellow ? " says she to me.

I spoke loud enough to be heard down the street—" If you mean, ma'am, my master, Mr. Frederic Altamont, esquire, he's just stept in, and is puttin on clean shoes in his bed-room."

She said nothink in answer, but flumps past me, and opening the parlor-door, sees master looking very queer, and Miss Mary a drooping down her head like a pale lily.

" Did you come into my family," says she, " to corrupt my daughters, and to destroy the hinnocence of that infamous gal ? Did you come here, sir, as a seducer, or only as a lodger ? Speak, sir, speak ! "—and she folded her arms quite fierce, and looked like Mrs. Siddums in the Tragic Mews.

"I came here, Mrs. Shum," said he, "because I loved your daughter, or I never would have condescended to live in such a beggarly hole. I have treated her in every respect like a genlmn, and she is as hinnocent now, mam, as she was when she was born. If she'll marry me, I am ready; if she'll leave you, she shall have a home where she shall be neither bullyd nor starved; no hangry frumps of sisters, no cross mother-in-law, only an affeckshnat husband, and all the pure pleasures of Hyming."

Mary flung herself into his arms—"Dear, dear Frederic," says she, "I'll never leave you."

"Miss," says Mrs. Shum, "You ain't a Slamcoe nor yet a Buckmaster, thank God. You may marry this person if your pa thinks proper, and he may insult me—brave me—trample on my feelinx in my own house—and there's no-o-o-obody by to defend me."

I knew what she was going to be at: on came her histarrix agen, and she began screechin and roarin like mad. Down comes of course the eleven gals and old Shum. There was a pretty row. "Look here, sir," says she, "at the conduck of your precious trull of a daughter—alone with this man, kissin and dandlin, and Lawd knows what besides."

"What, he?" cries Miss Betsy—"he in love with Mary! O, the wretch, the monster, the deceiver!"—and she falls down too, screeching away as loud as her mamma; for the silly creature fancied still that Altamont had a fondness for her.

"*Silence these women!*" shouts out Altamont, thundering loud. "I love your daughter, Mr. Shum. I will take her without a penny, and can afford to keep her. If you don't give her to me, she'll come of her own will. Is that enough?—may I have her?"

"We'll talk of this matter, sir," says Mr. Shum, looking as high aud mighty as an alderman. "Gals go up stairs with your dear mamma."—And they all trooped up again, and so the skrimmage ended.

You may be sure that old Shum was not very sorry to get a husband for his daughter Mary, for the old creatur loved her better than all the pack which had been brought him or born to him by Mrs. Buckmaster. But, strange to say, when he came to talk of settlements and so forth, not a word would my master answer. He said he made four hundred a-year reg'lar—he wouldn't tell how—but Mary, if she married him, must share all that he had, and ask no questions ; only this he would say, as he'd said before, that he was a honest mau.

They were married in a few days, and took a very genteel house at Islington; but still my master went away to business, and nobody knew where. Who could he be ?

CHAPTER III.

IF ever a young kipple in the middlin classes began life with a chance of happiness, it was Mr. and Mrs. Frederick Altamont. There house at Cannon Row, Islington, was as comfortable as house could be. Carpited from top to to; pore's rates small ; furnitur elygant; and three deomestix, of which I, in course, was one. My life wasn't so easy as in Mr. A.'s bachelor days; but, what then ? The three Ws. is my maxum ; plenty of work, plenty of wittles, and plenty of wages. Altamont kep his gig no longer, but went to the city in an omlibuster.

One would have thought, I say, that Mrs. A., with such an effeckshnut husband, might have been as happy as her blessid majisty. Nothink of the sort. For the fust six months it was all very well; but then she grew gloomier and gloomier, though A. did everythink in life to please her.

Old Shum used to come reglarly four times a wick to Cannon Row, where he lunched, and dined, and teed, and supd. The poor little man was a thought too fond of wine and spirits; and many and many's the night that I've had to support him home. And you may be sure that Miss Betsy did not now desert her sister : she was at our place mornink, noon, and night, not much to my mayster's liking, though he was too good natured to wex his wife in trifles.

But Betsy never had forgotten the recollection of old days, and hated Altamont like the foul feind. She put all kind of bad things into the head of poor innocent missis ; who, from being all gaiety and cheerfulness, grew to be quite melumcolly and pale, and retchid, just as if she had been the most misrable woman in the world.

In three months more, a baby comes, in course, and with it old Mrs. Shum, who stuck to Mrs. side as close as a wampire, and made her retchider and retchider. She used to bust into tears when Altamont came home; she used to sigh and wheep over the pore child, and say, "My child, my child, your father is false to me;" or, "your father deceives me;" or, "what will you do when your poor mother is no more?" or such like sentimeutal stuff.

It all came from Mother Shum, and her old trix, as I soon found out. The fact is, when there is a mistry of this kind in the house, its a servant's *duty* to listen; and listen I did, one day when Mrs. was cryin as usual, and fat Mrs. Shum a sittin consolin her, as she called it, though, Heaven knows, she only grew wuss and wuss for the consolation.

Well, I listened; Mrs. Shum was a rockin the baby, and missis cryin as yousual.

"Pore dear innocint," says Mrs. S., heavin a great sigh, "you're the child of a unknown father, and a misrabble mother."

"Don't speak ill of Frederic, mamma," says missis; "he is all kindness to me."

"All kindness, indeed! yes, he gives you a fine house, and a fine gownd, and a ride in a fly whenever you please; but *where does all his money come from?* Who is he—what is he? Who knows that he mayn't be a murderer, or a housebreaker, or a utterer of forged notes? How can he make his money honestly, when he won't say where he gets it? Why does he leave you eight hours every blessid day, and won't say where he goes to? Oh, Mary, Mary, you are the most injured of women!"

And with this Mrs. Shum began sobbin; and Miss Betsy began yowling like a cat in a gitter; and pore missis cried, too—tears is so remarkable infeckshus.

"Perhaps, mamma," wimpered out she, "Frederic is a shopboy, and don't like me to know that he is not a gentleman."

"A shopboy," says Betsy; "he a shopboy! O no, no, no! more likely a wretched willain of a murderer, stahbin and robing all day, and feedin you with the fruits of his ill-gotten games!"

More cryin and screechin here took place, in which the baby joined; and made a very pretty consort, I can tell you.

"He can't be a robber," cries missis; "he's too good, too kind, for that; besides, murdering is done at night, and Frederic is always home at eight."

"But he can be a forger," says Betsy, "a wicked, wicked *forger*. Why does he go away every day? to forge notes, to be sure. Why does he go to the city? to be near banks and places, and so do it more at his convenience."

"But he brings home a sum of money every day—about thirty shillings—sometimes fifty: and then he smiles, and says its a good day's work. This is not like a forger," said pore Mrs. A.

"I have it—I have it!" screams out Mrs. S. "The villain—the sneaking, double-faced Jonas! he's married to somebody else, he is, and that's why he leaves you, the base biggymist?"

At this, Mrs. Altamont, struck all of a heap, fainted clean 'away. A dreadful business it was—histarrix; then hystarrix, in course, from Mrs. Shum; bells ringin, child squalin, suvvants tearin up and down stairs with hot water! If ever there is a noosance in the world, it's a house where faintain is always goin on. I wouldn't live in one,—no, not to be groom of the chambers, and git two hundred a year.

It was eight o'clock in the evenin when this row took place; and such a row it was, that nobody but me heard master's knock. He came in, and heard the hooping, and screeching, and roaring. He seemed very much frightened at first, and said, "What is it?"

"Mrs. Shum's here," says I, "and Mrs. in astarrix."

Altamont looked as black as thunder, and growled out a word which I don't like to name,—let it suffice that it begins with a *d* and ends with a *nation;* and he tore up stairs like mad.

He bust open the bed-room door; missis lay quite pale and stony on the sofy; the babby was screechin from the craddle; Miss Betsy was sprawlin over missis; and Mrs. Shum half on the bed and half on the ground: all howlin and squeelin, like so many dogs at the moond.

When A. came in, the mother and daughter stopped all of a sudding. There had been one or two tiffs before between them, and they feared him as if he had been a hogre.

"What's this infernal screeching and crying about?" says he.

" Oh, Mr. Altamont," cries the old woman, " you know too well; it's about you that this darling child is misrabble !"

" And why about me, pray, madam ?"

" Why, sir, dare you ask why ? Because you deceive her, sir ; because you are a false, cowardly traitor, sir ; because *you have a wife elsewhere, sir ?* " And the old lady and Miss Betsy began to roar again as loud as ever.

Altamont pawsed for a miunit, and then flung the door wide open ; nex he seized Miss Betsy as if his hand were a vice, and he world her out of the room ; then up he goes to Mrs. S. " Get up," says he, thundering loud, " you lazy, trollopping, mischief-making, lying old fool ! Get up, and get out of this house. You have been the cuss and bain of my happyniss since you entered it. With your d—d lies, and novvle reading, and his-terrix, you have perwerted Mary, and made her almost as mad as yourself."

" My child ! my child ! " shriex out Mrs. Shum, and clings round missis. But Altamont ran between them, and griping the old lady by her arm, dragged her to the door. " Follow your daughter, ma'm," says he, and down she went. " *Chawls, see those ladies to the door,*" he hollows out, " and never let them pass it again." We walked down together, and off they went : and master locked and double-locked the bed-room door after him, intendin, of course, to have a *tator tator* (as they say) with his wife. You may be sure that I followed up stairs again pretty quick, to hear the result of their confidence.

As they say at St. Stevenses, it was rayther a stormy debate. " Mary," says master, " you're no longer the merry grateful gal, I knew and loved at Pentonwill : there's some secret a pressin on you —there's no smilin welcom for me now, as there used formly to be ! Your mother and sister-in-law have perwerted you, Mary : and that's why I've drove them from this house, which they shall not re-enter in my life."

" O, Frederic ! it's *you* is the cause, and not I. Why do you have any mistry from me ? Where do you spend your days ? Why did you leave me, even on the day of your marridge, for eight hours, and continue to do so every day ?"

" Because," says he, " I makes my livelihood by it. I leave

you, and don't tell you *how* I make it : for it would make you none
the happier to know."

It was in this way the convysation ren on—more tears and
questions on my missises part, more sturmness and silence on my
my master's: it ended for the first time since their marridge, in
a reglar quarrel. Wery difrent, I can tell you, from all the
hammerous billing and kewing which had proceeded their
nupshuls.

Master went out, slamming the door in a fury ; as well he might.
Says he, "If I can't have a comforable life, I can have a jolly
one ; " and so he went off to the hed tavern, and came home that
evening beesly intawsicated. When high words begin in a family
drink generally follows on the genlman's side ; and then, fearwell
to all conjubial happyniss ! These two pipple, so fond and loving
were now sirly, silent, and full of il wil. Master went out earlier,
and came home later ; missis cried more, and looked even paler
than before.

Well, things went on in this uncomfortable way, master still in
the mopes, missis tempted by the deamons of jellosy and curosity ;
until a singlar axident brought to light all the goings on of
Mr. Altamont.

It was the tenth of January ; I recklect the day, for old Shum
gev me half-a-crownd (the fust and last of his money I ever see, by
the way) : he was dining along with master, and they were making
merry together.

Master said, as he was mixing his fifth tumler of punch and little
Shum his twelfth, or so—master said, "I see you twice in the City
to-day, Mr. Shum."

"Well that's curous!" says Shum. "I *was* in the City. To
day's the day when the divvydins (God bless 'em) is paid ; and me
and Mrs. S. went for our half-year's inkem. But we only got out
of the coach, crossed the street to the Bank, took our money, and
got in agen. How could you see me twice ? "

Altamont stuttered, and stammered, and hemd, and hawd.
"O!" says he, "I was passing—passing as you went in and out.'
And he instantly turned the conversation, and began talking about
pollytix, or the weather or some such stuff.

"Yes, my dear," said my missis "but how could you see papa

twice?" Master didn't answer, but talked pollytix more than ever. Still she would continy on. "Where was you, my dear, when you saw pa? What were you doing, my love, to see pa twice?" and so forth. Master looked augrier and angrier, and his wife only pressed him wuss and wuss.

This was, as I said, little Shum's twelfth tumler; and I knew pritty well that he could git very little further; for, as reglar as the thirteenth came, Shum was drunk. The thirteenth did come, and its consquinzes. I was obliged to leed him home to John Street, where I left him in the hangry arms of Mrs. Shum.

"How the d—," sayd he all the way, "how the d dd—the deddy —deddy—devil—could he have seen me *twice?*"

CHAPTER IV.

IT was a sad slip on Altamont's part, for no sooner did he go out the next morning than missis went out too. She tor down the street, and never stopped till she came to her pa's house at Pentonwill. She was clositid for an hour with her ma, and when she left her she drove straight to the City. She walked before the Bank, and behind the Bank, and round the Bank: she came home disperryted, having learned nothink.

And it was now an extraordinary thing that from Shum's house for the next ten days there was nothink but expyditions into the City. Mrs. S., tho her dropsicle legs had never carred her half so fur before, was eternally on the *key veve*, as the French say. If she didn't go, Miss Betsy did, or misses did: they seemed to have an attrackshun to the Bank, and went there as natral as an omlibus.

At last one day, old Mrs. Shum comes to our house—(she wasn't admitted when master was there, but came still in his absints)—and she wore a hair of tryumph, as she entered. "Mary," says she, "where is the money your husbind brought to you yesterday?" My master used always to give it to missis when he returned.

"The money, ma!" says Mary. "Why here!" And pulling

out her puss, she shewed a sovrin, a good heap of silver, and an odd-looking little coin.

"THAT'S IT! that's it!" cried Mrs. S. "A Queene Anne's sixpence, isn't it dear—dated seventeen hundred and three?"

It was so sure enough: a Queen Ans sixpence of that very date.

"Now, my love," says she, "I have found him! Come with me to-morrow, and you shall KNOW ALL!"

And now comes the end of my story.

*   *   *   *   *   *

The ladies nex morning set out for the City, and I walked behind, doing the genteel thing, with a nosegy and a goold stick. We walked down the New Road—we walked down the City Road—we walked to the Bank. We were crossing from that heddyfiz to the other side of Cornhill, when all of a sudden missis shreeked, and fainted spontaceously away.

I rushed forrard, and raised her to my arms: spiling thereby a new weskit, and a pair of crimson smalcloes. I rushed forrard, I say, very nearly knocking down the old sweeper who was hobling away as fast as posibil. We took her to Birch's; we provided her with a hackney-coach and every lucksury, and carried her home to Islington.

*   *   *   *   *   *

That night master never came home. Nor the nex night, nor the nex. On the fourth day, an octioneer arrived; he took an infantry of the furnitur, and placed a bill in the window.

At the end of the wick Altamont made his appearance. He was haggard and pale; not so haggard, however, not so pale, as his misrable wife.

He looked at her very tendrilly. I may say, it's from him that I coppied *my* look to Miss ——. He looked at her very tendrilly and held out his arms. She gev a suffycating shreek, and rusht into his umbraces.

"Mary," says he, "you know all now. I have sold my place; I have got three thousand pounds for it, and saved two more. I've sold my house and furnitur, and that brings me another. We'll go abroad and love each other, has formly."

And now you ask me, Who he was? I shudder to relate.—

Mr. Haltamont SWEP THE CROSSIN FROM THE BANK TO CORN-HILL!!

Of cors, I left his servis. I met him, few years after, at Badden-Badden, where he and Mrs. A. were much respectid, and pass for pipple of propaty.

THE AMOURS OF MR. DEUCEACE.

DIMOND CUT DIMOND.

THE name of my nex master was, if posbil, still more ellygant and youfonious than that of my fust. I now found myself boddy servant to the Honrabble Halgernon Percy Deuceace, youngest and fifth son of the Earl of Crabs.

Halgernon was a barrystir—that is, he lived in Pump Cort, Temple; a wulgar naybrood, witch praps my readers don't no. Suffiz to say, its on the confines of the citty, and the choasen aboad of the lawyers of this metrappolish.

When I say that Mr. Deuceacre was a barrystir, I don't mean that he went sesshums or surcoats (as they call 'em), but simply that he kep chambers, lived in Pump Cort, and looked out for a commitionarship, or a revisinship, or any other place that the Wig guvvyment could give him. His father was a Wig pier (as the landriss told me), and had been a Toary pier. The fack is, his lordship was so poar, that he would be anythink or nothink, to get provisions for his sons and an inkum for himself.

I phansy that he aloud Halgernon two hundred a-year; and it would have been a very comforable maintenants, only he knever paid him.

Owever, the young gnlmn was a genlmn, and no mistake; he got his allowents of nothink a-year, and spent it in the most honrabble and fashnabble manner. He kep a kab—he went to Holmax—and Crockfud's—he moved in the most xquizzit suckles and trubbld the law boox very little, I can tell you. Those fashnabble gents have ways of getten money, witch comman pipple doant understand.

Though he only had a therd floar in Pump Cort, he lived as if he had the welth of Cresas. The tenpun notes floo abowt as common as haypince—clarrit and shampang was at his house as vulgar as gin ; and verry glad I was, to be sure, to be a valley to a zion of the nobillaty.

. Deuceace had, in his sittin-room, a large pictur on a sheet of paper. The names of his family was wrote on it ; it was wrote in the shape of a tree, a groin out of a man-in-arıner's stomick, and the names were on little plates among the bows. The pictur said that the Deuceaces kem into England in the year 1066, along with William Conqueruns. My master called it his podygree. I do bleev it was because he had this pictur, and because he was the *Honrabble* Deuceace, that he mannitched to live as he did. If he had been a common man, you'd have said he was no better than a swinler. It's only rank and buth that can warrant such singularities as my master show'd. For it's no use disgysing it —the Honrabble Halgernon was a GAMBLER. For a man of wulgar family, it's the wust trade that can be—for a man of common feelinx of honesty, this profession is quite imposbil ; but for a real thorough-bread genlmn, it's the esiest and most prophetable line he can take.

It may praps appear curous that such a fashnahble man should live in the Temple ; but it must be recklected, that it's not only lawyers who live in what's called the Ins of Cort. Many batchylers, who have nothink to do with lor, have here their loginx ; and many sham barrysters, who never put on a wig and gownd twise in their lives, kip apartments in the Temple, instead of Bon Street, Pickledilly, or other fashnabble places.

Frinstance, on our stairkis (so these houses are called), there was 8 sets of chamberses, and only 3 lawyers. These was bottom floar, Screwson, Hewson, and Jewson, attorneys ; fust floar, Mr. Sergeant Flabber—opsite, Mr. Counslor Bruffy ; and secknd pair, Mr. Haggerstony, an Irish counslor, praktising at the Old Baly, and lickwise what they call reporter to the *Morning Post* nyouspapper. Opsite him was wrote   .

Mr. RICHARD BLEWITT ;

and on the thud floar, with my master, lived one Mr. Dawkins. This young fellow was a new comer into the Temple, and unlucky it was for him too—he'd better have never been born; for it's my firm apinion that the Temple ruined him—that is, with the help of my master and Mr. Dick Blewitt, as you shall hear.

Mr. Dawkins, as I was gave to understand by his young man, had jest left the Universary of Oxford, and had a pretty little fortn of his own—six thousand pound, or so—in the stox. He was jest of age, an orfin who had lost his father and mother; and having distinkwished hisself at collitch, where he gained seffral prices, was come to town to push his fortn, and study the barryster's bisness.

Not bein of a very high fammly hisself—indeed, I've heard say his father was a chismonger, or somethink of that lo sort—Dawkins was glad to find his old Oxford frend, Mr. Blewitt, yonger son to rich Squire Blewitt, of Listershire, and to take rooms so near him.

Now, tho' there was a considdrable intimacy between me and Mr. Blewitt's gentleman, there was scarcely any betwixt our masters,—mine being too much of the aristoxy to associate with one of Mr. Blewitt's sort. Blewitt was what they call a bettin man; he went reglar to Tattlesall's, kep a pony, wore a white hat, a blue berd's-eye handkercher, and a cut-away coat. In his manners he was the very contrary of my master, who was a slim, ellygant man as ever I see—he had very white hands, rayther a sallow face, with sharp dark ise, and small wiskus neatly trimmed and as black as Warren's jet—he spoke very low and soft—he seemed to be watchin the person with whom he was in convysation, and always flatterd every body. As for Blewitt, he was quite of another sort. He was always swearin, singing, and slappin people on the back, as hearty as posbill. He seemed a merry, careless, honest cretur, whom one would trust with life and soul. So thought Dawkins, at least; who, though a quiet young man, fond of his boox, novvles, Byron's poems, floot-playing, and such like scientafic amusemints, grew hand in glove with honest Dick Blewitt, and soon after with my master, the Honrabble Halgernon. Poor Daw! he thought he was makin good connexions, and real frends—he had fallen in with a couple of the most etrocious swinlers that ever lived.

Before Mr. Dawkins's arrival in our house, Mr. Deuceace had barely condysended to speak to Mr. Blewitt: it was only about a month after that suckumstance that my master, all of a sudding, grew very friendly with him. The reason was pretty clear,—Deuceace *wanted him.* Dawkins had not been an hour in master's company before he knew that he had a pidgin to pluck.

Blewitt knew this too : and bein very fond of pidgin, intended to keep this one entirely to himself. It was amusin to see the Honrabble Halgernon manuvring to get this pore bird out of Blewitt's clause, who thought he had it safe. In fact, he'd brought Dawkins to these chambers for that very porpus, thinking to have him under his eye, and strip him at leisure.

My master very soon found out what was Mr. Blewitt's game. Gamblers know gamblers, if not by instink, at least by reputation; and though Mr. Blewitt moved in a much lower spear than Mr. Deuceace, they knew each other's dealins and caracters puffickly well.

" Charles, you scoundrel," says Deuceace to me one day (he always spoak in that kind way), " who is this person that has taken the opsit chambers, and plays the flute so industrusly ? "

" It's Mr. Dawkins, a rich young gentleman from Oxford, and a great frend of Mr. Blewittses, sir," says I, " they seem to live in each other's rooms."

Master said nothink, but he *grin'd*—my eye, how he did grin. Not the fowl find himself could snear more satannickly.

I knew what he meant:

Imprimish. A man who plays the floot is a simpleton.

Secknly. Mr. Blewitt is a raskle.

Thirdmo. When a raskle and a simpleton is always together, and when the simpleton is *rich*, one knows pretty well what will come of it.

I was but a lad in them days, but I knew what was what, as well as my master; it's not gentlemen only that's up to snough. Law bless us! there was four of us on this stairkes, four as nice young men as you ever see; Mr. Bruffy's young man, Mr. Dawkinses, Mr. Blewitt's, and me—and we knew what our masters was about as well as they did theirselfs. Frinstance, I

can say this for *myself*, there wasn't a paper in Deucéace's desk
or drawer, not a bill, a note, or mimerandum, which I hadn't read
as well as he: with Blewitt's it was the same—me and his young
man used to read 'em all.   There wasn't a bottle of wine that
we didn't get a glas, nor a pound of sugar that we didn't have,
some lumps of it.   We had keys to all the cubbards—we pipped
into all the letters that kem and went—we pored over all the
bill-files—we'd the best pickens out of the dinners, the livvers of
the fowls, the force-mit balls out of the soup, the egs from the
sallit. As for the coals and candles, we left them to the landrisses.
You may call this robry—nonsince—it's only our rights—a
suvvant's purquizzits is as sacred as the laws of Hengland.

Well, the long and short of it is this. Richard Blewitt,
esquire, was sityouated as follows: He'd an incum of three
hunderd a-year from his father. Out of this he had to pay one
hunderd and ninety for money borrowed by him at collidge,
seventy for chambers, seventy more for his hoss, aty for his
suvvant on bord wagis, and about three hunderd and fifty for a
sepprat establishmint in the Regency Park; besides this, his
pockit money, say a hunderd, his eatin, drinkin, and wine-
marchant's bill, about two hunderd moar. So that you see he
laid by a pretty handsome sum at the end of the year.

My master was diffrent; and being a more fashnabble man
than Mr. B., in course he owed a deal more money. There was
fust:

Account *contray*, at Crockford's . . .	£3711 0 0
Bills of xchange and I. O. U.'s (but he didn't	
pay these in most cases)	4963 0 0
21 tailors' bills, in all	1306 11 9
3 hossdealers' do.	402 0 0
2 coachbilder	506 0 0
Bills contracted at Cambritch	2193 6 8
Sundries	987 10 0
	£14069 8 5

I give this as a curosity—pipple doant know how in many cases
fashnabble life is carried on; and to know even what a real
gnlmn *owes* is somethink instructif and agreeable.

But to my tail. The very day after my master had made
the inquiries concerning Mr. Dawkins, witch I mentioned already,

he met Mr. Blewitt on the stairs; and byoutiffle it was to see how this gnlmn, who had before been almost cut by my master, was now received by him. One of the sweatest smiles I ever saw was now vizzable on Mr. Deuceace's countenance. He held out his hand, covered with a white kid glove, and said in the most frenly tone of vice posbill, "What? Mr. Blewitt? It is an age since we met. What a shame that such near naybors should see each other so seldom!"

Mr. Blewitt, who was standing at his door, in a pe-green dressing-gown, smoakin a segar, and singin a hunting coarus, looked surprised, flattered, and then suspicious.

"Why, yes," says he, "it is, Mr. Deuceace, a long time."

"Not, I think, since we dined at Sir George Hookey's. By the by, what an evening that was—hay, Mr. Blewitt? What wine! what capital songs! I recollect your ' May-day in the morning '—cuss me, the best comick song I ever heard. I was speaking to the Duke of Doncaster about it only yesterday. You know the duke, I think."

Mr. Blewitt said, quite surly, "No, I don't."

"Not know him!" cries master; "why, hang it, Blewitt! he knows *you*, as every sporting man in England does, I should think. Why, man, your good things are in everybody's mouth at Newmarket."

And so master went on chaffin Mr. Blewitt. That genlmn at fust answered him quite short and angry: but, after a little more flumery, he grew as pleased as posbill, took in all Deuceace's flatry, and bleeved all his lies. At last the door shut, and they both went into Mr. Blewitt's chambers together.

Of course I can't say what past there; but in an hour master kem up to his own room as yaller as mustard, and smellin sadly of backo smoke. I never see any genlmn more sick than he was; *he'd been smoakin seagars* along with Blewitt. I said nothink, in course, tho' I'd often heard him xpress his horrow of backo, and knew very well he would as soon swallow pizon as smoke. But he wasn't a chap to do a thing without a reason: if he'd been smoakin, I warrant he had smoked to some porpus.

I didn't hear the convysation between 'em; but Mr. Blewitt's man did: it was,—" Well, Mr. Blewitt, what capital seagars!

Have you one for a friend to smoak?" (The old fox, it wasn't only the *seagars* he was a smoakin!) "Walk in," says Mr. Blewitt; and they began a chaffin together; master very ankshous about the young gintleman who had come to live in our chambers, Mr. Dawkins, and always coming back to that subject, —saying that people on the same stairkis ot to be frenly; how glad he'd be, for his part, to know Mr. Dick Blewitt, and *any friend of his*, and so on. Mr. Dick, howsever, seamed quite aware of the trap laid for him. "I really don't no this Dawkins," says he: "he's a chismonger's son, I hear; and tho' I've exchanged visits with him, I doant intend to continyou the acquaintance,— not wishin to assoshate with that kind of pipple." So they went on, master fishin, and Mr. Blewitt not wishin to take the hook at no price.

"Confound the vulgar thief!" muttard my master, as he was laying on his sophy, after being so very ill; "I've poisoned myself with his infernal tobacco, and he has foiled me. The cursed swindling boor! he thinks he'll ruin this poor cheese-monger, does he? I'll step in, and *warn* him."

I thought I should bust a laffin, when he talked in this style. I knew very well what his "warning" meant,—lockin the stable-door, but stealin the hoss fust.

Next day, his strattygam for becoming acquainted with Mr. Dawkins, we exicuted, and very pritty it was.

Besides potry and the floot, Mr. Dawkins, I must tell you, had some other parshallities—wiz., he was very fond of good eatin and drinkin. After doddling over his music and boox all day, this young genlmn used to sally out of evenings, dine sumptiously at a tavern, drinkin all sots of wine along with his friend Mr. Blewitt. He was a quiet young fellow enough at fust; but it was Mr. B. who (for his own porpuses, no doubt,) had got him into this kind of life. Well, I needn't say that he who eats a fine dinner, and drinks too much overnight, wants a bottle of soda-water, and a gril, praps, in the morning. Such was Mr. Dawkinses case; and reglar almost as twelve o'clock came, the waiter from Dix Coffy-House was to be seen on our stairkis, bringing up Mr. D.'s hot breakfast.

No man would have thought there was anythink in such a

trifling cirkumstance; master did, though, and pounced upon it like a cock on a barlycorn.

He sent me out to Mr. Morell's in Pickledilly, for wot's called a Strasbug-pie—in French, a "*patty defau graw.*" He takes a card, and nails it on the outside case (patty defaw graws come generally in a round wooden box, like a drumb); and what do you think he writes on it? why, as follos :—"*For the Honourable Algernon Percy Deuceace, &c. &c. &c.   With Prince Talleyrand's compliments.*"

Prince Tallyram's complimints, indeed! I laff when I think of it, still, the old surpint! He *was* a surpint, that Deuceace, and no mistake.

Well, by a most extrornary piece of ill-luck, the nex day punctially as Mr. Dawkinses brexfas was coming *up* the stairs, Mr. Halgernon Percy Deuceace was going *down.* He was as gay as a lark, humming an Oppra tune, and twizzting round his head his hevy gold-headed cane. Down he went very fast, and by a most unlucky axdent struck his cane against the waiter's tray, and away went Mr. Dawkinses gril, kayann, kitchup, soda-water, and all! I can't think how my master should have choas such an exact time; to be sure, his windo looked upon the cort, and he could see every one who came into our door.

As soon as the axdent had took place, master was in such a rage as, to be sure, no man ever was in befor; he swoar at the waiter in the most dreddfle way; he threatened him with his stick, and it was only when he see that the waiter was rayther a bigger man than hisself that he was in the least pazzyfied. He returned to his own chambres; and John, the waiter, went off for more gril to Dixes Coffy-House.

"This is a most unlucky axdent, to be sure, Charles," says master to me, after a few minits paws, during witch he had been and wrote a note, put it into an anvelope, and sealed it with his bigg seal of arms. "But stay—a thought strikes me—take this note to Mr. Dawkins, and that pye you brought yesterday; and hearkye, you scoundrel, if you say where you got it I will break every bone in your skin!"

These kind of prommises were among the few which I knew him to keep: and as I loved boath my skinn and my boans, I carried

the noat, and, of cors, said nothink. Waiting in Mr. Dawkinses
chambus for a few minnits, I returned to my master with an anser.
I may as well give both of these documence, of which I happen
to have taken coppies.

I.

"THE HON. A. P. DEUCEACE TO T. S. DAWKINS, ESQ.

"Temple, Tuesday.

"Mr. Deuceace presents his compliments to Mr. Dawkins, and
begs at the same time to offer his most sincere apologies and
regrets for the accident which has just taken place.

"May Mr. Deuceace be allowed to take a neighbour's privilege,
and to remedy the evil he has occasioned to the best of his power ?
If Mr. Dawkins will do him the favour to partake of the contents
of the accompanying case (from Strasburg direct, and the gift of
a friend, on whose taste as a gourmand Mr. Dawkins may rely),
perhaps he will find that it is not a bad substitute for the *plat*
which Mr. Deuceace's awkwardness destroyed.

"It will, also, Mr. Deuceace is sure, be no small gratification
to the original donor of the *pâté*, when he learns that it has fallen
into the hands of so celebrated a *bon vivant* as Mr. Dawkins.

"*T. S. Dawkins, Esq., &c. &c. &c.*"

II.

FROM T. S. DAWKINS, ESQ., TO THE HON. A. P. DEUCEACE.

"Mr. Thomas Smith Dawkins presents his grateful compliments to the Hon. Mr. Deuceace, and accepts with the greatest
pleasure Mr. Deuceace's generous proffer.

"It would be one of the *happiest moments* of Mr. Smith
Dawkins's life, if the Hon. Mr. Deuceace would *extend his
generosity* still further, and condescend to partake of the repast
which his *munificent politeness* has furnished.

"Temple, Tuesday."

Many and many a time, I say, have I grind over these letters,
which I had wrote from the original by Mr. Bruffy's copyin

clark. Deuceace's flam about Prince Tallyram was puffickly suc-
cessful. I saw young Dawkins blush with delite as he red the
note; he toar up for or five sheets before he composed the
answer to it, which was as you red abuff, and roat in a hand quite
trembling with pleasyer. If you could but have seen the look of
triumph in Deuceace's wicked black eyes, when he read the noat!
I never see a deamin yet, but I can phansy 1, a holding a writhing
soal on his pitchfrock, and smilin like Deuceace. He dressed
himself in his very best clothes, and in he went, after sending me
over to say that he would xcept with pleasyour Mr. Dawkins's invite.

The pie was cut up, and a most frenly conversation begun
betwixt the two genlmin. Deuceace was quite captivating. He
spoke to Mr. Dawkins in the most respeckful and flatrin manner,
—agread in every think he said,—prazed his taste, his furniter,
his coat, his classick nolledge, and his playin on the floot; you'd
have thought, to hear him, that such a polygon of exlens as
Dawkins did not breath,—that such a modist, sinsear, honrabble
genlmn as Deuceace was to be seen no where xcept in Pump Cort.
Poor Daw was complitly taken in. My master said he'd intro-
duce him to the Duke of Doncaster, and Heaven knows how many
nobs more, till Dawkins was quite intawsicated with pleasyour.
I know as a fac (and it pretty well shows the young genlmn's
carryter), that he went that very day and ordered 2 new coats,
on porpos to be introjuiced to the lords in.

But the best joak of all was at last. Singin, swagrin, and
swarink—up stares came Mr. Dick Blewitt. He flung open
Mr. Dawkins's door, shouting out, "Daw, my old buck, how are
you?" when, all of a sudden, he sees Mr. Deuceace: his jor
dropt, he turned chocky white, and then burnin red, and looked
as if a stror would knock him down. "My dear Mr. Blewitt,"
says my master, smilin, and offring his hand, "how glad I am to
see you. Mr. Dawkins and I were just talking about your
pony! Pray sit down."

Blewitt did; and now was the question, who should sit the
other out; but, law bless you! Mr. Blewitt was no match for my
master; all the time he was fidgetty, silent, and sulky; on the
contry, master was charmin. I never herd such a flo of conver-
satin, or so many wittacisms as he uttered. At last, completely

beat, Mr. Blewitt took his leaf; that instant master followed
him; and passin his arm through that of Mr. Dick, led him into
our chambers, and began talkin to him in the most affabl and
affeckshnat manner.

But Dick was too angry to listen; at last, when master was
telling him some long story about the Duke of Doncaster, Blewitt
burst out—

"A plague on the Duke of Doncaster! Come, come, Mr.
Deuceace, don't you be running your rigs upon me; I an't the
man to be bamboozl'd by long-winded stories about dukes and
duchesses. You think I don't know you; every man knows you,
and your line of country. Yes, you're after young Dawkins there,
and think to pluck him; but you shan't,—no, by —— you shant."
(The reader must recklect that the oaths which interspussed Mr.
B's convysation I have lift out.)   Well, after he'd fired a wolley
of em, Mr. Deuceace spoke as cool as possbill.

"Heark ye, Blewitt. I know you to be one of the most infernal
thieves and scoundrels unhung. If you attempt to hector with
me, I will cane you; if you want more, I'll shoot you; if
you meddle between me and Dawkins, I will do both. I
know your whole life, you miserable swindler and coward.
I know you have already won two hunderd pounds of this lad,
and want all. I will have half, or you never shall have a
penny." It's quite true that master knew things; but how was
the wonder.

I couldn't see Mr. B's. face during this dialogue, bein on the
wrong side of the door; but there was a considdrable paws after
thuse complymints had passed between the two genlmn,—one
walkin quickly up and down the room,—tother, angry and stupid
sittin down, and stampin with his foot.

"Now listen to this, Mr. Blewitt," continues master at last;
"if you're quiet, you shall half this fellow's money: but venture
to win a shilling from him in my absence, or without my consent,
and you do it at your peril."

"Well, well, Mr. Deuceace," cries Dick, "it's very hard, and
I must say, not fair: the game was of my startin, and you've no
right to interfere with my friend."

"Mr. Blewitt, you are a fool! You professed yesterday not to know this man, and I was obliged to find him out for myself. I should like to know by what law of honour I am bound to give him up to you ? "

It was charmin to hear this pair of raskles talkin about *honour*. I declare I could have found it in my heart to warn young Dawkins of the precious way in which these chaps were going to serve him. But if *they* didn't know what honour was, *I* did ; and never, never did I tell tails about my masters when in their sarvice—*out*, in cors, the hobligation is no longer binding.

Well, the nex day there was a gran dinner at our chambers. White soop, turbit, and lobstir sos ; saddil of Scoch muttn, grous, and M'Arony ; wines, shampang, hock, maderia, a bottle of poart, and ever so many of clarrit. The compny present was three ; wiz., the Honrabble A. P. Deuceace, R. Blewitt, and Mr. Dawkins, Exquires. My i, how we genlmn in the kitchin did enjy it. Mr. Blewittes man eat so much grous (when it was brot out of the parlor), that I reely thought he would be sik ; Mr. Dawkinses gelnmn (who was only abowt 13 years of age) grew so il with M'Arony and plumb-puddn, as to be obleeged to take sefral of Mr. D's. pils, which ½ kild him. But this is all promiscuous : I an't talkin of the survants now, but the masters.

Would you bleeve it ? After dinner and praps 8 bottles of wine between the 3, the genlm sat down to *écarty*. It's a game where only 2 plays, and where, in coarse, when there's ony 3, one looks on.

Fust, they playd crown pints, and a pound the bett. At this game they were wonderful equill ; and about supper-time (when grilled am, more shampang, devld biskits, and other things, was brot in) the play stood thus : Mr. Dawkins had won 2 pounds ; Mr. Blewitt, 30 shillings ; the Honrabble Mr. Deuceace having lost 3*l*. 10*s*. After the devvle and the shampang the play was a little higher. Now it was pound pints, and five pound the bet. I thought, to be sure, after hearing the complymints between Blewitt and master in the morning, that now poor Dawkins's time was come.

Not so : Dawkins won always, Mr. B. betting on his play, and giving him the very best of advice. At the end of the evening (which was abowt five o'clock the nex morning) they stopt. Master was counting up the skore on a card.

"Blewitt," says he, "I've been unlucky. I owe you—let me see—yes, five-and-forty pounds?"

"Five-and-forty," says Blewitt, "and no mistake!"

"I will give you a cheque," says the honrabble genlmn.

"Oh! don't mention it, my dear sir!" But master got a grate sheet of paper, and drew him a check on Messeers. Pump, Algit, and Co., his bankers.

"Now," says master, "I've got to settle with you, my dear Mr. Dawkins. If you had backd your luck, I should have owed you a very handsome sum of money. *Voyons*, thirteen points at a pound—it is easy to calculate;" and drawin out his puss, he clinked over the table 13 goolden suverings, which shon till they made my eyes wink.

So did pore Dawkinses, as he put out his hand, all trembling, and drew them in.

"Let me say," added master, "let me say (and I've had some little experience), that you are the very best *écarté* player with whom I ever sat down."

Dawkinses eyes glissened as he put the money up, and said, "Law, Deuceace, you flatter me."

Flatter him! I should think he did. It was the very think which master ment.

"But mind you, Dawkins," continyoud he, "I must have my revenge; for I'm ruined—positively ruined—by your luck."

"Well, well," says Mr. Thomas Smith Dawkins, as pleased as if he had gained a millium, "shall it be to-morrow? Blewitt, what say you?"

Mr. Blewitt agreed, in course. My master, after a little demurring, consented too. "We'll meet," says he, "at your chambers. But mind, my dear fello, not too much wine: I can't stand it at any time, especially when I have to play *écarté* with *you*."

Pore Dawkins left our rooms as happy as a prins. "Here, Charles," says he, and flung me a sovring. Pore fellow! pore fellow! I knew what was a comin!

But the best of it was, that these 13 sovrings which Dawkins won, *master had borrowed them from Mr. Blewitt!* I brought 'em, with 7 more, from that young genlmn's chambers that very morning : for, since his interview with master, Blewitt had nothing to refuse him.

Well, shall I continue the tail? If Mr. Dawkins had been the least bit wiser, it would have taken him six months befoar he lost his money; as it was, he was such a confounded ninny, that it took him a very short time to part with it.

Nex day (it was Thursday, and master's acquaintance with Mr. Dawkins had only commenced on Tuesday), Mr. Dawkins, as I said, gev his party,—dinner at 7. Mr. Blewitt and the two Mr. D.'s as befoar. Play begins at 11. This time I knew the bisniss was pretty serious, for we suvvants was packed off to bed at 2 o'clock. On Friday, I went to chambers—no master—he kem in for 5 minutes at about 12, made a little toilit, ordered more devvles and soda-water, and back again he went to Mr. Dawkins's.

They had dinner there at 7 again, but nobody seamed to eat, for all the vittles came out to us genlmn : they had in more wine though, and must have drunk at least 2 dozen in the 36 hours.

At ten o'clock, however, on Friday night, back my master came to his chambers. I saw him as I never saw him before, namly, reglar drunk. He staggered about the room, he danced, he hickipd, he swoar, he flung me a heap of silver, and, finely, he sunk down exosted on his bed ; I pullin off his boots and close, and making him comfrabble.

When I had removed his garmints, I did what it's the duty of every servant to do—I emtied his pockits, and looked at his pockit-book and all his letters : a number of axdents have been prevented that way.

I found there, among a heap of things, the following pretty dockyment :

I. O. U.

£4700.

THOMAS SMITH DAWKINS.

Friday, 16th January.

D

There was another bit of paper of the same kind—"I. O. U. four hundred pounds, Richard Blewitt: " but this, in cors, ment nothink.

*   *   *   *   *

Nex mornin, at nine, master was up, and as sober as a judg. He drest, and was off to Mr. Dawkins. At 10, he ordered a cab, and the two genlmn went together.

" Where shall he drive, sir ?" says I.

" Oh, tell him to drive to THE BANK."

Pore Dawkins ! his eyes red with remors and sleepliss drunkenniss, gave a shudder and a sob, as he sunk back in the wehicle; and they drove on.

That day he sold out every hapny he was worth, xcept five hundred pounds.

*   *   *   *   *

Abowt 12 master had returned, and Mr. Dick Blewitt came stridin up the stairs with a sollum and important hair.

" Is your master at home ? " says he.

" Yes, sir," says I ; and in he walks. I, in coars, with my ear to the keyhole, listning with all my mite.

" Well," says Blewitt, " we maid a pretty good night of it, Mr. Deuceace. You've settled, I see, with Dawkins."

" Settled !" says master. " Oh, yes—yes—I've settled with him."

" Four thousand seven hundred, I think ?"

" About that—yes."

" That makes my share—let me see—two thousand three hundred and fifty ; which I'll thank you to fork out."

" Upon my word—why—Mr. Blewitt," says master, " I don't really understand what you mean."

" *You don't know what I mean !* " says Blewitt, in an axent such as I never before heard ; " You don't know what I mean ! Did you not promise me that we were to go shares ? Didn't I lend you twenty sovereigns the other night to pay our losings to Dawkins ? Didn't you swear, on your honour as a gentleman, to give me half of all that might be won in this affair ?"

" Agreed, sir," says Deuceace ; " agreed."

" Well, sir, and now what have you to say ?"

" Why, *that I don't intend to keep my promise !* You infernal fool and ninny! do you suppose I was labouring for *you?* Do you fancy I was going to the expense of giving a dinner to that jackass yonder, that you should profit by it? Get away, sir! Leave the room, sir! Or, stop—here—I will give you four hundred pounds—your own note of hand, sir, for that sum, if you will consent to forget all that has passed between us, and that you have never known Mr. Algernon Deuceace."

I've seen pipple angery before now, but never any like Blewitt. He stormed, groaned, belloed, swoar! At last, he fairly began blubbring ; now cussing and nashing his teeth, now praying dear Mr. Deuceace to grant him mercy.

At last, master flung open the door (Heavn bless us! it's well I didn't tumble, hed over eels, into the room!), and said, " Charles, show the gentleman down stairs!" My master looked at him quite steddy. Blewitt slunk down, as misrabble as any man I ever see. As for Dawkins, Heaven knows where he was!

    *   *   *   *   *

" Charles," says my master to me, about an hour afterwards, " I'm going to Paris ; you may come, too, if you please."

SKIMMINGS FROM "THE DAIRY OF GEORGE IV."

CHARLES YELLOWPLUSH, ESQ., TO OLIVER YORKE, ESQ.*

DEAR WHY,—Takin advantage of the Crismiss holydays, Sir John and me (who is a member of parlyment) had gone down to our place in Yorkshire for six wicks, to shoot grows and wood-cox, and enjoy old English hospatalaty. This ugly Canady bisniss unluckaly put an end to our sports in the country, and brot us up to Buckly Square as fast as four posterses could gallip. When there, I found your parcel, containing the two vollumes of a new book, witch, as I have been away from the literary world, and emplied solely in athlatic exorcises, have been laying neglected in

* These Memoirs were originally published in *Frazer's Magazine*, and it may be stated for the benefit of the unlearned in such matters, that " Oliver Yorke " is the assumed name of the editor of that periodical.

my pantry, among my knife-cloaths, and dekanters, and blacking-bottles, and bed-room candles, and things.

This will, I'm sure, account for my delay in notussing the work. I see sefral of the papers and magazeens have been befoarhand with me, and have given their apinions concerning it : specially the *Quotly Revew*, which has most mussilessly cut to peases the author of this *Dairy of the Times of George IV.**

That it's a woman who wrote it is evydent from the style of the writing, as well as from certain proofs in the book itself. Most suttnly a femail wrote this *Dairy*; but who this *Dairy-maid* may be, I, in coarse, cant conjecter : and indeed, common galliantry forbids me to ask. I can only judge of the book itself, which, it appears to me, is clearly trenching upon my ground and favrite subjicks, viz. fashnabble life, as igsibited in the houses of the nobility, gentry, and rile fammly.

But I bare no mallis—infamation is infamation, and it doesn't matter where the infamy comes from ; and whether the *Dairy* be from that distinguished pen to witch it is ornarily attributed—whether, I say, it comes from a lady of honor to the late quean, or a scullion to that diffunct majisty, no matter ; all we ask is nollidge, never mind how we have it. Nollidge, as our cook says, is like trikel-possit—its always good, though you was to drink it out of an old shoo.

Well, then, although this *Dairy* is likely searusly to injur my pussonal intrests, by fourstalling a deal of what I had to say in my private memoars—though many, many guineas, is taken from my pockit, by cuttin short the tail of my narratif—though much that I had to say in souperior languidge, greased with all the ellygance of my orytory, the benefick of my classicle reading, the chawms of my agreble wit, is thus abruply brot befor the world by an inferior genus, neither knowing nor writing English, yet I say, that nevertheless I must say, what I am puffickly pre-paired to say, to gainsay which no man can say a word—yet I

---

* Diary illustrative of the Times of George the Fourth, interspersed with original Letters from the late Queen Caroline, and from various other distinguished Persons.

        "Tôt ou tard, tout se sçait."—MAINTENON.

In 2 vols.   London, 1838.   Henry Colburn.

say, that I say I consider this publication welkom. Far from viewing it with enfy, I greet it with applaws ; because it increases that most exlent specious of nollidge, I mean " FASHNABBLE NOLLIDGE;" compayred to witch all other nollidge is nonsince—a bag of goold to a pare of snuffers.

Could Lord Broom, on the Canady question, say moar? or say what he had to say better? We are marters, both of us, to prinsple; and every body who knows eather knows that we would sacrafice anythiuk rather than that. Fashion is the goddiss I adoar. This delightful work is an offring on her srine ; and as sich all her wushippers are bound to hail it. Here is not a question of trumpry lords and honrabbles, generals and barronites, but the crown itself, and the king and queen's actions ; witch may be considered as the crown jewels. Here's princes, and grand-dukes and airsparent, and Heaven knows what; all with blood-royal in their veins, and their names mentioned in the very fust page of the peeridge. In this book you become so intmate with the Prince of Wales, that you may follow him, if you please, to his marridge-bed; or, if you prefer the Princiss Charlotte, you may have with her an hour's tator-tator.*

Now, though most of the remarkable extrax from this book have been given already (the cream of the *Dairy*, as I wittily say), I shall trouble you, nevertheless, with a few ; partly because they can't be repeated too often, and because the toan of obsyvation with witch they have been genrally received by the press, is not igsackly such as I think they merit. How, indeed, can these common magaseen and newspaper pipple know anythink of fashnabble life, let alone ryal?

Conseaving, then, that the publication of the *Dairy* has done reel good on this scoar, and may probly do a deal moor, I shall look through it, for the porpus of selecting the most ellygant passidges, and which I think may be peculiarly adapted to the reader's benefick.

For you see, my dear Mr. Yorke, that in the fust place, that this is no common catchpny book, like that of most authors and authoresses who write for the base looker of gain. Heaven bless

---

* Our estimable correspondent means, we presume, *tête-à-tête.*—O. Y.

you! the Dairy-maid is above anything musnary. She is a woman of rank, and no mistake; and is as much above doin a common or vulgar action as I am superaor to taking beer after dinner with my cheese. She proves that most satisfackarily, as we see in the following passidge :—

"Her royal highness came to me, and having spoken a few phrases on different subjects, produced all the papers she wishes to have published : her whole correspondence with the prince relative to Lady J——'s dismissal ; his subsequent neglect of the princess ; and, finally, the acquittal of her supposed guilt, signed by the Duke of Portland, &c., at the time of the secret inquiry : when, if proof could have been brought against her, it certainly would have been done ; and which acquittal, to the disgrace of all parties concerned, as well as to the justice of the nation in general, was not made public at the time. A common criminal is publicly condemned or acquitted. Her royal highness commanded me to have these letters published forthwith, saying, 'You may sell them for a great sum.' At first (for she had spoken to me before concerning this business), I thought of availing myself of the opportunity ; but upon second thoughts, I turned from this idea with detestation : for, if I do wrong by obeying her wishes and endeavouring to serve her, I will do so at least from good and disinterested motives, not from any sordid views. The princess commands me, and I will obey her, whatever may be the issue ; but not for fare or fee. I own I tremble, not so much for myself, as for the idea that she is not taking the best and most dignified way of having these papers published. Why make a secret of it at all? If wrong it should not be done ; if right it should be done openly, and in the face of her enemies. In her royal highness's case, as in that of wronged princes in general, why do they shrink from straightforward dealings, and rather have recourse to crooked policy? I wish, in this particular instance, I could make her royal highness feel thus : but she is naturally indignant at being falsely accused, and will not condescend to an avowed explanation."

Can anythink be more just and honrabble than this? The Dairy-lady is quite fair and abovebored. A clear stage, says she, and no faviour! " I won't do behind my back what I am ashamed of before my face : not I!" No more she does; for you see that, though she was offered this manyscrip by the princess *for nothink*, though she knew that she could actially get for it a large sum of money, she was above it, like an honest, noble, grateful, fashnabble woman, as she was. She aboars secrecy, and never will have recors to disguise or crookid polacy. This ought to be an ansure to them *Radicle sneerers*, who pretend that they are the equals of fashnabble pepple ; whereas it's a well-known fact, that the vulgar roagues have no notion of honour.

And after this positif declaration, which reflex honor on her ladyship (long life to her! I've often waited behind her chair!)—after this positif declaration, that, even for the porpus of *defending* her missis, she was so hi-mindid as to refuse anythink like a peculiarly consideration, it is actually asserted in the public prints by a booxeller, that he has given her *a thousand pound* for the *Dairy*. A thousand pound! nonsince!—it's a phigment! a base lible! This woman take a thousand pound, in a matter where her dear mistriss, frend, and benyfactriss was concerned! Never! A thousand baggonits would be more prefrabble to a woman of her xqizzit feelins and fashion.

But, to proceed. It's been objected to me, when I wrote some of my expearunces in fashnabble life, that my languidge was occasionally vulgar, and not such as is generally used in those exquizzit famlies which I frequent. Now, I'll lay a wager that there is in this book, wrote as all the world knows, by a rele lady, and speakin of kings and queens as if they were as common as sand-boys—there is in this book more wulgarity than ever I displayed, more nastiness than ever I would dare *to think on*, and more bad grammar than ever I wrote since I was a boy at school. As for authografy, evry genlmn has his own: never mind spellin, I say, so long as the sence is right.

Let me here quot a letter from a corryspondent of this charming lady of honour; and a very nice corryspondent he is, too, without any mistake:

"Lady O——, poor Lady O——! knows the rules of prudence, I fear me, as imperfectly as she doth those of the Greek and Latin Grammars: or she hath let her brother, who is a sad swine, become master of her secrets, and then contrived to quarrel with him. You would see the outline of the *mélange* in the newspapers; but not the report that Mr. S—— is about to publish a pamphlet, as an addition to the Harleian Tracts, setting forth the amatory adventures of his sister. We shall break our necks in haste to buy it, of course crying 'Shameful' all the while; and it is said that Lady O —— is to be cut, which I cannot entirely believe. Let her tell two or three old women about town that they are young and handsome, and give some well-timed parties, and she may still keep the society which she hath been used to. The times are not so hard as they once were, when a woman could not construe Magna Charta with anything like impunity. People were full as gallant many years ago. But the days are gone by wherein my lord-protector of the commonwealth of England was wont to go a love-making to Mrs. Fleetwood, with the Bible under his arm.

"And so Miss Jacky Gordon is really clothed with a husband at last, and. Miss Laura Manners left without a mate ! She and Lord Stair should marry and have children, in mere revenge. As to Miss Gordon, she's a Venus well suited for such a Vulcan,—whom nothing but money and a title could have rendered tolerable, even to a kitchen wench. It is said that the matrimonial correspondence between this couple is to be published, full of sad scandalous relations, of which you may be sure scarcely a word is true. In former times, the Duchess of St. A——'s made use of these elegant epistles in order to intimidate Lady Johnstone : but that *ruse* would not avail ; so in spite, they are to be printed. What a cargo of amiable creatures ! Yet will some people scarcely believe in the existence of Pandemonium.

"*Tuesday morning.*—You are perfectly right respecting the hot rooms here, which we all cry out against, and all find very comfortable—much more so than the cold sands and bleak neighbourhood of the sea ; which looks vastly well in one of Vander Velde's pictures hung upon crimson damask, but hideous and shocking in reality. H—— and his '*elle*' (talking of parties) were last night at Cholmondeley House, but seem not to ripen in their love. He is certainly good-humoured, and I believe, good-hearted, so deserves a good wife ; but his *cara* seems a genuine London miss, made up of many affectations. Will she form a comfortable helpmate? For me, I like not her origin, and deem many strange things to run in blood, besides madness and the Hanoverian evil.

"*Thursday.*—I verily do believe that I shall never get to the end of this small sheet of paper, so many unheard of interruptions have I had ; and now I have been to Vauxhall, and caught the tooth-ache. I was of Lady E. B——m and H——'s party : very dull—the Lady giving us all a supper after our promenade—

'Much ado was there, God wot
She would love, but he would not.'

He ate a great deal of ice, although he did not seem to require it ; and she '*faisoit les yeux doux*,' enough not only to have melted all the ice which he swal lowed, but his own hard heart into the bargain. The thing will not do. In the mean time, Miss Long hath become quite cruel to Wellesley Pole, and divides her favour equally between Lords Killeen and Kilworth, two as simple Irishmen as ever gave birth to a bull. I wish to Hymen that she were fairly married, for all this pother gives one a disgusting picture of human nature."

A disgusting pictur of human nature, indeed—and isn't he who moralises about it, and she to whom he writes, a couple of pretty heads in the same piece ? Which, Mr. Yorke, is the wust, the scandle or the scandle-mongers ? See what it is to be a moral man of fashn. Fust, he scrapes togither all the bad stoaries about all the people of his acquentance—he goes to a ball, and laffs or snears at everybody there—he is asked to a dinner, and brings away, along with meat and wine to his heart's content, a sour stomick filled with nasty stories of all the people present there.

·He has such a squeamish appytite, that all the world seems to *disagree* with him. And what has he got to say to his dellicate female frend? Why that—

Fust. Mr. S. is going to publish indescent stoaries about Lâdy O——, his sister, which everybody's goin to by.

Nex. That Miss Gordon is going to be cloathed with an usband; and that all their matrimonial corryspondins is to be published too.

8. That Lord H. is goin to be married; but there's something rong, in his wife's blood.

4. Miss Long has cut Mr. Wellesley, and is gone after two Irish lords.

Wooden you phancy, now, that the author of such a letter, instead of writin about pipple of tip-top qualaty was describin Vinegar Yard? Would you beleave that the lady he was a ritin to was a chased, modist lady of honour, and mothcr of a famly? *O trumpery! O_morris!* as Homer says, this is a higeous pictur of manners, such as I weap to think of, as evry morl man must weap.

The above is one pritty pictur of mearly fashnabble life : what follows is about families even higher situated than the most fashnabble. Here we have the princessregient, her daughter the Princess Sharlot, her grandmamma the old quean, and her madjisty daughters the two princesses. If this is not high life, I don't know where it is to be found; and it's pleasing to see what affeckshn and harmny rains in such an exolted spear.

"*Sunday* 24*th.*—Yesterday, the princess went to meet the Princess Charlotte at Kensington. Lady —— told me that, when the latter arrived, she rushed up to her mother, and said, 'For God's sake, be civil to her,' meaning the Duchess of Leeds, who followed her. Lady —— said she felt sorry for the latter; but when the Princess of Wales talked to her, she soon became so free and easy, that one could not have any *feeling* about her *feelings*. Princess Charlotte, I was told, was looking handsome, very pale, but her head more becomingly dressed,—that is tó say, less dressed than usual. Her figure is of that full round shape which is now in its prime; but she disfigures herself by wearing her boddice so short, that she literally has no waist. Her feet are very pretty; and so are her hands and arms, and her ears, and the shape of her head. Her countenance is expressive, when she allows her passions to play upon it; and I never saw any face, with so little shade, express so many powerful and varied emotions. Lady —— told me that the Princess Charlotte talked to her about her situation, and said, in a very quiet, but determined

way, she *would not bear it*, and that as soon as parliament met, she intended to
come to Warwick House, and remain there; that she was also determined not
to consider the Duchess of Leeds as her *governess* but only as her *first lady*.
She made many observations on other persons and subjects; and appears to
be very quick, very penetrating, but imperious and wilful. There is a tone of
romance, too, in her character, which will only serve to mislead her.

"She told her mother that there had been a great battle at Windsor between
the queen and the prince, the former refusing to give up Miss Knight from her
own person to attend on Princess Charlotte as sub-governess. But the prince-
regent had gone to Windsor himself, and insisted on her doing so; and the
'old Beguin' was forced to submit, but has been ill ever since: and Sir Henry
Halford declarod it was a complete breaking up of her constitution—to the
great delight of the two princesses, who were talking about this affair. Miss
Knight was the very person they wished to have; they think they can do as
they like with her. It has been ordered that the Princess Charlotte should
not see her mother alone for a single moment; but the latter went into her
room, stuffed a pair of large shoes full of papers, and having given them to
her daughter, she went home. Lady —— told me every thing was written
down and sent to Mr. Brougham *next day*."

See what diskcord will creap even into the best regulated
famlies. Here are six of 'em—viz., the quean and her two
daughters, her son, and his wife and daughter; and the manner
in which they hate one another is a compleat puzzle.

$$\text{The Prince hates} \dots \dots \left\{ \begin{array}{l} \text{his mother.} \\ \text{his wife.} \\ \text{his daughter.} \end{array} \right.$$

Princess Charlotte hates her father.
Princess of Wales hates her husband.

The old quean, by their squobbles, is on the pint of death;
and her two jewtiful daughters are delighted at the news. What
a happy, fashnabble, Christian famly! O Mr. Yorke, Mr. Yorke,
if this is the way in the drawin rooms, I'm quite content to live
below, in pease and charaty with all men; writin, as I am now,
in my pantry, or els havin a quite game at cards in the servants-
all. With *us* there's no bitter, wicked, quarling of this sort.
We don't hate our children, or bully our mothers, or wish em
ded when they're sick, as this Dairy-woman says kings and
queans do. When we're writing to our friends or sweethearts,
we don't fill our letters with nasty stoaries, takin away the
carricter of our fellow-servants, as this maid of honour's amusin,
moral, frend does. But, in coarse, its not for us to judge of our

betters ;—these great people are a supearur race, and we can't comprehend their ways.

Do you recklect—it's twenty years ago now—how a bewtiffle princess died in givin buth to a poar baby, and how the whole nation of Hengland wep, as though it was one man, over that sweet woman and child, in which were sentered the hopes of every one of us, and of which each was as proud as of his own wife or infnt? Do, you recklet how pore fellows spent their last shillin to buy a black crape for their hats, and clergymen cried in the pulpit, and the whole country through was no better than a great dismal funeral? Do you recklect, Mr. Yorke, who was the person that we all took on so about? We called her the Princis Sharlot of Wales; and we valyoud a single drop of her blood more than the whole heartless body of her father. Well, we looked up to her as a kind of saint or angle, and blest God (such foolish loyal English pipple as we ware in those days) who had sent this sweet lady to rule over us. But Heaven bless you! it was only souperstition. She was no better than she should be, as it turns out—or at least the Dairy-maid says so—no better ?—if my daughters or yours was ½ so bad, we'd as leaf be dead ourselves, and they hanged. But listen to this pritty charritable story, and a truce to reflexshuns :—

"*Sunday, January 9*, 1814.—Yesterday, according to appointment, I went to Princess Charlotte. Found at Warwick House the harp-player, Dizzi; was asked to remain and listen to his performance, but was talked to during the whole time, which completely prevented all possibility of listening to the music. The Duchess of Leeds and her daughter were in the room, but left it soon. Next arrived Miss Knight, who remained all the time I was there. Princess Charlotte was very gracious—showed me all her *bonny dyes*, as B—— would have called them—pictures, and cases, and jewels, &c. She talked in a very desultory way, and it would be difficult to say of what. She observed her mother was in very low spirits. I asked her how she supposed she could be otherwise? This *questioning* answer saves a great deal of trouble, and serves two purposes—*i. e.* avoids committing oneself, or giving offence by silence. There was hung in the apartment one portrait, amongst others, that very much resembled the Duke of D——. I asked Miss Knight whom it represented. She said that was not known; it had been supposed a likeness of the Pretender, when young. This answer suited my thoughts so comically I could have laughed, if one ever did at courts anything but the contrary of what one was inclined to do.

"Princess Charlotte has a very great variety of expression in her countenance—a play of features, and a force of muscle, rarely seen in connection with such soft and shadeless colouring. Her hands and arms are beautiful; but I think her figure is already gone, and will soon be precisely like her mother's in short it is the very picture of her, and *not in miniature.* I could not help analysing my own sensations during the time I was with her, and thought more of them than I did of her. Why was I at all flattered, at all more amused, at all more supple to this young princess, than to her who is only the same sort of person set in the shade of circumstances and of years? It is that youth, and the approach of power, and the latent views of self-interest, sway the heart and dazzle the understanding. If this is so with a heart not, I trust, corrupt, and a head not particularly formed for interested calculations, what effect must not the same causes produce on the generality of mankind?

"In the course of the conversation, the Princess Charlotte contrived to edge in a good deal of *tum-de-dy,* and would, if I had entered into the thing, have gone on with it, while looking at a little picture of herself, which had about thirty or forty different dresses to put over it, done on *isinglass,* and which allowed the general colouring of the picture to be seen through its transparency. It was, I thought, a pretty enough conceit, though rather like dressing up a doll. 'Ah!' said Miss Knight, 'I am not content though, madame—for I yet should have liked one more dress—that of the favourite Sultana.'

"'No, no!' said the princess, 'I never was a favourite, and never can be one,'—looking at a picture which she said was her father's, but which I do not believe was done for the regent any more than for me, but represented a young man in a hussar's dress—probably a former favourite.

"The Princess Charlotte seemed much hurt at the little notice that was taken of her birthday. After keeping me for two hours and a half she dismissed me; and I am sure I could not say what she said, except that it was an *olio* of *décousus* and heterogeneous things, partaking of the characteristics of her mother, grafted on a younger scion. I dined *tête-à-tête* with my dear old aunt; hers is always a sweet and soothing society to me."

There's a pleasing, lady-like, moral extrack for you! An innocent young thing of fifteen has picturs of *two* lovers in her room, and expex a good number more. This dellygate young creature *edges* in a good deal of *tumdedy* (I can't find it in Johnson's Dixonary), and would have *gone on with the thing* (ellygence of languidge), if the dairy-lady would have let her.

Now, to tell you the truth, Mr. Yorke, I doant beleave a single syllible of this story. This lady of honner says, in the fust place, that the princess would have talked a good deal of *tumdedy:* which means, I suppose, indeasnsy, if she, the lady of honner *would have let her.* This *is* a good one! Why, she lets every body else talk tumdedy to their hearts' content; she lets her friends *write* tumdedy, and, after keeping it for a quarter of a sentry, she *prints* it. Why, then, be so squeamish about *hearing* a little! And, then, there's the stoary of the two portricks. This woman has the honner to be received in the frendlyest manner by a British princess; and what does the grateful loyal creature do? 2 picturs of the princess's relations are hanging in her room, and the dairy-woman swears away the poor young princess's carrickter, by swearing they are picturs of her *lovers.* For shame, oh, for shame! you slanderin backbitin dairy-woman you! If you told all them things to your "dear old aunt," on going to dine with her, you must have had very "sweet and soothing society," indeed.

I had marked out many moar extrax, which I intended to write about; but I think I have said enough about this Dairy: in fack, the butler, and the gals in the servants' hall are not well pleased that I should go on readin this naughty book; so we'll have no more of it, only one passidge about Pollytics, witch is sertnly quite new :—

"No one was so likely to be able to defeat Bonaparte as the Crown Prince, from the intimate knowledge he possessed of his character. Bernadotte was also instigated against Bonaparte by one who not only owed him a personal hatred, but who possessed a mind equal to his, and who gave the Crown Prince both information and advice how to act. This was no less a person than Madame de Staël. It was not, as some have asserted, *that she was in love with Berna-dotte;* for, at the time of their intimacy, *Madame de Staël was in love with Rocca.* But she used her influence (which was not small), with the Crown Prince, to make him fight against Bonaparte, and to her wisdom may be attributed much of the success which accompanied his attack upon him. Berna-dotte has raised the flame of liberty, which seems fortunately to blaze all around. May it liberate Europe; and from the ashes of the laurel may olive branches spring up, and overshadow the earth!"

There's a discuvery! that the overthrow of Boneypart is owing to *Madame de Staël!* What nonsince for Colonel Southey or Doctor Napier to write histories of the war with that Capsican hupstart and murderer, when here we have the whole affair explaned by the lady of honour!

"*Sunday, April* 10, 1814.—The incidents which take place every hour are miraculous. Bonaparte is deposed, but alive; subdued, but allowed to choose his place of residence. The island of Elba is the spot he has selected for his ignominious retreat. France is holding forth repentant arms to her banished sovereign. The Poissardes who dragged Louis XVI. to the scaffold are presenting flowers to the Emperor of Russia, the restorer of their legitimate king ! What a stupendous field for philosophy to expatiate in ! What an endless material for thought ! What humiliation to the pride of mere human greatness ! How are the mighty fallen ! Of all that was great in Napoleon, what remains? Despoiled of his usurped power, he sinks to insignificance. There was no moral greatness in the man. The meteor dazzled, scorched, is put out,—utterly, and for ever. But the power which rests in those who have delivered the nations from bondage, is a power that is delegated to them from Heaven ; and the manner in which they have used it is a guarantee for its continuance. The Duke of Wellington has gained laurels unstained by any useless flow of blood. He has done more than conquer others—he has conquered himself: and in the midst of the blaze and flush of victory, surrounded by the homage of nations, he has not been betrayed into the commission of any act of cruelty or wanton offence. He was as cool and self-possessed under the blaze and dazzle of fame as a common man would be under the shade of his garden-tree, or by the hearth of his home. But the tyrant who kept Europe in awe is now a pitiable object for scorn to point the finger of derision at: and humanity shudders as it remembers the scourge with which this man's ambition was permitted to devastate every home tie, and every heartfelt joy."

And now, after this sublime passidge, as full of awfle reflections and pious sentyments as those of Mrs. Cole in the play, I shall only quot one little extrak more :—

" All goes gloomily with the poor princess. Lady Charlotte Campbell told me she regrets not seeing all these curious personages ; but she says, the more the princess is forsaken, the more happy she is at having offered to attend her at this time. *This is very amiable in her*, and cannot fail to be gratifying to the princess."

So it is—wery amiable, wery kind and considdrate in her, indeed. Poor Princess ; how lucky you was to find a frend who loved you for your own sake, and when all the rest of the wuld turned its back kep steady to you. As for beleaving that Lady Sharlot had any hand in this book,* Heaven forbid ! she is all gratitude, pure gratitude, depend upon it. *She* would not go for to blacken her old frend and patron's carrickter, after having

---

* The "authorised" announcement, in the *John Bull* newspaper, sets this question at rest. It is declared that her ladyship is not the writer of the *Diary*.—O. Y.

been so outragusly faithful to her; *she* wouldn't do it, at no price, depend upon it. How sorry she must be that others an't quite so squemish, and show up in this indesent way the follies of her kind, genrus, foolish bennyfactris!

FORING PARTS.

It was a singular proof of my master's modesty, that though he had won this andsome sum of Mr. Dawkins, and was inclined to be as extravygant and osntatious as any man I ever seed, yet, wen he determined on going to Paris, he didn't let a single freud know of all them winnings of his, didn't acquaint my Lord Crabs, his father, that he was about to leave his natiff shoars—neigh—didn't even so much as call together his tradesmin, and pay off their little bills befor his departure.

On the contry, "Chawles," said he to me, "stick a piece of paper on my door," which is the way that lawyers do, "and write 'Back at seven' upon it." Back at seven I wrote, and stuck it on our outer oak. And so mistearus was Deuceace about his continental tour (to all except me), that when the landriss brought him her account for the last month (amountain, at the very least, to 2*l.* 10*s.*), master told her to leave it till Monday mornin, when it should be properly settled. It's extrodny how ickonomical a man becomes, when he's got five thousand lbs. in his pockit.

Back at 7 indeed! At 7 we were a roalin on the Dover Road, in the Reglator Coach—master inside, me out. A strange company of people there was, too, in that wehicle,—3 sailors; an Italyin, with his music-box and munky; a missionary, going to convert the heathens in France; 2 oppra girls (they call 'em figure-aunts), and the figure-aunts' mothers inside; 4 Frenchmin, with gingybred caps, and mustashes, singing, chattering, and jesticklating in the most vonderful vay. Such compliments as passed between them and the figure-aunts! such a munchin of biskits and sippin of brandy! such *O mong Jews*, and *O sacrrrés*, and *kill fay frwaws!* I didn't understand their languidge at

that time, so of course can't igsplain much of their conwersa-
tion; but it pleased me, nevertheless, for now I felt that I
was reely going into foring parts, which, ever sins I had had
any edication at all, was always my fondest wish.   Heavin bless
us! thought I, if these are specimeens of all Frenchmen, what
a set they must be.   The pore Italyin's monky, sittin mopin and
meluncolly on his box was not half so ugly, and seamed quite as
reasonabble.

Well, we arrived at Dover—Ship Hotel—weal cutlets half a
ginny, glas of ale a shilling, glas of neagush, half-a-crownd, a
hapn'y-worth of wax-lites four shillings, and so on.   But master
paid without grumbling; as long as it was for himself he never
minded the expens: and nex day we embarked in the packit for
Balong sir-mare—which means in French, the town of Balong
sityouated on the sea.   I who had heard of foring wonders, expected this to be the fust and greatest: phansy, then, my disapint-
ment, when we got there, to find this Balong, not situated on the
sea, but on the *shoar.*

But, oh! the gettin there was the bisniss.   How I did wish
for Pump Court agin, as we were tawsing abowt in the Channel!
Gentle reader, av you ever been on the otion?—"The sea, the
sea, the open sea!" as Barry Cromwell says.   As soon as we
entered our little vessel, and I'd looked to master's luggitch and
mine (mine was rapt up in a very small hankercher), as soon, I
say, as we entered our little wessel, as soon as I saw the waives,
black and frothy, like fresh drawn porter, a dashin against the
ribbs of our galliant bark, the keal like a wedge, splittin the
billoes in two, the sales a flaffin in the hair, the standard of
Hengland floating at the mask-head, the steward a getting ready
the basins and things, the capting proudly tredding the deck and
giving orders to the salers, the white rox of Albany and the bathin-
masheens disappearing in the distans—then, then I felt, for the
first time, the mite, the madgisty of existence.   "Yellowplush, my
boy," said I, in a dialogue with myself, "your life is now about to
commens—your carear, as a man, dates from your entrans on
board this packit.   Be wise, be manly, be cautious, forgit the
follies of your youth.   You are no longer a boy now, but a FOOT-
MAN.   Throw down your tops, your marbles, your boyish games

—throw off your childish habbits with your inky clerk's jackit—throw up your—"

*　　*　　*　　*　　*

Here, I recklect, I was obleeged to stopp. A fealin, in the fust place singlar, in the next place painful, and at last compleatly overpowering, had come upon me while I was making the abuff speach, and now I found myself in a sityouation which Dellixy for Bids me to describe. Suffis to say, that now I dixcovered what basins was made for—that for many, many hours, I lay in a hagony of exostion, dead to all intense and porpuses, the rain pattering in my face, the salers tramplink over my body—the panes of purgatory going on inside. When we'd been about four hours in this sityouation (it seam'd to me four ears), the steward comes to that part of the deck where we servants were all huddled up together, and calls out "Charles!"

"Well," says I, gurgling out a faiut "yes, what's the matter?"

"You're wanted."

"Where?"

"Your master's wery ill," says he, with a grin.

"Master be hanged!" says I, turning round more misrable than ever. I woodn't have moved that day for twenty thousand masters—no, not for the Empror of Russia or the Pop of Room.

Well, to cut this sad subjik short, many and many a voyitch have I sins had upon what Shakspur calls "the wasty dip," but never such a retched one as that from Dover to Balong, in the year Anna Domino 1818. Steamers were scarce in those days; and our journey was made in a smack. At last, when I was in a stage of despare and exostion as reely to phansy myself at Death's doar, we got to the end of our journy. Late in the evening we hailed the Gaelic shoars, and hankered in the arbour of Balong sir Mare.

It was the entrans of Parrowdice to me and master; and as we entered the calm water, and saw the comfrabble lights gleaming in the houses, and felt the roal of the vessel degreasing, never was two mortials gladder, I warrant, than we were. At length our capting drew up at the key, and our journey was down. But such a bustle and clatter, such jabbering, such shrieking and swaring, such wollies of oafs and axicrations as saluted us on

B

landing, I never knew! We were boarded, in the fust place, by custom-house officers in cock-hats, who seased our luggitch, and called for our passpots: then a crowd of inn-waiters came, tumbling and screaming on deck—"Dis way, sare," cries one; "Hotel Meurice," says another; "Hotel de Bang," screeches another chap—the tower of Babyle was nothink to it. The fust thing that struck me on landing was a big fellow with ear-rings, who very nigh knock me down, in wrenching master's carpet-bag out of my hand, as I was carrying it to the hotell. But we got to it safe at last; and, for the fust time in my life, I slep in a foring country.

I shan't describe this town of Balong, which, as it has been visited by not less (on an avaridg) than two milliums of English since I fust saw it twenty years ago, is tolrabbly well known already. It's a dingy, mellumcolly place, to my mind; the only thing moving in the streets is the gutter which runs down 'em. As for wooden shoes, I saw few of 'em; and for frogs, upon my honour, I never see a single Frenchman swallow one, which I had been led to beleave was their reglar, though beastly, custom. One thing which amazed me was the singlar name which they give to this town of Balong. It's divided, as every boddy knows, into an upper town (sitouate on a mounting, and surrounded by a wall, or *bullyvar*), and a lower town, which is on the level of the sea. Well, will it be believed that they call the upper town the *Hot Veal*, and the other the *Base Veal*, which is, on the contry, genrally good in France, though the beaf it must be confest, is exscrabble.

It was in the Base Veal that Deuceace took his lodgian, at the Hotel de Bang, in a very crooked street called the Rue del Ascew; and if he'd been the Archbishop of Devonshire, or the Duke of Canterbury, he could not have given himself greater hairs, I can tell you. Nothink was too fine for us now; we had a sweet of rooms on the first floor, which belonged to the prime minister of France (at least the landlord said they were the *premier's*); and the Hon. Algernon Percy Deuceace, who had not paid his landriss, and came to Dover in a coach, seamed now to think that goold was too vulgar for him, and a carridge and six would break down with a man of his weight. Shampang flew about like ginger-pop, besides bordo, clarit, burgundy, burgong, and other wines, and all the delixes of the Balong kitchins. We stopped a fortnit at this dull place, and did nothing from morning till night excep walk on the beach, and watch the ships going in and out of arber: with one of them long, sliding opra-glasses, which they call, I don't know why, tallow-scoops. Our amusements for the fortnit we stopped here were boath numerous and daliteful: nothink, in fact, could be more *pickong*, as they say. In the morning before breakfast we boath walked on the Peer; master in a blue mareen jackit, and me in a slap-up new livry; both provided with long sliding opra-glasses, called as I said (I don't know Y, but I spose it's a scientafick term) tallow-scoops. With these we igsamined, very attentively, the otion, the sea-weed, the pebbles, the dead cats, the fishwimmin, and the waives (like little children playing at leap-frog), which came tumbling over 1 and other on to the shoar. It seemed to me as if they were scrambling to get there, as well they might, being sick of the sea, and anxious for the blessid, peaceable *terry firmy*.

After brexfast, down we went again (that is, master on his beat, and me on mine,—for my place in this foring town was a complete *shinycure*), and putting our tally-scoops again in our eyes, we egsamined a little more the otion, pebbils, dead cats, and so on; and this lasted till dinner, and dinner till bed-time, and bed-time lasted till nex day, when came brexfast, and dinner, and tally-scooping, as befoar. This is the way with all people of this town, of which, as I've heard say, there is ten thousand happy English, who lead this plesnt life from year's end to year's end.

Besides this, there's billiards and gambling for the gentlemen, a little dancing for the gals, and scandle for the dowygers. In none of these amusements did we partake. We were a *little* too good to play crown pints at cards, and never get paid when we won; or to go dangling after the portionless gals, or amuse our-selves with slops and penny-wist along with the old ladies. No, no; my master was a man of fortn now, and behayved himself as sich. If ever he condysended to go into the public room of the Hotel de Bang—the French—(doubtless for reasons best known to themselves) call this a sallymanjy—he swoar more and lowder than any one there; he abyoused the waiters, the wittles, the

E 2

wines. With his glas in his i, he staired at every body. He took always the place before the fire. He talked about " My carridge," " My currier," " My servant ; " and he did wright. I've always found through life, that if you wish to be respected by English people, you must be insalent to them, especially if you are a sprig of nobiliaty. We *like* being insulted by noablemen,—it shows they're familiar with us. Law bless us ! I've known many and many a genlmn about town who'd rather be kicked by a lord than not be noticed by him ; they've even had an aw of *me*, because I was a lord's footman. While my master was hectoring in the parlor, at Balong, pretious airs I gave myself in the kitching, I can tell you ; and the consequints was, that we were better served, and moar liked, than many pipple with twice our merit.

Deuceace had some particklar plans, no doubt, which kep him so long at Balong ; and it clearly was his wish to act the man of fortune there for a little time before he tried the character of Paris. He purchased a carridge, he hired a currier, he rigged me in a fine new livry blazin with lace, and he past through the Balong bank a thousand pounds of the money he had won from Dawkins, to his credit at a Paris house ; showing the Balong bankers at the same time, that he'd plenty moar in his potfolie. This was killin two birds with one stone ; the bankers' clerks spread the nuse over the town, and in a day after master had paid the money every old dowyger in Balong had looked out the Crab's family podigree in the Peeridge, and was quite intimate with the Deuceace name and estates. If Sattn himself were a Lord, I do beleave there's many vurtuous English mothers would be glad to have him for a son-in-law.

Now, though my master had thought fitt to leave town without excommunicating with his father on the subject of his intended continental tripe, as soon as he was settled at Balong he roat my lord Crabbs a letter, of which I happen to have a copy. It run thus :—

" Boulogne, January, 25.

" My dear Father,—I have long, in the course of my legal studies, found the necessity of a knowledge of French, in which language all the early history of our profession is written, and have determined to take a little relaxation from chamber reading, which has seriously injured my health. If my modest finances can bear a two months' journey, and a residence at Paris, I propose to remain there that period.

" Will you have the kindness to send me a letter of introduction to Lord Bobtail, our ambassador ? My name, and your old friendship with him, I know would secure me a reception at his house; but a pressing letter from yourself would at once be more courteous, and more effectual.

" May I also ask you for my last quarter's salary ? I am not an expensive man, my dear father, as you know; but we are no chameleons, and fifty pounds (with my little earnings in my profession) would vastly add to the *agrémens* of my continental excursion.

" Present my love to all my brothers and sisters. Ah! how I wish the hard portion of a younger son had not been mine, and that I could live without the dire necessity for labour, happy among the rural scenes of my childhood, and in the society of my dear sisters and you! Heaven bless you, dearest father, and all those beloved ones now dwelling under the dear old roof at Sizes. Ever your affectionate son.

" ALGERNON.

" *The Right Hon. the Earl of Crabs, &c.*
" *Sizes Court, Bucks.*"

To this affeckshnat letter his lordship replied, by return of poast, as follos :

" My dear Algernon,—Your letter came safe to hand, and I enclose you the letter for Lord Bobtail as you desire. He is a kind man, and has one of the best cooks in Europe.

" We were all charmed with your warm remembrances of us, not having seen you for seven years. We cannot but be pleased at the family affection which, in spite of time and absence, still clings so fondly to home. It is a sad, selfish world, and very few who have entered it can afford to keep those fresh feelings which you have, my dear son.

" May you long retain them, is a fond father's earnest prayer. Be sure, dear Algernon, that they will be through life your greatest comfort, as well as your best worldly ally; consoling you in misfortune, cheering you in depression, aiding and inspiring you to exertion and success.

" I am sorry, truly sorry, that my account at Coutts's is so low, just now, as to render a payment of your allowance for the present impossible. I see by my book that I owe you now nine quarters, or 450*l*. Depend on it, my dear boy, that they shall be faithfully paid over to you on the first opportunity.

" By the way, I have enclosed some extracts from the newspapers, which may interest you: and have received a very strange letter from a Mr. Blewitt, about a play transaction, which, I suppose, is the case alluded to in these prints. He says you won 4700*l*. from one Dawkins; that the lad paid it; that he, Blewitt, was to go what he calls 'snacks' in the winning; but that you refused to share the booty. How can you, my dear boy, quarrel with these vulgar people, or lay yourself in any way open to their attacks ? I have played myself a good deal, and there is no man living who can accuse me of a doubtful act. You should either have shot this Blewitt or paid him. Now, as the matter stands, it is too late to do the former; and, perhaps, it would be Quixotic to perform the latter. My dearest boy! recollect through life that *you never can afford to be dishonest with a rogue.* Four thousand seven hundred pounds was a great *coup* to be sure.

" As you are now in such high feather, can you, dearest Algernon! lend me five hundred pounds ? Upon my soul and honour, I will repay you. Your brothers and sisters send you their love. I need not add, that you have always the blessings of your affectionate father.

" CRABS.

" P.S.—Make it 500, and I will give you my note of hand for a thousand."

*   *   *   *   *

I neednt say that this did not *quite* enter into Deuceace's eyedears. Lend his father 500 pound, indeed! He'd as soon have lent him a box on the year! In the fust place, he hadn seen old Crabs for seven years, as that nobleman remarked in his epistol; in the secknd he hated him, and they hated each

other; and nex, if master had loved his father ever so much, he
loved somebody else better—his father's son, namely: and
sooner than deprive that exlent young man of a penny, he'd have
sean all the fathers in the world hangin at Newgat, and all the
"beloved ones," as he called his sisters, the Lady Deuceacisses,
so many convix at Bottomy Bay.

The newspaper parrografs showed that, however secret *we*
wished to keep the play transaction, the public knew it now
full well. Blewitt, as I found after, was the author of the libels
which appeared right and left:

"GAMBLING IN HIGH LIFE:—the *Honorable* Mr. De—c—ce again !—This
celebrated whist-player has turned his accomplishments to some profit. On
Friday, the 16th January, he won five thousand pounds from a *very* young
gentleman, Th—m—s Sm—th D—wk—ns, Esq., and lost two thousand five
hundred to R. Bl—w—tt, Esq., of the T—mple. Mr. D. very honourably paid
the sum lost by him to the honourable whist-player, but we have not heard
that, *before his sudden trip to Paris*, Mr. D—uc—ce paid *his* losings to Mr.
Bl—w—tt."

Nex came a " Notice to Corryspondents: "

"Fair Play asks us, if we know of the gambling doings of the notorious
Deuceace? We answer, WE DO; and, in our very next Number, propose to
make some of them public."

*   *   *   *   *

They didn't appear, however; but, on the contry, the very
same newspeper, which had been before so abusiff of Deuceace,
was now loud in his praise. It said:

" A paragraph was inadvertently admitted into our paper of last week, most
unjustly assailing the character of a gentleman of high birth and talents, the
son of the exemplary E—rl of Cr—ba. We repel, with scorn and indignation,
the dastardly falsehoods of the malignant slanderer who vilified Mr.
De—ce—ce, and beg to offer that gentleman the only reparation in our
power for having thus tampered with his unsullied name. We disbelieve
the *ruffian* and *his story*, and most sincerely regret that such a tale, or
such a writer, should ever have been brought forward to the readers of this
paper."

This was satisfactory, and no mistake: and much pleased we
were at the denial of this conshentious editor. So much pleased
that master sent him a ten-pound noat, and his complymints.

He'd sent another to the same address, *before* this parrowgraff was printed; *why,* I can't think: for I woodnt suppose any thing musnary in a littery man.

Well, after this bisniss was concluded, the currier hired, the carridge smartened a little, and me set up in my new livries, we bade ajew to Bulong in the grandest state posbill. What a figure we cut! and, my i, wbat a figger the postillion cut! A cock-hat, a jackit made out of a cow's skin (it was in cold weather), a pig-tale about 3 fit in length, and a pair of boots! Oh, sich a pare! A bishop might almost have preached out of one, or a modrat-sized famly slep in it. Me and Mr. Schwig-shhnaps, the currier, sate behind, in the rumbill; master aloan in the inside, as grand as a Turk, and rapt up in his fine fir-cloak. Off we sett, bowing gracefly to the crowd; the harniss-bells jinglin, the great white hosses snortin, kickin, and squeelin, and the postilium cracking his wip, as loud as if he'd been drivin her majesty the quean.

＊　　＊　　＊　　＊　　＊

Well, I shant describe our voyitch. We passed sefral sitties, willitches, and metrappolishes; sleeping the fust night at Amiens, witch, as everyboddy knows, is famous ever since the year 1802 for what's called the Pease of Amiens. We had some, very good, done with sugar and brown sos, in the Amiens way. But after all the boasting about them, I think I like our marrowphats better.

Speaking of wedgytables, another singler axdent happened here concarning them. Master, who was brexfasting before going away, told me to go and get him his fur travling-shoes. I went and toald the waiter of the inn, who stared, grinned (as these chaps always do), said *"Bong"* (which means, very well), and presently came back.

I'm blest if he didnt bring master a plate of cabbitch! Would you bleave it, that now, in the nineteenth sentry, when they say there's schoolmasters abroad, these stewpid French jackasses are so extonishingly ignorant as to call a *cabbidge* a *shoo!* Never, never let it be said, after this, that these benighted, souperstitious, misrabble *savidges,* are equill, in any respex, to the great Brittish people. The moor I travvle, the moor I see of the world, and other natiums, I am proud of my own, and despise and deplore the retchid ignorance of the rest of Yourup.

* * * * *

My remark on Parris you shall have by an early opportunity. Me and Deuceace played some curious pranx there, I can tell you.

MR. DEUCEACE AT PARIS.

CHAPTER I.

THE TWO BUNDLES OF HAY.

LIEUTENANT-GENERAL SIR GEORGE GRIFFIN, K.C.B., was about seventy-five years old when he left this life, and the East Ingine army, of which he was a distinguished ornyment. Sir George's first appearance in Injar was in the character of a cabbingboy to a vessel; from which he rose to be clerk to the owners at Calcutta, from which he became all of a sudden a capting in the Company's service; and so rose and rose, until he rose to be a leftenant-general, when he stopped rising altogether—hopping the twig of this life, as drummers, generals, dustmen, and emperors, must do.

Sir George did not leave any mal hair to perpetuate the name of Griffin. A widow of about twenty-seven, and a daughter avaritching twenty-three, was left behind to deploar his loss, and share his proppaty. On old Sir George's deth, his intresting widdo and orfan, who had both been with him in Injer, returned home—tried London for a few months, did not like it, and resolved on a trip to Paris, where very small London people become very great ones, if they've money, as these Griffinses had. The intelligent reader need not be told that Miss Griffin was not the daughter of Lady Griffin; for though marritches are made tolrabbly early in Injer, people are not quite so precoashoos as all that: the fact is, Lady G. was Sir George's second wife. I need scarcely add, that Miss Matilda Griffin wos the offspring of his fust marritch.

Miss Leonora Kicksey, a ansum, lively Islington gal, taken out

to Calcutta, and, amongst his other goods, very comfortably disposed of by her uncle, Capting Kicksey, was one-and-twenty when
she married Sir George at seventy-one; and the 13 Miss Kickseys,
nine of whom kep a school at Islington (the other 4 being married
variously in the city), were not a little envius of my lady's luck,
and not a little proud of their relationship to her. One of 'em,
Miss Jemima Kicksey, the oldest, and by no means the least
ugly of the sett, was staying with her ladyship, and gev me all
the partecklars. Of the rest of the famly, being of a lo sort, I
in course no nothink; *my* acquaintance, thank my stars, don't lie
among them, or the likes of them.

Well, this Miss Jemima lived with her younger and more
fortnat sister, in the qualaty of companion, or toddy. Poar thing!
I'd a soon be a gally slave, as lead the life she did! Every body
in the house despised her; her ladyship insulted her; the very
kitching gals scorned and flouted her. She roat the notes, she
kep the bills, she made the tea, she whipped the chocklate, she
cleaned the Canary birds, and gev out the linning for the wash.
She was my lady's walking pocket, or rettycule; and fetched and
carried her handkercher, or her smell-bottle, like a well-bred
spaniel. All night, at her ladyship's swarries, she thumped
kidrills (nobody ever thought of asking *her* to dance!); when
Miss Griffing sung, she played the piano, and was scolded because
the singer was out of tune; abommanating dogs, she never drove
out without her ladyship's puddle in her lap; and, reglarly unwell
in a carriage, she never got any thing but the back seat. Poar
Jemima! I can see her now in my lady's *secknd-best* old clothes
(the ladies-maids always got the prime leavings): a liloc sattn
gown, crumpled, blotched, and greasy; a pair of white sattn shoes,
of the colour of Inger rubber; a faded yellow velvet hat, with a
wreath of hartifishl flowers run to sead, and a bird of Parrowdice
perched on the top of it, melumcolly and moulting, with only a
couple of feathers left in his unfortunate tail.

Besides this ornyment to their saloon, Lady and Miss Griffin
kept a number of other servants in the kitching; 2 ladies-maids;
2 footmin, six feet high each, crimson coats, goold knots, and
white cassymear pantyloons; a coachmin to match; a page: and
a Shassure, a kind of servant only known among forriners, and

who looks more like a major-general than any other mortial, wearing a cock-hat, a unicorn covered with silver lace, mustashos, eplets, and a sword by his side. All these to wait upon two ladies; not counting a host of the fair six, such as cooks, scullion, housekeepers, and so forth.

My Lady Griffin's lodging was at forty pound a week, in a grand sweet of rooms in the Plas Vandome at Paris. And, having thus described their house, and their servants' hall, I may give a few words of description concerning the ladies themselves.

In the fust place, and in coarse, they hated each other. My lady was twenty-seven—a widdo of two years—fat, fair, and rosy. A slow, quiet, cold-looking woman, as those fair-haired gals generally are, it seemed difficult to rouse her either into likes or dislikes; to the former, at least. She never loved any body but *one*, and that was herself. She hated, in her calm, quiet way, almost every one else who came near her—every one, from her neighbour the duke, who had slighted her at dinner, down to John the footman, who had torn a hole in her train. I think this woman's heart was like one of them lithograffic stones, you *can't rub out any thing* when once it's drawn or wrote on it; nor could you out of her ladyship's stone—heart, I mean—in the shape of an affront, a slight, or real or phansied injury. She boar an exlent, irreprotchable character, against which the tongue of scandal never wagged. She was allowed to be the best wife posbill—and so she was; but she killed her old husband in two years, as dead as ever Mr. Thurtell killed Mr. William Weare. She never got into a passion, not she—she never said a rude word; but she'd a genius—a genius which many women have—of making *a hell* of a house, and tort'ring the poor creatures of her family, until they were wellnigh drove mad.

Miss Matilda Griffin was a good deal uglier, and about as amiable as her mother-in-law. She was crooked, and squinted; my lady, to do her justice, was straight, and looked the same way with her i's. She was dark, and my lady was fair—sentimental, as her ladyship was cold. My lady was never in a passion—Miss Matilda always; and awfille were the scenes which used to pass between these 2 women, and the wickid, wickid quarls which took place. Why did they live together? There was the mistry. Not

related, and hating each other like pison, it would surely have
been easier to remain seprat, and so have detested each other at a
distaus.

As for the fortune which old Sir George had left, that, it was
clear, was very considrabble—300 thowsnd lb. at the least, as I
have heard say. But nobody knew how it was disposed of. Some
said that her ladyship was sole mistriss of it, others that it was
divided, others that she had only a life inkum, and that the money
was all to go (as was natral) to Miss Matilda. These are subjix
which are not, praps, very interesting to the British public; but
were mighty important to my muster, the Honrable Algernon
Percy Deuceace, esquire, barrister-at-law, etsettler, etsettler.

For I've forgot to inform you that my master was very intimat
in this house; and that we were now comfortably settled at the
Hotel Mirabew (pronounced Marobo in French), in the Rew delly
Pay, at Paris. We had our cab, and two riding horses; our
banker's book, and a thousand pound for a balants at Lafitt's; our
club at the corner of the Rew Gramong; our share in a box at
the oppras ; our apartments, spacious and elygant; our swarries
at court; our dinners at his excellency Lord Bobtail's and elsewhere. Thanks to poar Dawkins's five thousand pound, we were
as complete gentlemen as any in Paris.

Now my master, like a wise man as he was, seaing himself at
the head of a smart sum of money, and in a country where his
debts could not bother him, determined to give up for the present
every think like gambling—at least, high play ; as for losing or
winning a ralow of Napoleums at whist or ecarty, it did not
matter: it looks like money to do such things, and gives a kind of
respectabilaty. "But as for play, he wouldn't—O no! not for
worlds!—do such a thing." He *had* played, like other young men
of fashn and won and lost [old fox! he didn't say he had *paid*] ;
but he had given up the amusement, and was now determined, he
said, to live on his inkum. The fact is, my master was doing
his very best to act the respectable man: and a very good game
it is, too ; but it requires a precious great roag to play it.

He made his appearans reglar at church—me carrying a handsome large black marocky Prayer-book and Bible, with the psalms
and lessons marked out with red ribbings ; and you'd have thought,

as I graivly laid the volloms down before him, and as he berried his head in his nicely brushed hat, before service began, that such a pious, proper, morl, young nobleman was not to be found in the whole of the peeridge. It was a comfort to look at him. Efry old tabby and dowyger at my Lord Bobtail's turned up the wights of their i's when they spoke of him, and vowed they had never seen such a dear, daliteful, exlent young man. What a good son he must be, they said; and, oh, what a good son-in-law! He had the pick of all the English gals at Paris before we had been there 3 months. But, unfortunately, most of them were poar; and love and a cottidge was not quite in master's way of thinking.

Well, about this time my Lady Griffin and Miss G. made their appearants at Parris, and master, who was up to snough, very soon changed his noat. He sate near them at chapple, and sung hims with my lady: he danced with 'em at the embassy balls; he road with them in the Boy de Balong and the Shandeleasies (which is the French High Park); he roat potry in Miss Griffin's halbim, and sang jewets along with her and Lady Griffin; he brought sweat-meats for the puddle-dog; he gave money to the footmin, kissis and gloves to the sniggering ladies-maids; he was sivvle even to poar Miss Kicksey; there wasn't a single soal at the Griffinses that didn't adoar this good young man.

The ladies, if they hated befoar, you may be sure detested each other now wuss than ever. There had been always a jallowsy between them; miss jellows of her mother-in-law's bewty; madam of miss's espree: miss taunting my lady about the school at Islington, and my lady snearing at miss for her squint and her crookid back. And now came a stronger caws. They both fell in love with Mr. Deuceace—my lady, that is to say, as much as she could, with her cold selfish temper. She liked Deuceace, who amused her and made her laff. She liked his manners, his riding, and his good loox; and being a *pervinew* herself, had a dubble respect for real aristocratick flesh and blood. Miss's love, on the contry, was all flams and fury. She'd always been at this work from the time she had been at school, where she very nigh run away with a Frentch master; next with a footman (which I may say, in con-fidence, is by no means unnatral or unusyouall, as I *could show if*

I liked); and so had been going on sins fifteen. She reglarly flung herself at Deuceace's head—such sighing, crying, and ogling, I never see. Often was I ready to bust out laffin, as I brought master skoars of rose-coloured *billydoos*, folded up like cockhats, and smellin like barber's shops, which this very tender young lady used to address to him. Now, though master was a scoundrill, and no mistake, he was a gentlemin, and a man of good breading; and miss *came a little too strong* (pardon the wulgarity of the xpression) with her hardor and attachmint, for one of his taste. Besides, she had a crookid spine, and a squint; so that (supposing their fortns tolrabbly equal) Deuceace reely preferred the mother-in-law.

Now, then, it was his bisniss to find out which had the most money. With an English famly this would have been easy: a look at a will at Doctor Commons'es would settle the matter at once. But this India naybob's will was at Calcutty, or some outlandish place; and there was no getting sight of a coppy of it. I will do Mr. Algernon Deuceace the justass to say, that he was so little musnary in his love for Lady Griffin, that he would have married her gladly, even if she had ten thousand pounds less than Miss Matilda. In the mean time, his plan was to keep 'em both in play, until he could strike the best fish of the two—not a difficult matter for a man of his genus; besides, Miss was hooked for certain.

CHAPTER II.

"HONOUR THY FATHER."

I SAID that my master was adoared by every person in my Lady Griffin's establishmint. I should have said by every person excep one,—a young French gnlmn, that is, who, before our appearants, had been mighty partiklar with my lady, ockupying by her side exackly the same pasition, which the Honrable Mr. Deuceace now held. It was bewtiffle and headifying to see how coolly that young nobleman kicked the poar Shevalliay de L'Orge out of his shoes, and how gracefully he himself stept into 'em. Munseer de L'Orge was a smart young French jentleman, of about my master's age and good looks, but not possest of half my

master's impidince. Not that that quallaty is uncommon in
France; but few, very few, had it to such a degree as my exlent
employer, Mr. Deuceace. Besides De L'Orge was reglarly and
reely in love with Lady Griffin, and master only pretending: he
had, of coars, an advantitch, which the poar Frentchman never
could git. He was all smiles and gaty, while Delorge was
ockward and melumcolly. My master had said twenty pretty
things to Lady Griffin, befor the shevalier had finished smoothing
his hat, staring at her, and sighing fit to bust his weskit. O luv,
luv! *This* is'nt the way to win a woman, or my name's not
Fitzroy Yellowplush! Myself, when I begun my carcar among
the fair six, I was always sighing and moping, like this poar
Frenchman. What was the consquints? The foar fust women I
adoared lafft at me, and left me for something more lively. With
the rest I have edopted a diffrent game, and with tolrable suxess,
I can tell you. But this is eggatism, which I aboar.

Well, the long and the short of it is, that Munseer Ferdinand
Hyppolite Xavier Stanislas, Shevalier de L'Orge, was reglar cut
out by Munseer Algernon Percy Deuceace, Exquire. Poar
Ferdinand did not leave the house—he hadn't the heart to do
that—nor had my lady the desire to dismiss him. He was usefle
in a thousand different ways, gitting oppra boxes, and invitations
to Frentch swarries, bying gloves, and O de Colong, writing
French noats, and such like. Always let me recommend an
English famly, going to Paris, to have at least one young man of
the sort about them. Never mind how old your ladyship is, he
will make love to you; never mind what errints you send him
upon, he'll trot off and do them. Besides, he's always quite and
well-dresst, and never drinx moar than a pint of wine at dinner,
which (as I say) is a pint to consider. Such a conveniants of
a man was Munseer de L'Orge—the greatest use and comfort to
my lady posbill; if it was but to laff at his bad pronunciatium of
English, it was somethink amusink: the fun was to pit him
against poar Miss Kicksey, she speakin French, and he our naytif
British tong.

My master, to do him justace, was perfickly sivvle to this poar
young Frenchman; and having kicked him out of the place which
he occupied, sertingly treated his fallen anymy with every respect

and consideration. Poar modist down-hearted little Ferdinand adoared my lady as a goddice; and so he was very polite, likewise, to my master—never ventring once to be jellows of him, or to question my Lady Griffin's right to chauge her lover, if she choase to do so.

Thus, then, matters stood; master had two strinx to his bo, and might take either the widdo or the orfn, as he preferred: *com bong lwee somblay*, as the Frentch say. His only pint was to discover how the money was disposed off, which evidently belonged to one or other, or boath. At any rate he was sure of one; as sure as any mortial man can be in this sublimary spear, where nothink is suttn except unsertnty.

* * * * *

A very unixpected insdint here took place, which in a good deal changed my master's calkylations.

One night, after conducting the two ladies to the oppra, after suppink of white soop, sammy-deperdrow, and shampang glassy (which means, eyced), at their house in the Plas Vandom, me and master droav hoam in the cab, as happy as possbill.

"Chawls, you d—d scoundrel," says he to me (for he was in an exlent humer), "when I'm married, I'll dubbil your wagis."

This he might do, to be sure, without injaring himself, seing that he had as yet never paid me any. But, what then? Law bless us! things would be at a pretty pass if we suvvants only lived on our *wagis;* our puckwisits is the thing, and no mistake.

I ixprest my gratatude as best I could; swoar that it wasnt for wagis I served him—that I would as leaf weight upon him for nothink; and that never, never, so long as I livd, would I, of my own accord, part from such an exlent master. By the time these two spitches had been made—my spitch and his—we arrived at the Hotel Mirabeu; which, as every body knows, aint very distant from the Plas Vandome. Up we marched to our apartmince, me carrying the light and the cloax, master hummink a hair out of the oppra, as merry as a lark.

I opened the door of our salong. There was lights already in the room; an empty shampang bottle roaling on the floar, another on the table; near which the sofy was drawn, and on it lay a stout old genlmn, smoaking seagars as if he'd bean in an inn tap-room.

Deuceace (who abommanates seagars, as I've already shown) bust into a furious raige against the genlmn, whom he could hardly see for the smoak; and, with a number of oaves quite unnecessary to repeat, asked him what bisniss he'd there.

The smoaking chap rose, and, laying down his seagar, began a ror of laffin, and said, "What Algy! my boy! don't you know me ?"

The reader may, praps recklect a very affecting letter which was published in the last chapter of these memoars; in which the writer requested a loan of five hundred pound from Mr. Algernon Deuceace, and which boar the respected signatur of the Earl of Crabs, Mr. Deuceace's own father. It was that distinguished arastycrat who was now smokin and laffin in our room.

My Lord Crabs was, as I preshumed, about 60 years old. A stowt, burly, red-faced, bald-headed nobleman, whose nose seemed blushing at what his mouth was continually swallowing; whose hand, praps, trembled a little; and whose thy and legg was not quite so full or as steddy as they had been in former days. But he was a respecktabble, fine-looking, old nobleman; and though it must be confest, ½ drunk when we fust made our appearance in the salong, yet by no means moor so than a reel noblemin ought to be.

"What, Algy! my boy!" shouts out his lordship, advancing and seasing master by the hand, "doan't you know your own father ?"

Master seemed anythink but overhappy. "My lord," says he, looking very pail, and speakin rayther slow, "I didn't—I confess —the unexpected pleasure—of seeing you in Paris. The fact is, sir," said he, recovering himself a little; "the fact is, there was such a confounded smoke of tobacco in the room, that I really could not see who the stranger was who had paid me such an unexpected visit."

"A bad habit, Algernon; a bad habit," said my lord, lighting another seagar: "a disgusting and filthy practice, which you, my dear child, will do well to avoid. It is at best, dear Algernon but a nasty, idle pastime, unfitting a man as well for mental exertion as for respectable society; sacrificing, at once, the vigour

of the intellect and the graces of the person. By-the-by, what
infernal bad tobacco they have, too, in this hotel. Could not you
send your servant to get me a few seagars at the Café de Paris?
Give him a five-franc piece, and let him go at once, that's a good
fellow."

Here his lordship hiccupt, and drank off a fresh tumbler of
shampang. Very sulkily, master drew out the coin, and sent me
on the errint.

Knowing the Café de Paris to be shut at that hour, I didn't
say a word, but quietly establisht myself in the anteroom; where,
as it happened by a singler coinstdints, I could hear every word
of the conversation between this exlent pair of relatifs.

"Help yourself, and get another bottle," says my lord, after a
sollum paws. My poar master, the king of all other compnies in
which he moved, seamed here but to play secknd fiddill, and went
to the cubbard, from which his father had already igstracted two
bottils of his prime Sillary.

He put it down before his father, coft, spit, opened the
windows, stirred the fire, yawned, clapt his hand to his forehead,
and suttnly seamed as uneezy as a genlmn could be. But it was
of no use; the old one would not budg. "Help yourself," says
he again, "and pass me the bottil."

"You are very good, father," says master; "but really, I
neither drink nor smoke."

"Right, my boy: quite right. Talk about a good conscience in
this life—a good *stomack* is everythink. No bad nights, no
headachs—eh? Quite cool and collected for your law studies in
the morning?—eh?" And the old nobleman here grinned, in a
manner which would have done creddit to Mr. Grimoldi.

Master sate pale and wincing, as I've seen a pore soldier under
the cat. He didn't anser a word. His exlent pa went on,
warming as he continued to speak, and drinking a fresh glas at
evry full stop.

"How you must improve, with such talents and such principles! Why, Algernon, all London talks of your industry and
perseverance: You're not merely a philosopher, man; hang it!
you've got the philosopher's stone. Fine rooms, fine horses,
champagne, and all for 200 a-year!"

"I presume, sir," says my master, "that you mean the two hundred a-year which *you* pay me?"

"The very sum, my boy; the very sum!" cries my lord, laffin as if he would die. "Why, that's the wonder! I never pay the two hundred a-year, and you keep all this state up upon nothing. Give me your secret, O you young Trismegistus! Tell your old father how such wonders can be worked, and I will—yes, then, upon my word, I will—pay you your two hundred a-year!"

"*Enfin*, my lord," says Mr. Deuceace, starting up, and losing all patience, "will you have the goodness to tell me what this visit means? You leave me to starve, for all you care; and you grow mighty facetious because I earn my bread. You find me in prosperity, and——"

"Precisely, my boy; precisely. Keep your temper, and pass that bottle. I find you in prosperity; and a young gentleman of your genius and acquirements asks me why I seek your society? Oh, Algernon! Algernon! this is not worthy of such a profound philosopher. *Why* do I seek you? Why, because you *are* in prosperity, O my son! else, why the devil should I bother myself about you? Did I, your poor mother, or your family, ever get from you a single affectionate feeling? Did we, or any other of your friends or intimates, ever know you to be guilty of a single honest or generous action? Did we ever pretend any love for you, or you for us? Algernon Deuceace, you don't want a father to tell you that you are a swindler and a spendthrift! I have paid thousands for the debts of yourself and your brothers; and, if you pay nobody else, I am determined you shall repay me. You would not do it by fair means, when I wrote to you and asked you for a loan of money. I knew you would not. Had I written again to warn you of my coming, you would have given me the slip; and so I came, uninvited, to *force* you to repay me. *That's* why I am here, Mr. Algernon; and so help yourself and pass the bottle."

After this speach, the old genlmn sunk down on the sofa, and puffed as much smoke out of his mouth as if he'd been the chimley of a steam-injian. I was pleased, I confess, with the sean, and liked to see this venrabble and virtuous old man a nocking his son about the hed; just as Deuceace had done with Mr. Richard

ϝ 2

Blewitt, as I've before shown. Master's face was, fust, red-hot; next, chawk-white; and then, sky-blew. He looked, for all the world, like Mr. Tippy Cooke in the tragady of *Frankinstang*. At last, he mannidged to speek.

" My lord," says he, " I expected when I saw you that some such scheme was on foot. Swindler and spendthrift as I am, at least it is but a family failing; and I am indebted for my virtues to my father's precious example. Your lordship has, I perceive, added drunkenness to the list of your accomplishments ; and, I suppose, under the influence of that gentlemanly excitement, has come to make these preposterous propositions to me. When you are sober, you will, perhaps, be wise enough to know, that, fool as I may be, I am not such a fool as you think me ; and that if I have got money, I intend to keep it—every farthing of it, though you were to be ten times as drunk, and ten times as threatening, as you are now."

" Well, well, my boy," said Lord Crabs, who seemed to have been half-asleep during his son's oratium, and received all his sneers and surcasms with the most complete good-humour ; " well, well, if you will resist—*tant pis pour toi*—I've no desire to ruin you, recollect, and am not in the slightest degree angry; but I must and will have a thousand pounds. You had better give me the money at once; it will cost you more if you don't."

" Sir," says Mr. Deuceace, " I will be equally candid. I would not give you a farthing to save you from ——"

Here I thought proper to open the door, and, touching my hat, said, " I have been to the Café de Paris, my lord, but the house is shut."

" *Bon:* there's a good lad; you may keep the five francs. And now, get me a candle and show me down stairs."

But my master seized the wax taper. " Pardon me, my lord," says he. " What ! a servant do it, when your son is in the room ? Ah, *par exemple*, my dear father," said he, laughing, " you think there is no politeness left among us." And he led the way out.

" Good night, my dear boy," said Lord Crabs.

" God bless you, sir," says he. " Are you wrapped warm ? Mind the step ! "

And so this affeckshnate pair parted.

CHAPTER III.

MINEWVRING.

MASTER rose the nex morning with a dismal countinants—he saamed to think that his pa's visit boded him no good. I heard him muttering at his brexfast, and fumbling among his hundred pound notes; once he had laid a parsle of them aside (I knew what he meant), to send 'em to his father. "But, no," says he at last, clutching them all up together again, and throwing them into his escritaw, "what harm can he do me? If he is a knave, I know another who's full as sharp. Let's see if we cannot beat him at his own weapons." With that, Mr. Deuceace drest himself in his best clothes, and marched off to the Plas Vandom, to pay his cort to the fair widdo and the intresting orfn.

It was abowt ten o'clock, and he propoased to the ladies, on seeing them, a number of planns for the day's rackryation. Riding in the Body Balong, going to the Twillaries to see King Looy Disweet (who was then the raining sufferin of the French crownd) go to Chapple, and, finely, a dinner at 5 o'clock at the Caffy de Parry; whents they were all to adjourn, to see a new peace at the theatre of the Pot St. Martin, called *Susannar and the Elders*.

The gals agread to everythink, exsep the two last prepositiums. "We have an engagement, my dear Mr. Algernon," said my lady. "Look—a very kind letter from Lady Bobtail." And she handed over a pafewmd noat from that exolted lady. It ran thus :—

"*Fbg. St. Honoré, Thursday, Feb. 15, 1817.*

"My dear Lady Griffin,—It is an age since we met. Harassing public duties occupy so much myself and Lord Bobtail, that we have scarce time to see our private friends; among whom, I hope, my dear Lady Griffin will allow me to rank her. Will you excuse so very unceremonious an invitation, and dine with us at the Embassy to-day? We shall be *en petit comité*, and shall have the pleasure of hearing, I hope, some of your charming daughter's singing in the evening. I ought, perhaps, to have addressed a separate note to dear Miss Griffin; but I hope she will pardon a poor *diplomate*, who has so many letters to write, you know.

"Farewell till seven, when I *positively must* see you both. Ever, dearest Lady Griffin, your affectionate

"ELIZA BOBTAIL."

Such a letter from the ambassdriss, brot by the ambasdor's Shassure, and sealed with his seal of arms, would affect anybody in the middling ranx of life. It droav Lady Griffin mad with delight; and, long before my master's arrivle, she'd sent Mortimer and Fitzclarence, her two footmin, along with a polite reply in the affummatiff.

Master read the noat with no such fealinx of joy. He felt that there was somethink a-going on behind the seans, and, though he could not tell how, was sure that some danger was near him. That old fox of a father of his had begun his M'Inations pretty early!

Deuceace handed back the letter; sneared, and poohd, and hinted that such an invitation was an insult at best (what he called a *pees ally*); and, the ladies might depend upon it, was only sent because Lady Bobtail wanted to fill up two spare places at her table. But Lady Griffin and miss would not have his insin-wations; they knew too fu lords ever to refuse an invitatium from any one of them. Go they would; and poor Deuceace must dine alone. After they had been on their ride, and had had their other amusemince, master came back with them, chatted, and laft; he was mighty sarkastix with my lady; tender and sentry-mentle with miss; and left them both in high sperrits to perform their twollet, before dinner.

As I came to the door (for I was as famillyer as a servnt of the house), as I came into the drawing-room to announts his cab, I saw master very quietly taking his pocket-book (or *pot fool*, as the French call it) and thrusting it under one of the cushinx of the sofa. What game is this? thinx I.

Why, this was the game. In abowt two hours, when he knew the ladies were gon, he pretends to be vastly anxious abowt the loss of his potfolio; and back he goes to Lady Griffinses, to seek for it there.

" Pray," says he, on going in, "ask Miss Kicksey if I may see
her for a single moment." And down comes Miss Kicksey, quite
smiling, and happy to see him.

"Law, Mr. Deuceace!" says she, trying to blush as hard as
ever she could, "you quite surprise me! I don't know whether
I ought, really, being alone, to admit a gentleman."

"Nay, don't say so, dear Miss Kicksey! for do you know, I
came here for a double purpose—to ask about a pocket-book
which I have lost, and may, perhaps, have left here; and then, to
ask you if you will have the great goodness to pity a solitary
bachelor, and give him a cup of your nice tea?"

Nice tea! I thot I should have split; for, I'm blest if master
had eaten a morsle of dinner!

Never mind: down to tea they sate. "Do you take cream and
sugar, dear sir?" says poar Kicksey, with a voice as tender as
a tuttle-duff.

"Both, dearest Miss Kicksey!" answers master; and stowed
in a power of sashong and muffinx which would have done honour
to a washawoman.

I shan't describe the conversation that took place betwigst
master and this young lady. The reader, praps, knows y Deuceace took the trouble to talk to her for an hour, and to swallow all
her tea. He wanted to find out from her all she knew about the
famly money matters, and settle at once which of the two
Griffinses he should marry.

The poar thing, of cors, was no match for such a man as my
master. In a quarter of an hour, he had, if I may use the
igspression, "turned her inside out." He knew every thing that
she knew, and that, poar creature, was very little. There was
nine thousand a year, she had heard say, in money, in houses, in
banks in Injar, and what not. Boath the ladies signed papers for
selling or buying, and the money seemed equilly divided betwigst
them.

Nine thousand a year! Deuceace went away, his cheex tingling,
his heart beating. He, without a penny, could nex morning, if
he liked, be master of five thousand per hannum!

Yes. But how? Which had the money, the mother or the
daughter? All the tea-drinking had not taught him this piece of

nollidge; and Deuceace thought it a pity that he could not
marry both.

   *   *   *   *   *   *

The ladies came back at night, mightaly pleased with their
reception at the ambasdor's; and, stepping out of their carridge,
bid coachmin drive on with a gentlemin, who had handed them
out—a stout old gentlemin, who shook hands most tenderly at
parting, and promised to call often upon my Lady Griffin. He
was so polite, that he wanted to mount the stairs with her ladyship; but no, she would not suffer it. "Edward," says she to
the coachmin, quite loud, and pleased that all the people in the
hotel should hear her, "you will take the carriage, and drive *his*
lordship home." Now, can you guess who his lordship was? The
Right Hon. the Earl of Crabs, to be sure; the very old genlmn
whom I had seen on such charming terms with his son the day
before. Master knew this the nex day, and began to think he had
been a fool to deny his pa the thousand pound.

Now, though the suckmstansies of the dinner at the ambasdor's
only came to my years some time after, I may as well relate 'em
here, word for word, as they was told me by the very genlmn who
waited behind Lord Crabseses chair.

There was only a "*petty comity*" at dinner, as Lady Bobtail
said; and my Lord Crabs was placed betwigst the two Griffinses,
being mighty ellygant and palite to both. "Allow me," says he
to Lady G. (between the soop and the fish), "my dear madam, to
thank you—fervently thank you, for your goodness to my poor
boy. Your ladyship is too young to experience, but, I am sure,
far too tender not to understand the gratitude which must fill a
fond parent's heart for kindness shown to his child. Believe me,"
says my lord, looking her full and tenderly in the face, "that the
favours you have done to another have been done equally to
myself, and awaken in my bosom the same grateful and affectionate feelings with which you have already inspired my son
Algernon."

Lady Griffin blusht, and droopt her head till her ringlets fell
into her fish-plate: and she swallowed Lord Crabs's flumry just
as she would so many musharuins. My lord (whose powers of
slack-jaw was notoarious) nex addrast another spitch to Miss

Griffin. He said he'd heard how Deuceace was *situated*. Miss blusht—what a happy dog he was—Miss blusht crimson, and then he sighed deeply, and began eating his turbat and lobster sos. Master was a good un at flumry, but, law bless you! he was no moar equill to the old man than a molehill is to a mounting. Before the night was over, he had made as much progress as another man would in a ear. One almost forgot his red nose and his big stomick, and his wicked leering i's, in his gentle insiniwating woice, his fund of annygoats, and, above all, the bewtifle, morl, religious, and honrabble toan of his genral conversation. Praps you will say that these ladies were, for such rich pipple, mightily esaly captivated; but recklect, my dear sir, that they were fresh from Injar,—that they'd not sean many lords,—that they adoared the peeridge, as every honest woman does in England who has proper feelinx, and has read the fashnabble novvles,—and that here at Paris was their fust step into fashnabble sosiaty.

Well, after dinner, while Miss Matilda was singing "*Die tantie*," or "*Dip your chair*," or some of them sellabrated Italyian hairs (when she began this squall, hang me if she'd ever stop), my lord gets hold of Lady Griffin again, and gradgaly begins to talk to her in a very different strane.

"What a blessing it is for us all," says he, "that Algernon has found a friend so respectable as your ladyship."

"Indeed, my lord; and why? I suppose I am not the only respectable friend that Mr. Deuceace has?"

"No, surely; not the only one he *has had*: his birth, and, permit me to say, his relationship to myself, have procured him many. But—" (here my lord heaved a very affecting and large sigh.)

"But what?" says my lady, laffing at the igspression of his dismal face. "You don't mean that Mr. Deuceace has lost them or is unworthy of them?"

"I trust not, my dear madam, I trust not; but he is wild, thoughtless, extravagant, and embarrassed: and you know a man under these circumstances is not very particular as to his associates."

"Embarrassed? Good heavens! He says he has two thousand a-year left him by a god-mother; and he does not seem even to spend his income—a very handsome independence, too, for a bachelor."

My lord nodded his head sadly, and said,—" Will your ladyship give me your word of honour to be secret ?   My son has but a thousand a-year, which I allow him, and is heavily in debt.   He has played, madam, I fear; and for this reason I am so glad to hear that he is in a respectable domestic circle, where he may learn, in the presence of far greater and purer attractions, to forget the dice-box, and the low company which has been his bane."

My lady Griffin looked very grave indeed.   Was it true ?   Was Deuceace sincere 'in his professions of love, or was he only a sharper wooing her for her money?   Could she doubt her informer ? his own father, and, what's more, a real flesh and blood pear of parlyment ?   She determined she would try him.   Praps she did not know she had liked Deuceace so much, until she kem to feel how much she should *hate* him, if she found he'd been playing her false.

The evening was over, and back they came, as wee've seen,—my lord driving home in my lady's carridge, her ladyship and Miss walking up stairs to their own apartmince.

Here, for a wonder, was poar Miss Kicksy quite happy and smiling, and evidently full of a secret,—something mighty plea- sant to judge from her loox.   She did not long keep it.   As she was making tea for the ladies (for in that house they took a cup regular before bedtime), " Well, my lady," says she, " who do you think has been to drink tea with me ? "   Poar thing, a frendly face was an event in her life—a tea-party quite a hera !

" Why, perhaps, Lenoir, my maid," says my lady, looking grave. "I wish, Miss Kicksy, you would not demean yourself by mixing with my domestics.   Recollect, madam, that you are sister to Lady Griffin."

" No, my lady, it was not Lenoir; it was a gentleman, and a handsome gentleman, too."

" Oh, it was Monsieur de l'Orge, then," says miss ; " he pro- mised to bring me some guitar-strings."

" No, nor yet M. de l'Orge.   He came, but was not so polite as to ask for me.   What do you think of your own beau, the honourable Mr. Algernon Deuceace;" and, so saying, poar Kicksey clapped her hands together, and looked as joyfle as if she'd come into a fortin.

"Mr. Deuceace here; and why, pray?" says my lady, who reckleeted all that his exlent pa had been saying to her.

"Why, in the first place, he had left his pocket-book, and in the second, he wanted, he said, a dish of my nice tea, which he took, and stayed with me an hour, or moar."

"And pray Miss Kicksey," said Miss Matilda, quite contempshusly, "what may have been the subject of your conversation with Mr. Algernon? Did you talk politics, or music, or fine arts, or metaphysics?" Miss M. being what was called a *blue* (as most hump-backed women in sosiaty are), always made a pint to speak on these grand subjects.

"No, indeed; he talked of no such awful matters. If he had, you know, Matilda, I should never have understood him. First we talked about the weather, next about muffins and crumpets. Crumpets, he said, he liked best; and then we talked (here Miss Kicksy's voice fell) about poor dear Sir George in heaven! what a good husband he was, and——"

"What a good fortune he left,—eh, Miss Kicksy?" says my lady, with a hard, snearing voice, and a diabollicle grin.

"Yes, dear Leonora, he spoke so respectfully of your blessed husband, and seemed so anxious about you and Matilda, it was quite charming to hear him, dear man!"

"And pray, Miss Kicksy, what did you tell him?"

"Oh, I told him that you and Leonora had nine thousand a-year, and ——"

"What then?"

"Why nothing; that is all I know. I am sure, I wish I had ninety," says poor Kicksy, her eyes turning to heaven.

"Ninety fiddlesticks! Did not Mr. Deuceace ask how the money was left, and to which of us?"

"Yes; but I could not tell him."

"I knew it!" says my lady, slapping down her teacup,—"I knew it!"

"Well!" says Miss Matilda, "and why not Lady Griffin? There is no reason you should break your teacup, because Algernon asks a harmless question. *He* is not mercenary; he is all candour,

innocence, generosity! He is himself blest with a sufficient portion of the world's goods to be content; and often and often has
he told me, he hoped the woman of his choice might come to him
without a penny, that he might show the purity of his affection."

"I've no doubt," says my lady. "Perhaps the lady of his
choice is Miss Matilda Griffin!" and she flung out of the room,
slamming the door, and leaving Miss Matilda to bust into tears, as
was her reglar custom, and pour her loves and woas into the buzzom
of Miss Kicksy.

CHAPTER IV.

"HITTING THE NALE ON THE HEDD."

THE nex morning, down came me and master to Lady Griffinses,
—I amusing myself with the gals in the antyroom, he paying his
devours to the ladies in the salong. Miss was thrumming on her
gitter; my lady was before a great box of papers, busy with
accounts, bankers' books, lawyers' letters, and what not. Law
bless us! it's a kind of bisniss I should like well enuff, especially
when my hannual account was seven or eight thousand on the
right side, like my lady's. My lady in this house kep all these
matters to herself. Miss was a vast deal too sentrimentle to mind
business.

Miss Matilda's eyes sparkled as master came in; she pinted
gracefully to a place on the sofy beside her, which Deuceace took.
My lady only looked up for a moment, smiled very kindly, and
down went her head among the papers agen, as busy as a B.

"Lady Griffin has had letters from London," says miss, "from
nasty lawyers and people. Come here and sit by me, you naughty
man, you!"

And down sat master. "Willingly," says he, "my dear Miss
Griffin; why, I declare, it is quite a *tête-à-tête*."

"Well," says miss (after the prillimnary flumries, in coarse),
"we met a friend of yours at the embassy, Mr. Deuceace."

"My father, doubtless; he is a great friend of the ambassador,
and surprised me myself by a visit the night before last."

"What a dear delightful old man! how hn loves you, Mr.
Deuceace!"

"Oh, amazingly!" says master, throwing his i's to heaven. "He spoke of nothing but you, and such praises of you!"

Master breathed more freely. "He is very good, my dear father; but blind, as all fathers are, he is so partial and attached to me."

"He spoke of you being his favourite child, and regretted that you were not his eldest son. 'I can but leave him the small portion of a younger brother,' he said; 'but never mind, he has talents, a noble name, and an independence of his own.'"

"An independence? yes, oh yes! I am quite independent of my father."

"Two thousand pounds a-year left you by your godmother; the very same you told us you know."

"Neither more nor less," says master, bobbing his head; "a sufficiency, my dear Miss Griffin,—to a man of my moderate habits an ample provision."

"By-the-by," cries out Lady Griffin, interruping the conversation, "you who are talking about money matters there, I wish you would come to the aid of poor *me!* Come, naughty boy, and help me out with this long long sum."

Didnt he go—that's all! My i, how his i's shone, as he skipt across the room, and seated himself by my lady!

"Look!" said she, "my agents write me over that they have received a remittance of 7200 rupees, at 2*s.* 9*d.* a rupee. Do tell me what the sum is, in pounds and shillings;" which master did with great gravity.

"Nine hundred and ninety pounds. Good; I dare say you are right. I'm sure I can't go through the fatigue to see. And now comes another question. Whose money is this, mine or Matilda's? You see it is the interest of a sum in India, which we have not had occasion to touch; and, according to the terms of poor Sir George's will, I really don't know how to dispose of the money except to spend it. Matilda, what shall we do with it?"

"La, ma'am, I wish you would arrange the business yourself."

"Well, then, Algernon, *you* tell me;" and she laid her hand on his, and looked him most pathetickly in the face.

"Why," says he, "I don't know how Sir George left his money; you must let me see his will, first."

" Oh, willingly."

Master's chair seemed suddenly to have got springs in the cushns ; he was obliged to *hold himself down.*

" Look here, I have only a copy, taken by my hand from Sir George's own manuscript. Soldiers, you know, do not employ lawyers much, and this was written on the night before going into action." And she read, " ' I, George Griffin,' &c. &c.—you know how these things begin—' being now of sane mind '—um, um, um, —' leave to my friends, Thomas Abraham Hicks, a colonel in the H. E. I. Company's Service, and to John Monro Mackirkincroft (of the house of Huffle, Mackirkincroft, and Dobbs, at Calcutta), the whole of my property, to be realised as speedily as·they may (consistently with the interests of the property), in trust for my wife, Leonora Emilia Griffin (born L. E. Kicksy), and my only legitimate child, Matilda Griffin. The interest resulting from such property to be paid to them, share and share alike ; the principal to remain untouched, in the names of the said T. A. Hicks and J. M. Mackirkincroft, until the death of my wife, Leonora Emilia Griffin, when it shall be paid to my daughter, Matilda Griffin, her heirs, executors, or assigns.' "

" There," said my lady, " we won't read any more ; all the rest is stuff. But, now you know the whole business, tell us what is to be done with the money ? "

" Why, the money, unquestionably, should be divided between you."

" *Tant mieux,* say I, I really thought it had been all Matilda's."

    *   *   *   *   *   *

There was a paws for a minit or two after the will had been read. Master left the desk at which he had been seated with her ladyship, paced up and down the room for a while, and then came round to the place where Miss Matilda was seated. At last he said, in a low, trembling voice,

" I am almost sorry, my dear Lady Griffin, that you have read that will to me; for an attachment such as must seem, I fear, mercenary, when the object of it is so greatly favoured by worldly fortune. Miss Griffin—Matilda ! I know I may say the word; your dear eyes grant me the permission. I need not tell you, or you, dear mother-in-law, how long, how fondly, I have adored you.

My tender, my beautiful Matilda, I will not affect to say I have not read your heart ere this, and that I have not known the preference with which you have honoured me. *Speak it*, dear girl! from your own sweet lips, in the presence of an affectionate pareut, utter the sentence which is to seal my happiness for life. Matilda, dearest Matilda! say, oh say, that you love me!"

Miss M. shivered, turned pail, rowled her eyes about, and fell on master's neck, whispering hodibly, "*I do!*"

My lady looked at the pair for a moment with her teeth grinding, her i's glaring, her busm throbbing, and her face chock white, for all the world like Madam Pasty, in the oppra of *Mydear* (when she's goin to mudder her childring, you recklect), and out she flounced from the room, without a word, knocking down poar me, who happened to be very near the dor, and leaving my master along with his crook-back mistress.

I've repotted the speech he made to her pretty well. The fact is, I got it in a ruff copy, which, if any boddy likes, they may see at Mr. Frazierses, only on the copy it's wrote, "*Lady Griffin, Leonora!*" instead of "*Miss Griffin, Matilda*," as in the abuff, and so on.

Master had hit the right nail on the head this time, he thought; but his adventors an't over yet.

CHAPTER V.

THE GRIFFIN'S CLAWS.

WELL, master had hit the right nail on the head this time: thanx to luck—the crooked one, to be sure, but then it had the *goold nobb*, which was the part Deuceace most valued, as well he should; being a connyshure as to the relletiff valyou of pretious metals, and much preferring virging goold like this to poor old battered iron like my Lady Griffin.

And so, in spite of his father (at which old noblemin Mr. Deuceace now snapt his fingers), in spite of his detts (which, to do him Justas, had never stood much in his way), and in spite of his povatty, idleness, extravagans, swindling, and debotcheries of all kinds (which an't *generally* very favorabble to a young man who has to make his way in the world); in spite of all, there he was, I

say, at the topp of the trea, the fewcher master of a perfect
fortun, the defianced husband of a fool of a wife. What can
mortial man want more? Vishns of ambishn now occupied his
soal. Shooting boxes, oppra boxes, money boxes, always full;
hunters at Melton; a seat in the House of Commins, Heaven
knows what! and not a poar footman, who only describes what
he's seen, and can't in cors, pennytrate into the idears and the
busms of men.

You may be shore that the three-cornerd noats came pretty
thick now from the Griffinses. Miss was always a writing them
befoar; and now, nite, noon, and mornink, breakfast, dinner, and
sopper, in they came, till my pantry (for master never read 'em,
and I carried 'em out) was puffickly intolrabble from the odor of
musk, ambygrease, bargymot, and other sense with which they
were impregniated. Here's the contense of three on 'em, which
I've kep in my dex these twenty years as skewriosities. Faw! I
can smel 'em at this very minit, as I am copying them down.

BILLY DOO. No. I.

" Monday morning, 2 o'clock.

" 'Tis the witching hour of night. Luna illumines my chamber, and falls upon my sleepless pillow. By her light I am
inditing these words to thee, my Algernon. My brave and beautiful, my soul's lord! when shall the time come when the tedious
night shall not separate us, nor the blessed day? Twelve! one!
two! I have heard the bells chime, and the quarters, and never
cease to think of my husband. My adored Percy, pardon the
girlish confession,—I have kissed the letter at this place. Will
thy lips press it too, and remain for a moment on the spot which
has been equally saluted by your

" MATILDA ? "

This was the *fust* letter, and was brot to our house by one of
the poar footmin, Fitzclarence, at sicks o'clock in the morning.
I thot it was for life and death, and woak master at that extraor-
nary hour, and gave it to him. I shall never forgit him, when he
red it; he cramped it up, and he cust and swoar, applying to the

lady who roat, the genlmn that brought it, and me who introjuiced it to his notice, such a collection of epitafs as I seldum
hered, excep at Billinxgit. The fact is thiss, for a fust letter,
miss's noat was *rather* too strong, and sentymentle. But that
was her way; she was always reading melancholy stoary books—
Thaduse of Wawsaw, the Sorrows of Mac Whirter, and
such like.

After about 6 of them, master never yoused to read them; but
handid them over to me, to see if there was any think in them
which must be answered, in order to kip up appearuntses. The
next letter is

"No. II.

"Beloved! to what strange madnesses will passion lead one!
Lady Griffin, since your avowal yesterday, has not spoken a word
to your poor Matilda; has declared that she will admit no one
(heigho! not even you, my Algernon); and has locked herself in
her own dressing-room. I do believe that she is *jealous*, and
fancies that you were in love with *her!* Ha, ha! I could have
told her *another tale*—n'est-ce pas? Adieu, adieu, adieu! A
thousand, thousand, million kisses!

"M. G.

"*Monday afternoon, 2 o'clock.*"

There was another letter kem before bedtime; for though me
and master called at the Griffinses, we wairnt aloud to enter at
no price. Mortimer and Fitzclarence grind at me, as much as to
say we were going to be relations; but I dont spose master was
very sorry when he was obleached to come back without seeing
the fare objict of his affeckshns.

Well, on Chewsdy there was the same game; ditto on Wens-
day; only, when we called there, who should we see but our father,
Lord Crabs, who was waiving his hand to Miss Kicksey, and
saying *he should be back to dinner at* 7, just as me and master
came up the stares. There was no admittns for us though.
"Bah! bah! never mind," says my lord, taking his son affeckshn-
ately by the hand. "What, two strings to your bow; ay,
Algernon? The dowager a little jealous, miss a little lovesick.

ꝍ

But my lady's fit of anger will vanish, and I promise you, my boy, that you shall see your fair one to-morrow."

And, so saying, my lord walked master down stares, looking at him as tender and affeckshnat, and speaking to him as sweet as posbill. Master did not know what to think of it. He never new what game his old father was at; only he somehow felt that he had got his head in a net, in spite of his suxess on Sunday. I knew it—I knew it quite well, as soon as I saw the old genlmn igsammin him, by a kind of smile which came over his old face, and was somethink betwigst the angellic and the direbollicle.

But master's dowts were cleared up nex day, and every thing was bright again. At brexfast, in comes a note with inclosier, boath of witch I here copy:

"No. IX.

"Thursday morning.

"Victoria, Victoria! Mamma has yielded at last; not her consent to our union, but her consent to receive you as before; and has promised to forget the past. Silly woman, how could she ever think of you as anything but the lover of your Matilda? I am in a whirl of delicious joy and passionate excitement. I have been awake all this long night, thinking of thee, my Algernon, and longing for the blissful hour of meeting.

"Come!   M. G."

This is the inclosier from my lady:

"I will not tell you that your behaviour on Sunday did not deeply shock me. I had been foolish enough to think of other plans, and to fancy your heart (if you had any) was fixed elsewhere than on one at whose foibles you have often laughed with me, and whose person at least cannot have charmed you.

"My step-daughter will not, I presume, marry without at least going through the ceremony of asking my consent; I cannot, as yet, give it. Have I not reason to doubt whether she will be happy in trusting herself to you?

"But she is of age, and has the right to receive in her own house all those who may be agreeable to her,—certainly you, who are likely to be one day so nearly connected with her. If I have honest reason to believe that your love for Miss Griffin is sincere; if I find in a few months that you yourself are still desirous to marry her, I can, of course, place no further obstacles iu your way.

"You are welcome, then, to return to our hotel. I cannot promise to receive you as I did of old; you would despise me if I did. I can promise, however, to think no more of all that has passed between us, and yield up my own happiness for that of the daughter of my dear husband.

"L. E. G."

Well, now, an't this a manly, straitforard letter enough, and natral from a woman whom we had, to coufess the truth, treated most scuvvily? Master thought so, and went and made a tender, respeckful speach to Lady Griffin (a little flumry cqsts nothink). Grave and sorrofle he kist her hand, and, speakin in a very low adgitayted voice, calld Hevn to witness how he deplord that his conduct should ever have given rise to such an unfortnt ideer; but if he might offer her esteem, respect, the warmest and tenderest admiration, he trusted she would accept the same, and a deal moar flumry of the kind, with dark, sollum, glansis of thȯ eyes, and plenty of white pockit hankercher.

He thought he'd make all safe. Poar fool! he was in a net— sich a net as I never yet see set to ketch a roag in.

CHAPTER VI.

THE JEWEL.

THE Shevalier de l'Orge, the young Frenchmin whom I wrote of in my last, who had been rather shy of his visits while master was coming it so very strong, now came back to his old place by the side of Lady Griffin; there was no love now, though, betwigst him and master, although the shevallier had got his lady back agin, Deuceace being compleatly devoted to his crookid Veanus.

The shevalier was a little, pale, moddist, insinifishnt creature; and I shoodn't have thought, from his appearants, would have the

heart to do harm to a fli, much less to stand befor such a tre-
mendious tiger and fire-eater as my master. But I see putty
well, after a week, from his manner of going on—of speakin at
master, and lookin at him, and olding his lips tight when Deuceace
came into the room, and glaring at him with his i's, that he hated
the Honrabble Algernon Percy.

Shall I tell you why? Because my Lady Griffin hated him;
hated him wuss than pison, or the devvle, or even wuss than her
daughter-in-law. Praps you phansy that the letter you have juss
red was honest; praps you amadgin that the sean of the reading
of the wil came on by mere chans, and in the reglar cors of
suckinstansies: it was all a *game*, I tell you—a reglar trap; and
that extrodnar clever young man, my master, as neatly put his
foot into it, as ever a pocher did in fesnt preserve.

The shevalier had his q from Lady Griffin. When Deuceace
went off the feald, back came De l'Orge to her feet, not a witt
less tender than befor. Por fellow, por fellow! he really loved
this woman. He might as well have foln in love with a borecon-
structor! He was so blinded and beat by the power wich she
had got over him, that if she told him black was white he'd
beleave it, or if she ordered him to commit murder, he'd do it—
she wanted something very like it, I can tell you.

I've already said how, in the fust part of their acquaintance,
master used to laff at De l'Orge's bad Inglish, and funny
ways. The little creature had a thowsnd of these; and being
small, and a Frenchman, master, in cors, looked on him with
that good-humoured kind of contemp which a good Brittn ot
always to show. He rayther treated him like an intelligent
munky than a man, and ordered him about as if he'd bean my
lady's footman.

All this munseer took in very good part, until after the quarl
betwigst master and Lady Griffin; when that lady took care to
turn the tables. Whenever master and miss were not present
(as I've heard the servants say), she used to laff at shevalliay for
his obeajance and sivillatty to master. "For her part, she won-
dered how a man of his birth could act a servnt; how any man
could submit to such contemsheous behaviour from another; and
then she told him how Deuceace was always sneariug at him

behind his back; how, in fact, he ought to hate him corjaly, aud
how it was suttnly time to show his sperrit."

Well, the poar little man beleaved all this from his hart, and
was angry or pleased, gentle or quarlsum, igsactly as my lady
liked. There got to be frequiut rows betwigst him and master;
sharp words flung at each other across the dinner-table; dispewts
about handing ladies their smeling-botls, or seeing them to their
carridge; or going in and out of a roam fust, or any such
nonsince.

" For Hevn's sake," I heerd my lady, in the midl of one of these
tiffs, say, pail, and the tears trembling in her i's, " do, do be calm
Mr. Deuceace. Monsieur de l'Orge, I beseech you to forgive
him. You are, both of you, so esteemed, lov'd, by members of
this family, that for its peace as well as your own, you should
forbear to quarrel."

It was on the way to the Sally Mangy that this brangling had
begun, and it ended jest as they were seating themselves. I shall
never forgit poar little De l'Orge's eyes, when my lady said "*both*
of you." He stair'd at my lady for a momint, turned pail, red,
look'd wild, and then, going round to master, shook his hand as if
he would have wrung it off. Mr. Deuceace only bowd and grind,
and turned away quite stately; miss heaved a loud O from her
busm, and lookd up in his face with an igspreshn, jest as if she
could have eat him up with love; and the little shevalliay sate
down to his soop-plate, and wus so happy, that I'm blest if he
wasn't crying! He thought the widdow had made her declyra-
tion, and would have him; and so thought Deuceace, who lookd
at her for some time mighty bitter and contempshus, and then
fell a talking with miss.

Now, though master didn't choose to marry for Lady Griffin,
as he might have done, he yet thought fit to be very angry at the
notion of her marrying any body else: and so, consquintly, was
in a fewry at this confision which she had made regarding her
parshaleaty for the French shevaleer.

And this I've perseaved in the cors of my expearants through
life, that when you vex him, a roag's no longer a roag; you find
him out at onst when he's in a passion, for he shows, as it ware,
his cloven foot the very instnt you tread on it. At least, this is

what *young* roags do; it requires very cool blood and long practis
to get over this pint, and not to show your pashn when you feel
it, and snarl when you are angry.   Old Crabs wouldn't do it
being like another noblemin, of whom I heard the Duke of Wellington say, while waiting behind his graci's chair, that if you
were kicking him from behind, no one standing before him wuld
know it, from the bewtifle smiling igspreshn of his face.   Young
Master hadn't got so far in the thief's grammer, and, when he was
angry, showd it.   And it's also to be remarked (a very profownd
observatiu for a footmin, but we have i's though we *do* wear plush
britchis), it's to be remarked, I say, that one of these chaps is
much sooner maid angry than another, because honest men yield
to other people, roags never do ; honest men love other people,
roags only themselves ; and the slightest thing which comes in the
way of thir beloved objects sets them fewrious.   Master hadn't
led a life of gambling, swindling, and every kind of debotch to be
good tempered at the end of it, I prommis you.

He was in a pashun, and when he *was* in a pashn, a more insalent,
insuffrable, overbearing broot didn't live.

This was the very pint to which my lady wished to bring him;
for I must tell you, that though she had been trying all her might
to set master and the shevalliay by the years, she had suxcaded
only so far as to make them hate each profowndly ; but somehow
or other, the 2 cox wouldnt *fight.*

I doan't think Deuceace ever suspected any game on the part
of her ladyship, for she carried it on so admirally, that the quarls
which daily took place betwigst him and the Frenchman never
seemed to come from her ; on the contry, she acted as the reglar
pease-maker between them, as I've just shown in the tiff which
took place at the door of the Sally Mangy.   Besides, the 2 young
men, thoagh reddy enough to snarl, were natrally unwilling to cum
to bloes.   I'll tell you why : being friends, and idle, they spent
their mornins as young fashnabbles genrally do, at billiads, fensing,
riding, pistle-shooting, or some such improoving study.   In billiads,
master beat the Frenchmn hollow (and had won a pretious sight
of money from him, but that's neither here nor there, or, as the
French say, *ontry noo*) ; at pistle-shooting, master could knock
down eight immidges out of ten, and De l'Orge seven ; and in

fensing, the Frenchman could pink the Honorable Algernon down evry one of his weskit buttns. They'd each of them been out more than onst, for every Frenchman will fight, and master had been obleag'd to do so in the cors of his bisniss; and knowing each other's curridg, as well as the fact that either could put a hundrid bolls running into a hat at 30 yards, they wairn't *very* willing to try such exparrymence upon their own hats with their own heads in them. So you see they kep quiet, and only grould at each other.

But to-day Deuceace was in one of his thundering black humers; and when in this way he wouldnt stop for man or devvle. I said that he walked away from the shevalliay, who had given him his hand in his sudden bust of joyfle good-humour, and who, I do bleave, would have hugd a she-bear, so very happy was he. Master walked away from him pale and hotty, and, taking his seat at table, no moor mindid the brandishments of Miss Griffin, but only replied to them with a pshaw, or a dam at one of us servnts, or abuse of the soop, or the wine; cussing and swearing like a trooper, and not like a wel-bred son of a noble Brittish peer.

" Will your ladyship," says he, slivering off the wing of a *pully ally bashymall*, " allow me to help you ?' "

" I thank you! no; but I will trouble Monsieur de l'Orge." And towards that gnlmn she turned, with a most tender and fasnating smile.

" Your ladyship has taken a very sudden admiration for Mr. de l'Orge's carving. You used to like mine once."

" You are very skilful ; but to-day, if you will allow me, I will partake of something a little simpler."

The Frenchman helped ; and, being so happy, in cors, spilt the gravy. A great blob of brown sos spurted on to master's chick, and myandrewd down his shert collar and virging-white weskit.

" Confound you!" says he, " M. de l'Orge, you have done this on purpose." And down went his knife and fork, over went his tumbler of wine, a deal of it into poar Miss Griffinses lap, who looked fritened and ready to cry.

My lady bust into a fit of laffin, peel upon peel, as if it was the best joak in the world. De l'Orge giggled and grind too.

"*Pardong*," says he; "*meal pardong, mong share munseer.*"
And he looked as if he would have done it again for a penny.

The little Frenchman was quite in exstasis; he found himself
all of a suddn at the very top of the trea; and the laff for onst
turned against his rivle, he actialy had the ordassaty to propose
to my lady in English to take a glass of wine.

" Veal you," says he, in his jargin, " take a glas of Madére viz
me, mi ladi ? "   And he looked round, as if he'd igsackly hit the
English manner and pronunciation.

"With the greatest pleasure," says Lady G., most graciously
nodding at him, and gazing at him as she drank up the wine. She'd
refused master befor, and *this* didn't increase his good humer.

Well, they went on, master snarling, snapping, and swearing,
making himself, I must confess, as much of a blaggard as any I
ever see; and my lady employing her time betwigst him and the
shevalliay, doing every think to irritate master, and flatter the
Frenchmn.   Desert came; and by this time, miss was stock-still
with fright, the chevaleer half tipsy with pleasure and gratafied
vannaty.   My lady puffickly raygent with smiles, and master bloo
with rage.

" Mr. Deuceace," says my lady, in a most winning voice, after
a little chaffing (in which she only worked him up moar and
moar), " may I trouble you for a few of those grapes ? they look
delicious."

For answer, master seas'd hold of the grayp dish, and sent it
sliding down the table to De l'Orge; upsetting, in his way, fruit-
plates, glasses, dickanters, and Heaven knows what.

" Monsieur de l'Orge," says he, shouting out at the top of his
voice, " have the goodness to help Lady Griffin. She wanted *my*
grapes long ago, and has found out they are sour ! "

*   *   *   *   *   *

There was a dead paws of a moment or so.

*   *   *   *   *   *

"*Ah !* " says my lady, " *vous osez m'insulter, devant mes gens,
dans ma propre maison—c'est par trop fort, monsieur.*"   And up

---

* In the long dialogues, we have generally ventured to change the peculiar
spelling of our friend, Mr. Yellowplush.

she got, and flung out of the room. Miss followed her, screeching out, "Mamma—for God's sake—Lady Griffin!" and here the door slammed on the pair.

Her ladyship did very well to speak French. *De l'Orge would not have understood her else;* as it was he heard quite enough; and as the door clikt too, in the presents of me, and Messeers Mortimer and Fitzclarence, the family footmen, he walks round to my master, and hits him a slap on the face, and says, "*Prends ça menteur et lâche!*" Which means, "Take that, you liar and coward!"—rayther strong igspreshns for one genlmn to use to another.

Master staggered back, and looked bewildered; and then he gave a kind of a scream, and then he made a run at the Frenchman, and then me and Mortimer flung ourselves upon him, whilst Fitzclarence embraced the shevalliay.

"*A demain!*" says he, clinching his little fist, and walking away not very sorry to git off.

When he was fairly down stares, we let go of master: who swallowed a goblit of water, and then pawsing a little, and pulling out his pus, he presented to Messeers Mortimer and Fitzclarence a luydor each. "I will give you five more to-morrow," says he, "if you will promise to keep this secrit."

And then he walked into the ladies. "If you knew," says he, going up to Lady Griffin, and speaking very slow (in cors we were all at the keyhole), "the pain I have endured in the last minute, in consequence of the rudeness and insolence of which I have been guilty to your ladyship, you would think my own remorse was punishment sufficient, and would grant me pardon."

My lady bowed, and said she didn't wish for explanations. Mr. Deuceace was her daughter's guest, and not hers; but she certainly would never demean herself by sitting again at table with him. And so saying, out she boltid again.

"Oh! Algernon! Algernon!" says miss, in teers, "what is this dreadful mystery—these fearful, shocking quarrels? Tell me, has anything happened? Where, where is the chevalier?"

Master smiled, and said, "Be under no alarm, my sweetest Matilda. De l'Orge did not understand a word of the dispute;

he was too much in love for that. He is but gone away for half an hour, I believe; and will return to coffee."

I knew what master's game was, for if miss had got a hinkling of the quarrel betwigst him and the Frenchman, we should have had her screeming at the Hotel Mirabeu, and the juice and all to pay. He only stopt for a few minuits, and cumfitted her, and then drove off to his friend, Captain Bullseye, of the Rifles; with whom I spose, he talked over this unplesnt bisniss. We fownd, at our hotel, a note from De l'Orge, saying where his secknd was to be seen.

Two mornings after there was a parrowgraf in *Gallynanny's Messinger*, which I hear beg leaf to transcribe :—

"*Fearful Duel.*—Yesterday morning, at six o'clock, a meeting took place, in the Bois de Boulogne, between the Hon. A. P. D—ce—ce, a younger son of the Earl of Cr—bs, and the Chevalier de l'O——. The chevalier was attended by Major de M——, of the Royal Guard, and the Hon. Mr. D—— by Captain B—lls—ye, of the British Rifle Corps. As far as we have been able to learn the particulars of this deplorable affair, the dispute originated in the house of a lovely lady (one of the most brilliant ornaments of our embassy), and the duel took place on the morning ensuing.

"The chevalier (the challenged party, and the most accomplished amateur swordsman in Paris) waived his right of choosing the weapons, and the combat took place with pistols.

"The combatants were placed at forty paces, with directions to advance to a barrier which separated them only eight paces. Each was furnished with two pistols. Monsieur de l'O—— fired almost immediately, and the ball took effect in the left wrist of his antagonist, who dropped the pistol which he held in that hand. He fired, however, directly with his right, and the chevalier fell to the ground, we fear mortally wounded. A ball has entered above his hip-joint, and there is very little hope that he can recover.

"We have heard that the cause of this desperate duel was a blow, which the chevalier ventured to give to the Hon. Mr. D. If so, there is some reason for the unusual and determined manner in which the duel was fought.

"Mr. Deu—a—e returned to his hotel; whither his excellent father, the Right Hon. Earl of Cr—bs, immediately hastened on hearing of the sad news, and is now bestowing on his son the most affectionate parental attention. The news only reached his lordship yesterday at noon, while at breakfast with his excellency, Lord Bobtail, our ambassador. The noble earl fainted on receiving the intelligence; but in spite of the shock to his own nerves and health, persisted in passing last night by the couch of his son."

And so he did. "This is a sad business, Charles," says my lord to me, after seeing his son, and settling himself down in our salong. "Have you any segars in the house? And, hark ye, send me up a bottle of wine and some luncheon. I can certainly not leave the neighbourhood of my dear boy."

CHAPTER VII.

THE CONSQUINSIES.

THE shevalliay did not die, for the ball came out of it's own accord, in the midst of a violent fever and inflamayshn which was brot on by the wound. He was kept in bed for 6 weeks though, and did not recover for a long time after.

As for master, his lot, I'm sorry to say, was wuss than that of his advisary. Inflammation came on too; and, to make an ugly story short, they were obliged to take off his hand at the rist.

He bore it, in cors, like a Trojin, and in a month he too was well, and his wound heel'd; but I never see a man look so like a devvle as he used sometimes, when he looked down at the stump!

To be sure, in Miss Griffinses eyes, this only indeered him the mor. She sent twenty noats a day to ask for him, calling him her beloved, her unfortnat, her hero, her wictim, and I dono what. I've kep some of the noats as I tell you, and curiously sentimentle they are, beating the sorrows of Mac Whirter all to nothink.

Old Crabs used to come offen, and consumed a power of wine and seagars at our house. I bleave he was at Paris because there was an exycution in his own house in England; and his son was a sure find (as they say) during his illness, and couldn't deny himself to the old genlmn. His eveninx my lord spent reglar at Lady Griffin's, where, as master was ill, I didn't go any more now, and where the shevalier wasn't there to disturb him.

"You see how that woman hates you, Deuceace," says my lord, one day, in a fit of cander, after they had been talking about Lady Griffin: "*she has not done with you yet*, I tell you fairly."

"Curse her," says master, in a fury, lifting up his maim'd arm —"curse her, but I will be even with her one day. I am sure of

Matilda; I took care to put that beyond the reach of a failure. The girl must marry me for her own sake."

"*For her own sake!* O ho! Good, good!" My lord lifted his i's, and said, gravely, "I understand, my dear boy: it is an excellent plan."

"Well," says master, grinning fearcely and knowingly at his exlent old father, "as the girl is safe, what harm can I fear from the fiend of a stepmother?"

My lord only gev a long whizzle, and, soon after, taking up his hat, walked off. I saw him sawnter down the Plas Vandome, and go in quite calmly to the old door of Lady Griffinses hotel. Bless his old face! such a puffickly good-natured, kind hearted, merry, selfish old scoundrel, I never shall see again.

His lordship was quite right in saying to master that "Lady Griffin hadn't done with him." No moar she had. But she never would have thought of the nex game she was going to play, *if somebody hadn't put her up to it.* Who did? If you red the above passidge, and saw how a venrabble old genlmn took his hat, and sauntered down the Plas Vandome (looking hard and kind at all the nussary-maids—*buns* they call them in France—in the way), I leave you to guess who was the author of the nex skeam: a woman, suttnly, never would have pitcht on it.

In the fuss payper which I wrote concerning Mr. Deuceace's adventers, and his kind behayviour to Messeers Dawkins and Blewitt, I had the honor of laying before the public a skidewl of my masters detts, in witch was the following itim:

"Bills of xchange and I.O.U's., 4963*l*. 0*s*. 0*d*."

The I.O.U.se were trifling, say a thowsnd pound. The bills amountid to four thowsnd moar.

Now, the lor is in France, that if a genlmn gives these in England, and a French genlmn gits them in any way, he can pursew the Englishman who has drawn them, even though he should be in France. Master did not know this fact—labouring under a very common mistak, that, when onst out of England, he might wissle at all the debts he left behind him.

My Lady Griffin sent over to her slissators in London, who made arrangemints with the persons who possest the fine collection of ortografs on stampt paper which master had left behind him;

and they were glad enuff to take any oppertunity of getting back their moncy.

One fine morning, as I was looking about in the court-yard of our hotel, talking to the servant gals, as was my reglar custom, in order to improve myself in the French languidge, one of them comes up to me and says, " Tenez, Monsieur Charles, down below in the office there is a bailiff, with a couple of gendarmes, who is asking for your master—*a-t-il des dettes par hasard?*"

I was struck all of a heap—the truth flasht on my mind's hi. "Toinette," says I, for that was the gal's name—"Toinette," says I, giving her a kiss, "keep them for two minnits, as you valyou my affeckshn;" and then I gave her another kiss, and ran up stares to our chambers. Master had now pretty well recovered of his wound, and was aloud to drive abowt; it was lucky for him that he had the strength to move. "Sir, sir," says I, "the bailiffs are after you, and you must run for your life."

"Bailiffs," says he: "nonsense! I don't, thank Heaven, owe a shilling to any man."

"Stuff, sir," says I, forgetting my respeck; "don't you owe money in England? I tell you the bailiffs are here, and will be on you in a moment."

As I spoke, cling cling, ling ling, goes the bell of the anty-shamber, and there they were sure enough!

What was to be done? Quick as litening, I throws off my livry coat, claps my goold lace hat on master's head, and makes him put on my livry. Then I wraps myself up in his dressing-gown, and lolling down on the sofa, bids him open the dor.

There they were—the bailiff—two jondarms with him— Toinette, and an old waiter. When Toinette sees master, she smiles, and says: "Dis donc, Charles! où est, donc, ton maitre? Chez lui, n'est-ce pas? C'est le jeune homme à monsieur," says she, curtsying to the bailiff.

The old waiter was just a going to blurt out, "Mais ce n'est pas!" when Toinette stops him, and says, "Laissez donc passer ces messieurs, vieux bête; " and in they walk, the 2 jon d'arms taking their post in the hall.

Master throws open the salong doar very gravely, and touching *my* hat says, "Have you any orders about the cab, sir?"

"Why, no, Chawls," says I ; "I shan't drive out to-day."

The old bailiff grinned, for he understood English (having had plenty of English customers), and says in French, as master goes out, "I think, sir, you had better let your servant get a coach, for I am under the painful necessity of arresting you, *au nom de la loi*, for the sum of ninety-eight thousand seven hundred francs, owed by you to the Sieur Jacques François Lebrun, of Paris ;" and he pulls out a number of bills, with master's acceptances on them sure enough.

"Take a chair, sir," says I ; and down he sits ; and I began to chaff him, as well as I could, about the weather, my illness, my sad axdent, having lost one of my hands, which was stuck into my busum, and so on.

At last after a minnit or two, I could contane no longer, and bust out in a horse laff.

The old fellow turned quite pail, and began to suspect something. "Hola !" says he ; "gendarmes ! à moi ! à moi ! Je suis floué, volé," which means, in English, that he was reglar sold.

The jondarmes jumped into the room, and so did Toinette and the waiter. Grasefly rising from my arm-chare, I took my hand from my dressing-gownd, and, flinging it open, stuck up on the chair one of the neatest legs ever seen.

I then pinted myjestickly—to what do you think?—to my PLUSH TITES ! those sellabrated inigspressables which have rendered me faymous in Yourope.

Taking the hint, the jondarmes and the servnts rord out laffing ; and so did Charles Yellowplush, Esquire, I can tell you. Old Grippard, the bailiff, looked as if he would faint in his chare.

I heard a kab galloping like mad out of the hotel-gate, and knew then that my master was safe.

CHAPTER VIII.

THE END OF MR. DEUCEACE'S HISTORY. LIMBO.

MY tail is droring rabidly to a close : my suvvice with Mr. Deuceace didn't continyou very long after the last chapter, in which I described my admiral strattyjam, and my singlar self-devocean. There's very few servnts, I can tell you, who'd have

thought of such a contrivance, and very few few moar would have
eggsycuted it when thought of.

But, after all, beyond the trifling advantich to myself in selling
master's roab de sham, which you, gentle reader, may remember I
woar, and in dixcovering a fipun note in one of the pockets,—
beyond this, I say, there was to poar master very little advantich
in what had been done. It's true he had escaped. Very good.
But Frans is not like Great Brittin; a man in a livry coat, with 1
arm, is pretty easly known, and caught, too, as I can tell
you.

Such was the case with master. He coodn leave Paris, moar-
over, if he would. What was to become, in that case, of his bride
—his unchbacked hairis? He knew that young lady's *temprimong*
(as the Parishers say) too well to let her long out of his site.
She had nine thousand a-yer. She'd been in love a duzn times
befor, and mite be agin. The Honrabble Algernon Deuceace was
a little too wide awake to trust much to the constnsy of so very
inflammable a young creacher. Heavn bless us, it was a marycle
she wasn't earlier married! I do bleave (from suttn seans that
past betwigst us) that she'd have married me, if she hadn't been
sejuiced by the supearor rank and indianuity of the genlmn in
whose survace I was.

Well, to use a commin igspreshn, the beaks were after him.
How was he to manitch? He coodn get away from his debts,
and he wooden quit the fare objict of his affeckshns. He was
ableejd, then, as the French say, to lie perdew,—going out at
night, like a howl out of a hivy-bush, and returning in the daytime
to his roast. For its a maxum in France (and I wood it were
followed in Ingland), that after dark no man is lible for his detts;
and in any of the royal gardens—the Twillaries, the Pally Roil, or
the Lucksimbug, for example—a man may wander from sunrise to
evening, and hear nothing of the ojus dunns: they an't admitted
into these places of public enjyment and rondyvoo any more than
dogs; the centuries at the garden-gate having orders to shuit all
such.

Master, then, was in this uncomfrable situation—neither liking
to go nor to stay! peeping out at nights to have an interview with
his miss; ableagd to shuffle off her repeated questions as to the

reason of all this disgeise, and to talk of his two thowend a-year, jest as if he had it, and didn't owe a shilling in the world.

Of course, now, he began to grow mighty eager for the marritch.

He roat as many noats as she had done befor; swoar against delay and cerymony; talked of the pleasures of Hyming, the ard-ship that the ardor of two arts should be allowed to igspire, the folly of waiting for the consent of Lady Griffin. She was but a step-mother, and an unkind one. Miss was (he said) a major, might marry whom she liked; and suttnly had paid Lady G. quite as much attention as she ought, by paying her the compliment to ask her at all.

And so they went on. The curious thing was, that when master was pressed about his cause for not coming out till night-time, he was misterus; and Miss Griffin, when asked why she wooden marry, igsprest, or rather, *didn't* igspress, a simlar secrasy. Wasn't it hard? the cup seemed to be at the lip of both of 'em, and yet somehow, they could not manitch to take a drink.

But one morning, in reply to a most desprat epistol wrote by my master over night, Deuceace, delighted, gits an answer from his soal's beluffd, which ran thus:—

MISS GRIFFIN TO THE HON. A. P. DEUCEACE.

"Dearest,—You say you would share a cottage with me; there is no need, luckily, for that! You plead the sad sinking of your spirits at our delayed union. Beloved, do you think *my* heart rejoices at our separation? You bid me disregard the refusal of Lady Griffin, and tell me that I owe her no further duty.

"Adored Algernon! I can refuse you no more. I was willing not to lose a single chance of reconciliation with this unnatural stepmother. Respect for the memory of my sainted father bid me do all in my power to gain her consent to my union with you; nay, shall I own it, prudence dictated the measure; for to whom should she leave the share of money accorded to her by my father's will but to my father's child.

"But there are bounds beyond which no forbearance can go;

and, thank Heaven, we have no need of looking to Lady Griffin
for sordid wealth: we have a competency without her. Is it not
so, dearest Algernon ?

"Be it as you wish, then, dearest, bravest, and best. Your
poor Matilda has yielded to you her heart long ago ; she has no
longer need to keep back her name. Name the hour, and I will
delay no more ; but seek for refuge in your arms from the
contumely and insult which meet me ever here.

"MATILDA.

"P.S. O, Algernon ! if you did but know what a noble part
your dear father has acted throughout, in doing his best en-
deavours to further our plans, and to soften Lády Griffin ! It is
not *his* fault that she is inexorable as she is. I send you a note
sent by her to Lord Crabs ; we will laugh at it soon, *n'est ce pas ?* "

II.

" My Lord,—In reply to your demand for Miss Griffin's hand,
in favour of your son, Mr. Algernon Deuceace, I can only repeat
what I before have been under the necessity of stating to you,—
that I do not believe a union with a person of Mr. Deuceace's
character would conduce to my step-daughter's happiness, and
therefore *refuse my consent*. I will beg you to communicate the
contents of this note to Mr. Deuceace ; and implore you no more
to touch upon a subject which you must be aware is deeply
painful to me.

"I remain your lordship's most humble servant,
"L. E. GRIFFIN.
" *The Right Hon. the Earl of Crabs.*"

" Hang her ladyship ! " says my master, " what care I for it ? "
As for the old lord who'd been so afishous in his kindniss and
advice, master recknsiled that pretty well, with thinking that his
lordship knew he was going to marry ten thousand a-year, ana
igspected to get some share of it; for he roat back the following
letter to his father, as well as a flaming one to miss:

" Thank you, my dear father, for your kindness in that awkward
business. You know how painfully I am situated just now, and

H

can pretty well guess *both the causes* of my disquiet. A marriage with my beloved Matilda will make me the happiest of men. The dear girl consents, and laughs at the foolish pretensions of her mother-in-law. To tell you the truth, I wonder she yielded to them so long. Carry your kindness a step further, and find for us a parson, a license, and make us two into one. We are both major, you know; so that the ceremony of a guardian's consent is unnecessary.   Your affectionate

"ALGERNON DEUCEACE.

"How I regret that difference between us some time back! Matters are changed now, and shall be more still *after the marriage.*"

I knew what my master meant,—that he would give the old lord the money after he was married; and as it was probble that miss would see the letter he roat, he made it such as not to let her see two clearly in to his present uncomfrable situation.

I took this letter along with the tender one for miss, reading both of 'em, in course, by the way. Miss, on getting hers, gave an inegspressable look with the white of her i's, kist the letter, and prest it to her busm. Lord Crabs read his quite calm, and then they fell a talking together; and told me to wait awhile, and I should git an anser.

After a deal of counseltation, my lord brought out a card, and there was simply written on it,

> *To-morrow, at the Ambassador's, at Twelve.*

"Carry that back to your master, Chawls," says he, "and bid him not to fail."

You may be sure I stept back to him pretty quick, and gave him the card and the messinge. Master looked sattasfied with both; but suttnly not over happy; no man is the day before his marridge; much more his marridge with a hump-back, Harriss though she be.

Well, as he was a going to depart this bachelor life, he did what every man in such suckmstansies ought to do; he made his will,—that is, he made a dispasition of his property, and wrote letters to his creditors telling them of his lucky chance; and that after his marridge he would sutnly pay them every stiver. *Before*, they must know his povvaty well enough to be sure that paymint was out of the question.

To do him justas, he seam'd to be inclined to do the thing that was right, now that it didn't put him to any inkinvenients to do so.

" Chawls," says he, handing me over a tenpun note, " Here's your wagis, and thank you for getting me out of the scrape with the bailiffs: when you are married, you shall be my valet out of liv'ry, and I'll treble your salary."

His vallit! praps his butler! Yes, thought I, here's a chance —a vallit to ten thousand a-year. Nothing to do but to shave him, and read his notes, and let my wiskers grow; to dress in spick and span black, and a clean shut per day; muffings every night in the house-keeper's room; the pick of the gals in the servents' hall; a chap to clean my boots for me, and my master's oppra bone reglar once a-week. *I* knew what a vallit was as well as any genlmn in service; and this I can tell you, he's genrally a hapier, idler, hundsomer, mor genlmnly man than his master. He has more money to spend, for genlmn *will* leave their silver in their weskit pockets; more suxess among the gals; as good dinners, and as good wine—that is, if he's friends with the butler, and friends in corse they will be if they know which way their interest lies.

But these are only cassels in the air, what the French call *shutter d'Espang*. It wasn't roat in the book of fate that I was to be Mr. Deuceace's vallit.

Days will pass at last—even days befor a wedding, (the longist and unpleasantist day in the whole of a man's life, I can tell you, excep, may be, the day before his hanging); and at length Aroarer dawned on the suspicious morning which was to unite in the bonds of Hyming the Honrabble Algernon Percy Deuceace, Exquire, and Miss Matilda Griffin. My master's wardrobe wasn't so rich as it had been; for he'd left the whole of his nicknax and trumpry of dressing cases and rob dy shams, his bewtifle muscum of varnished boots, his curous colleckshn of Stulz and Staub coats when he had been ableaged to quit so sudnly our pore dear lodginx at the Hotel Mirabew; and, being incog at a friend's house, and contentid himself with ordring a coople of shoots of clovés from a common tailor, with a suffishnt quantaty of linning.

Well, he put on the best of his coats—a blue; and I thought it my duty to ask him whether he'd want his frock again; and he was good natured and said, "Take it and be hanged to you." And half-past eleven o'clock came, and I was sent to look out at the door, if there were any suspicious charicters (a precious good nose I have to find a bailiff out, I can tell you, and an i which will almost see one round a corner); and presuly a very modest green glass-coach droave up, and in master stept. I didn't, in corse, appear on the box; because, being known, my appearints might have compromised master. But I took a short cut, and walked as quick as posbil down to the Rue de Foburg St. Honoré, where his exlnsy the English ambasdor lives, and where marridges are always performed betwigst English folk at Paris.

*   *   *   *   *   *

There is, almost nex door to the ambasdor's hotel, another hotel, of that lo kind which the French call cabbyrays, or wine houses; and jest as master's green glass-coach pulled up, another coach drove off, out of which came two ladies, whom I knew pretty well,—suffiz, that one had a humpback, and the ingenious reader well knew why *she* came there; the other was poor Miss Kicksey, who came see her turned off.

Well, master's glass-coach droav up jest as I got within a few yards of the door; our carridge, I say, droav up, and stopt. Down gits coachmin to open the door, and comes I to give Mr. Deuceace an arm, when—out of the cabaray shoot four fellows, and draw up betwigst the coach and embassy-doar; two other chaps go to the other doar of the carridge, and, opening it, one says—"*Rendez vous, M. Deuceace ! Je vous arrête au nom de la loi !*" (which means, "Get out of that, Mr. D.; you are nabbed, and no mistake)." Master turned gashly pail, and sprung to the other side of the coach, as if a serpint had stung him. He flung open the door, and was for making off that way; but he saw the four chaps standing betwigst libbarty and him. He slams down the front window, and screams out, "*Fouettez, cocher !*" (which means, "Go it, coachmin !") in a despert loud voice ; but coachmin wooden go it, and besides, was off his box.

The long and short of the matter was, that jest as I came up to the door two of the bums jumped into the carridge. I saw all; I knew my duty, and so very mornfly I got up behind.

" *Tiens,*" says oue of the chaps in the street ; " *c'est ce drôle qui nous a loué l'autre jour.*" · I knew 'em, but was too melumcolly to smile.

" *Où irons-nous donc ?*" says coachmin to the genlmn who had got inside.

A deep woice from the intearor shouted out, in reply to the coachmin, "À SAINTE PELAGIN !"

*　　*　　*　　*　　*　　*

And now, praps, I ot to dixcribe to you the humours of the prizn qf Sainte Pelagie, which is the French for Fleat, or Queen's Bentch; but on this subject I'm rather shy of writing, partly because the admiral Boz has, in the history of Mr. Pickwick, made such a dixcripshun of a prizn, that mine wooden read very amyousingly afterwids; and, also, because, to tell you the truth, I didn't stay loug in it, being not in a humer to waist my igsistance by passing away the ears of my youth in such a dull place.

My fust erriut now was, as you may phansy, to carry a noat from master to his destiued bride. The poar thing was sadly taken aback, as I can tell you, when she found, after remaining two hours at the Embassy, that her husband didn't make his appearance. And so, after staying on and on, and yet seeing no husband, she was forsed at last to trudge dishconslit home, where I was already waiting for her with a letter from my master.

There was no use now denying the fact of his arrest, and so he confest it at onst; but he made a cock-and-bull story of treachery of a friend, infimous fodgery, and Heaven knows what. However, it didn't matter much; if he had told her that he had been betrayed by the man in the moon, she would have bleavd him.

Lady Griffin never used to appear now at any of my visits. She kep one drawing-room, and Miss dined and lived alone in another; they quarld so much that praps it was best they should live apart : only my Lord Crabs used to see both, comforting each with that winning and innsnt way he had. He came in as Miss, in tears, was lisning to my account of master's seazure, and hopin that the prisn wasn't a horrid place, with a nasty horrid dunjeon, and a dreadfle jailer, and nasty horrid bread and water. Law bless us! she had borrod her ideers from the novvles she had been reading!

"O my lord, my lord," says she, "have you heard this fatal story?"

"Dearest Matilda, what? For Heaven's sake, you alarm me! What—yes—no—is it—no, it can't be! Speak!" says my lord, seizing me by the choler of my coat, "what has happened to my boy?"

"Pleasé you, my lord," says I, "he's at this moment in prisn, no wuss,—having been incarserated about two hours ago."

"In prison! Algernon in prison! 'tis impossible! Imprisoned, for what sum? Mention it, and I will pay to the utmost farthing in my power."

"I'm sure your lordship is very kind," says I (recklecting the scan betwixgst him and master, whom he wanted to diddil out of a thowsand lb.); "and you'll be happy to hear he's only in for a trifle. Five thousand pound is, I think, pretty near the mark."

"Five thousand pounds!—confusion!" says my lord, clasping his hands, and looking up to heaven, "aud I have not five hundred! Dearest Matilda, how shall we help him?"

"Alas, my lord, I have but three guineas, and you know how Lady Griffin has the—— "

"Yes, my sweet child, I know what you would say; but be of good cheer—Algernon, you know, has ample funds of his own."

Thinking my lord meant Dawkins's five thousand, of which, to be sure, a good lump was left, I held my tung; but I cooden help wondering at Lord Crab's igstream compashn for his son, and miss, with her 10,000l. a-year, having only 3 guineas in her pockit.

I took home (bless us, what a home?) a long and very inflamble letter from miss, in which she dixscribed her own sorror at the disappointment; swoar she loy'd him only the moar for his misfortns; made light of them; as a pusson for a paltry sum of five thousand pound ought never to be cast down, 'specially as he had a certain independence in view; and vowd that nothing, nothing, should ever injuice her to part from him, etsettler, etsettler.

I told master of the conversation which had past betwigst me and my lord, and of his handsome offers, and his horrow at hearing of his son's being taken: and likewise mentioned how strange it was that miss should only have 3 guineas, and with such a fortn: bless us, I should have thot that she would always have carried a hundred thowsnd lb. in her pockit!

At this master only said Pshaw! But the rest of the story about his father seemed to dixquiet him a good deal, and he made me repeat it over agin.

He walked up and down the room agytated, and it seam'd as if a new lite was breaking in upon him.

"Chawls," says he, "did you observe—did miss—did my father seem *particularly intimate* with Miss Griffin?"

"How do you mean, sir?" says I.

"Did Lord Crabs appear very fond of Miss Griffin?"

"He was suttnly very kind to her."

"Come, sir, speak at once; did Miss Griffin seem very fond of his lordship?"

"Why, to tell the truth, sir, I must say she seemed *very* fond of him."

"What did he call her?"

"He called her his dearest gal."

"Did he take her hand?"

"Yes, and he—"

"And he what?"

"He kist her, and told her not to be so wery down-hearted about the misfortn which had hapnd to you."

"I have it now!" says he, clinching his fist, and growing gashly pail—"I have it now—the infernal old hoary scoundrel! the wicked unnatural wretch! He would take her from me!" And he poured out a volley of oaves which are impossbill to be repeatid here.

I thot as much long ago: and when my lord kem with his

vizits so pretious affeckshnt at my Lady Griffinses, I expected some such game was iu the wind. Indeed, I'd heard a some-think of it from the Griffinses servnts, that my lord was mighty tender with the ladies.

One thing, however, was evident to a man of his intleckshal capassaties ; he must either marry the gal at oust, or he stood very small chance of having her. He must git out of limbo immediantly, or his respectid father might be stepping into his vaykint shoes. Oh! he saw it all now—the fust attempt at arest, the marridge fixt at 12 o'clock, and the bayliffs fixt to come and intarup the marridge !—the jewel, praps, betwigst him and De l'Orge : but no, it was the *woman* who did that—a *man* don't deal such fowl blows, igspecially a father to his son : a woman may, poar thing !—she's no other means of reventch, and is used to fight with under-hand wepns all her life through.

Well, whatever the pint might be, this Deuceace saw pretty clear, that he'd been beat by his father at his own game—a trapp set for him onst, which had been defitted by my presnts of mind—another trap set afterwids, in which my lord had been suxesfle. Now, my lord, roag as he was, was much too good-naterd to do an unkind ackshn, mearly for the sake of doing it. He'd got to that pich that he didn't mind injuries—they were all fair play to him—he gave 'em, and reseav'd them, without a thought of mallis. If he wanted to injer his son, it was to bene-fick himself. And how was this to be done ? By getting the hairiss to himself, to be sure. The Honrabble Mr. D. didn't say so, but I knew his feelinx well enough—he regretted that he had not given the old genlmn the money he askt for.

Poar fello ! he thought he had hit it, but he was wide of the mark after all.

Well, but what was to be done ? It was clear that he must marry the gal at any rate—*cootky coot*, as the French say ; that is, marry her, and hang the igspence.

To do so he must first git out of prisn—to get out of prisn he must pay his debts—and to pay his debts, he must give every shilling he was worth. Never mind, four thousand pound is a small stake to a reglar gambler, igspecially when he must play it, or rot for life in prisn, and when, if he plays it well, it will give him ten thousand a-year.

So, seeing there was no help for it, he maid up his mind, and accordingly wrote the follying letter to Miss Griffin;—

"My adored Matilda,—Your letter has indeed been a comfort to a poor fellow, who had hoped that this night would have been the most blessed in his life, and now finds himself condemned to spend it within a prison wall! You know the accursed conspiracy which has brought these liabilities upon me, and the foolish friendship which has cost me so much. But what matters? We have, as you say, enough, even though I must pay this shameful demand upon me; and five thousand pounds are as nothing, compared to the happiness which I lose in being separated a night from thee! Courage, however! If I make a sacrifice, it is for you; and I were heartless indeed, if I allowed my own losses to balance for a moment against your happiness.

"Is it not so, beloved one? *Is* not your happiness bound up with mine, in a union with me? I am proud to think so—proud, too, to offer such a humble proof as this of the depth and purity of my affection.

"Tell me that you will still be mine; tell me that you will be mine to-morrow; and to morrow these vile chains shall be removed, and I will be free once more—or if bound, only bound to you! My adorable Matilda! my betrothed bride! write to me ere the evening closes, for I shall never be able to shut my eyes in slumber upon my prison couch, until they have been first blest by the sight of a few words from thee! Write to me, love! write to me! I languish for the reply which is to make or mar me for ever.

"Your affectionate, A. P. D."

Having polisht off this epistol, master intrustid it to me to carry, and bade me, at the same time to try and give it into Miss Griffin's hand alone. I ran with it to Lady Griffinses. I found miss, as I desired, in a sollatary condition; and I presented her with master's pafewmed Billy.

She read it, and the number of size to which she gave vint, and the tears which she shed, beggar digscription. She wep and sighéd until I thought she would bust. She claspt my hand even in her's, and said, " O Charles ! is he very, very miserable ? "

" He is, ma'am," says I; "very miserable indeed—nobody, upon my honour, could be miserablerer."

On hearing this pethetic remark, her mind was made up at onst: and sitting down to her eskrewtaw, she immediahtly ableaged master with an anser. Here it is in black and white.

" My prisoued bird shall pine no more, but fly home to its nest in these arms! Adored Algernon, I will meet thee to-morrow, at the same place, at the same hour. Then, then, it will be impossible for aught but death to divide us.   M. G."

This kind of flumry style comes, you see of reading novvles, and cultivating littery purshuits in a small way. How much better is it to be puffickly ignorant of the hart of writing, and to trust to the writing of the heart. This is *my* style: artyfiz I despise, and trust compleatly to natur : but *revnong a no mootong*, as our continental friends remark, to that nice white sheep, Algernon Percy Deuceace, Exquire; that wenrabble old ram, my Lord Crabs, his father ; and that tender and dellygit young lamb, Miss Matilda Griffin.

She had just foalded up into its proper triangular shape the noat transcribed abuff, and I was jest on the point of saying, according to my master's orders, " Miss, if you please, the Honrabble Mr. Deuceace, would be very much ableaged to you to keep the seminary which is to take place to morrow a profound se——," when my master's father entered, and I fell back to the door. Miss, without a word, rusht into his arms, bust into teers agin, as was her reglar way (it must be confest she was of a very mist constitution), and showing to him his son's note, cried, " Look my dear lord, how nobly your Algernon, *our* Algernon, writes to me. Who can doubt, after this, of the purity of his matchless affection ? "

My lord took the letter, read it, seamed a good deal amyoused, and returning it to its owner, said, very much to my surprise, " My dear Miss Griffin, he certainly does seem in earnest ; and if you

choose to make this match without the consent of your mother-
in-law, you know the consequence, and are of course your own
mistress."

" Consequences!—for shame, my lord! A little money, more
or less, what matters it to two hearts like ours ? "

" Hearts are very pretty things, my sweet young lady, but three
per cents. are better."

" Nay, have we not an ample income of our own, without the
aid of Lady Griffin ? "

My lord shrugged his shoulders. " Be it so, my love," says he.
" I'm sure I can have no other reason to prevent a union
which is founded upon such disinterested affection."

And here the conversation dropt. Miss retired, clasping her
hands, and making play with the whites of her i's. My lord
began trotting up and down the room, with his fat hands stuck in
his britchis pockits, his countnince lighted up with igstream joy,
and singing, to my inordnit igstonishment :

> "See the conquering hero comes !
> Tiddy diddy doll—tiddydoll, doll, doll."

He began singing this song, and tearing up and down the room
like mad. I stood amazd—a new light broke in upon me. He
wasn't going, then, to make love to Miss Griffin! Master might
marry her ! Had she not got the for—?

I say, I was just standing stock still, my eyes fixt, my hands
puppindicklar, my mouf wide open and these igstrordinary
thoughts passing in my mind, when my lord having got to the
last " doll " of his song, just as I came to the sillible " for " of my
ventriloquism, or inward speech—we had eatch jest reached the
pint digscribed, when the meditations of both were sudnly stopt,
by my lord, in the midst of his singin and trottin match, coming
bolt up aginst poar me, sending me up aginst one end of the room,
himself flying back to the other : and it was only after considrabble
agitation that we were at length restored to anything like a
liquilibrium.

" What, you here, you infernal rascal ? " says my lord.

" Your lordship's very kind to notus me," says I ; " I am here ; "
and I gave him a look.

He saw I knew the whole game.

And after whisling a bit, as was his habit when puzzled (I bleave he'd have only whisled if he had been told he was to be hauged in five minnits), after whisling a bit, he stops sudnly, and coming up to me, says :

" Hearkye, Charles, this marriage must take place to-morrow."

" Must it, sir," says I ; " now, for my part, I don't think——"

" Stop, my good fellow ; if it does not take place, what do you gain ?"

This stagger'd me. If it didn't take place, I only lost a situation, for master had but just enough money to pay his detts ; and it wooden soot my book to serve him in prisn or starving.

" Well," says my lord, " you see the force of my argument. Now, look here," and he lugs out a crisp, fluttering, snowy HUNDRED PUN NOTE ! " if my son and Miss Griffin are married to-morrow, you shall have this ; and I will, moreover, take you into my service, and give you double your present wages."

Flesh and blood cooden bear it. " My lord," says I, laying my hand upon my busm, " only give me security, and I'm yours for ever."

The old noblemin grind, and pattid me on the shoulder. " Right, my lad," says he, " right—you're a nice promising youth. Here is the best security," and he pulls out his pockit-book, returns the hundred pun bill, and takes out one for fifty—" here is half to-day ; to-morrow you shall have the remainder."

My fingers trembled a little as I took the pretty fluttering bit of paper, about five times as big as any sum of money I had ever had in my life. I cast my i upon the amount : it was a fifty sure enough—a bank poss-bill, made payable to *Leonora Emilia Griffin,* and indorsed by her. The cat was out of the bag. Now, gentle reader, I spose you begin to see the game.

" Recollect from this day, you are in my service."

" My lord, you overpoar me with your faviours."

" Go to the devil, sir," says he, " do your duty, and hold your tongue."

And thus I went from the service of the Honorabble Algernon Deuceace to that of his exlnsy the Right Honorabble Earl of Crabs.

●   ●   ●   ●   ●

On going back to prisn, I found Deuceace locked up in that oajus place to which his igstravygansies had deservedly led him, and felt for him, I must say, a great deal of eontemp. A raskle such as he—a swindler, who had robbed poar Dawkins of the means of igsistanee, who had cheated his fellow roag, Mr. Richard Blewitt, and who was making a musnary marridge with a disgusting creacher like Miss Griffin, didn merit any compashn on my purt; and I determined quite to keep secret the suckmstansies of my privit intervew with his exlnsy my presut master.

I gev him Miss Griffinses trianglar, which he read with a satasfied air. Then, turning to me, says he : "You gave this to Miss Griffin alone ?"

"Yes, sir."

"You gave her my message ?"

"Yes, sir."

"And you are quite sure Lord Crabs was not there when you gave either the message or the note ?"

"Not there upon my honour," says I.

"Hang your honour, sir ! Brush my hat and coat, and go *call a coach*, do you hear ?"

*   *   *   *   *   *

I did as I was ordered; and on coming back found master in what's called, I think, the *greffe* of the prisn. The officer in waiting had out a great register, and was talking to master in the French tongue, in coarse; a number of poar prisners were looking eagerly on.

"Let us see, my lor," says he; "the debt is 98,700 francs ; there are capture expenses, interest so much; and the whole sum amounts to a hundred thousand francs, *moins* 13."

Deuceace, in a very myjestic way, takes out of his pocket-book four thowsnd pun notes. "This is not French money, but I presume that you know it, M. Greffier," says he.

The greffier turned round to old Solomon, a money-changer, who had one or two clients in the prisn, and hapnd luckily to be there. "Les billets sont bons," says de, "je les prendrai pour cent mille douze cent francs, et j'éspère, my lor, de vous revoir."

"Good," says the greffier; "I know them to be good and I will give my lor the difference, and make out his release."

Which was done. The poar debtors gave a feeble cheer, as the great dubble iron gates swung open, and clang to again, and Deuceace stept out, and me after him to breathe the fresh hair.

He had been in the place but six hours, and was now free again —free, and to be married to ten thousand a-year nex day. But, for all that, he lookt very faint and pale. He *had* put down his great stake ; and when he came out of Sainte Pelagie, he had but fifty pounds left in the world!

Never mind—when onst the money's down, make your mind easy ; and so Deuceace did. He drove back to the Hotel Mirabew, where he ordered apartmince infinately more splendid than befor ; and I pretty soon told Toinette, and the rest of the suvvants, how nobly he behayved, and how he valyoud four thousnd pound no more than ditch water. And such was the consquincies of my praises, and the poplarity I got for us boath, that the delighted landlady immediantly charged him dubble what she would have done, if it hadn been for my stoaries.

He ordered splendid apartmince, then, for the nex week, a carridge and four for Fontainebleau to-morrow at 12 precisely ; and having settled all these things, went quietly to the Roshy de Cancale, where he dined, as well he might, for it was now eight o'clock. I didn't spare the shompang neither that night, I can tell you ; for when I carried the note he gave me for Miss Griffin in the evening, informing her of his freedom, that young lady remarked my hagitated manner of walking and speaking, and said, " Honest Charles ! he is flusht with the events of the day. Here, Charles, is a napoleon ; take it and drink to your mistress."

I pockitid it, but I must say, I didn't like the money—it went against my stomick to take it.

CHAPTER IX.

THE MARRIAGE.

WELL, the nex day came ; at 12 the carridge and four was waiting at the ambasdor's doar ; and Miss Griffin and the faithfle Kicksy were punctial to the apintment.

I don't wish to digscribe the marridge seminary—how the

embasy chapling jined the hands of this loving young couple—
how one of the embasy footmin was called in to witness the
marridge—how miss wep and fainted, as usial—and how Deuceace
carried her, fainting, to the brisky, and drove off to Fontingblo,
where they were to pass the fust weak of the honey-moon. They
took no servnts, because they wisht, they said, to be privit. And
so, when I had shut up the steps, and bid the postilion drive on,
I bid ajew to the Honrabble Algernon, ond went off strait to his
exlent father.

"Is it all over, Chawls?" said he.

"I saw them turned off at igsackly a quarter past 12, my lord,"
says I.

"Did you give Miss Griffin the paper, as I told you, before her
marriage?"

"I did, my lord, in the presents of Mr. Brown, Lord Bobtail's
man, who can swear to her having had it."

I must tell you that my lord had made me read a paper which
Lady Griffin had written, and which I was comishnd to give in
the manner menshnd abuff. It ran to this effect:—

"According to the authority given me by the will of my late
dear husband, I forbid the marriage of Miss Griffin with the
Honourable Algernon Percy Deuceace. If Miss Griffin persists
in the union, I warn her that she must abide by the consequences
of her act.

"LEONORA EMILIA GRIFFIN."

"*Rue de Rivoli,* *May* 8, 1818."

When I gave this to Miss as she entered the cortyard, a minnit
before my master's arrivle, she only read it contemptiously, and
said, "I laugh at the threats of Lady Griffin;" and she toar the
paper in two, and walked on, leaning on the arm of the faithful
and obleaging Miss Kicksey.

I picked up the paper for fear of axdents, and brot it to my
lord. Not that there was any necessaty, for he'd kep a copy, and
made me and another witniss (my Lady Griffin's solissator) read
them both, before he sent either away.

"Good!" says he; and he projuiced from his potfolio

the fello of that bewchus fifty-pun note, which he'd given me yesterday. "I keep my promise, you see Charles," says he. "You are now in Lady Griffin's service, in the place of Mr. Fitzclarence, who retires. Go to Frojé's, and get a livery."

"But, my lord," says I, "I was not to go into Lady Griffinses service, according to the bargain, but into ——"

"It's all the same thing," says he; and he walked off. I went to Mr. Frojé's, and ordered a new livry; and found, likwise, that our coachmin, and Munseer Mortimer had been there too. My lady's livery was changed, and was now of the same color as my old coat, at Mr. Deuceace's; and I'm blest if there wasn't a tremenjious great earl's corronit on the butins, instid of the Griffin rampint, which was worn befoar.

I asked no questions, however, but had myself measured; and slep that night at the Plas Vandome. I didn't go out with the carridge for a day or two, though; my lady only taking one footmin, she said, until *her new carridge* was turned out.

I think you can guess what's in the wind *now !*

I bot myself a dressing case, a box of Ody colong, a few duzen lawn sherts and neckcloths, and other things which were necessary for a genlmn in my rank. Silk stockings was provided by the rules of the house. And I completed the bisniss by writing the follying ginteel letter to my late master:—

"CHARLES YELLOWPLUSH, ESQUIRE, TO THE HONOURABLE
A. P. DEUCEACE.

"Sur,—Suckmstansies have acurd sins I last had the honner of wating on you, which render it impossbil that I should remane any longer in your suvvice, I'll thank you to leave out my thinx, when they come home on Sattady from the wash.

"Your obeajnt servnt,
"CHARLES YELLOWPLUSH."

"*Plas Vendome.*"

The athography of the abuv noat, I confess, is atrocious; but, *ke voolyvoo?* I was only eighteen, and hadn then the expearance in writing which I've eujide sins.

Having thus done my jewty in evry way, I shall prosead, in the nex chapter, to say what hapnd in my new place.

CHAPTER X.

THE HONEY-MOON.

THE weak at Fontingblow past quickly away ; and at the end of it, our son and daughter-in-law—a pare of nice young tuttle-duvs —returned to their nest, at the Hotel Mirabew. I suspeck that the *cock* turtle-dove was preshos sick of his barging.

When they arriv'd, the fust thing they found on their table was a large parsle wrapt up in silver paper, and a newspaper, and a couple of cards, tied up with a peace of white ribbing. In the parsle was a hansume piece of plum-cake, with a deal of sugar. On the cards was wrote, in Goffick characters,

𝕰𝖆𝖗𝖑 𝖔𝖋 𝕮𝖗𝖆𝖇𝖘.

And, in very small Italian,

Countess of Crabs.

And in the paper was the following parrowgraff :—

" MARRIAGE IN HIGH LIFE.—Yesterday, at the British embassy, the Right Honourable John Augustus Altamont Plantagenet, Earl of Crabbs, to Leonora Emilia, widow of the late Lieutenant-General Sir George Griffin, K. C. B. An elegant *dejeuné* was given to the happy couple, by his excellency Lord Bobtail, who gave away the bride. The *élite* of the foreign diplomacy the Prince Talleyrand, and Marshal the Duke of Dalmatia, on behalf of H. M. the King of France, honoured the banquet and the marriage ceremony Lord and Lady Crabbs intend passing a few weeks at Saint Cloud."

The above dockyments, along with my own triffling billy, of which I have also givn a copy, greated Mr. and Mrs. Deuceace on their arrivle from Fontingblo. Not being presnt, I can't say what Deuceace said, but I can fancy how he *lookt*, and how poor Mrs. Deuceace look't. They weren't much inclined to rest after the fiteeg of the junny, for, in ½ an hour after their arrival at Paris, the hosses were put to the carridge agen, and down they came thundering to our country-house, at St. Cloud (pronounst by those absud Frenchmin Sing Kloo), to interrup our chaste loves, and delishs marridge injyments.

My lord was sittn in a crimson satan dress, lolling on a sofa at an open windy, smoking seagars, as ushle; her ladyship, who, to du him justice, didn mind the smell, occupied another end of the room, and was working, in wusted, a pare of slippers, or an umbrel-lore case, or a coal skittle, or some such nonsints. You would have thought to have sean 'em that they had been married a sentry, at least. Well, I bust in upon this conjugal *tatortator*, and said, very much alarmed, " My lord, here's your son and daughter-in-law."

" Well," says my lord, quite calm, " and what then ? "

" Mr. Deuceace ! " says my lady, starting up, and looking fritened.

" Yes, my love, my son; but you need not be alarmed. Pray, Charles, say that Lady Crabs and I will be very happy to see Mr. and Mrs. Deuceace; and that they must excuse us receiving them *en famille*. Sit still, my blessing—take things coolly. Have you got the box with the papers ? "

My lady pointed to a great green box—the same from which she had takęn the papers, when Deuceace fust saw them,—and handed over to my lord a fine gold key. I went out, met Deuceace and his wife on the stepps, gave my messinge, and bowed them palitely in.

My lord didn't rise, but smoaked away as usual (praps a little quicker, but I can't say) ; my lady sate upright, looking handsum and strong. Deuceace walked in, his left arm tied to his breast, his wife and hat on the other. He looked very pale and frightened; his wife, poar thing ! had her head berried in her handkerchief, and sobd fit to break her heart.

Miss Kicksy,·who was in the room (but I didnt mention her, she was less than nothink in our house), went up to Mrs. Deuceace at onst, and held out her arms—she had a heart, that old Kicksey, and I respect her for it. The poor hunchback flung herself into miss's arms, with a kind of whooping screech, and kep there for some time, sobbing in quite a historical manner. I saw there was going to be a sean, and so, in cors, left the door ajar.

" Welcome to Saint Cloud, Algy, my boy !" says my lord, in a loud, hearty voice. " You thought you would give us the slip, eh, you rogue ? But we knew it, my dear fellow; we knew the whole affair—did we not, my soul ? And, you see, kept our secret better than you did yours."

" I must confess, sir," says Deuceace, bowing, "that I had no idea of the happiness which awaited me, in the shape of a mother-in-law."

" No, you dog; no, no," says my lord, giggling; "old birds, you know, not to be caught with chaff, like young ones. But, here we are, all spliced and happy, at last. Sit down, Algernon; let us smoke a segar, and talk over the perils and adventures of the last month. My love," says my lord, turning to his lady, " you have no malice against poor Algernon, I trust? Pray shake *his hand.*" (A grin.)

But my lady rose, and said, " I have told Mr. Deuceace, that I never wished to see him, or speak to him, more. I see no reason, now, to change my opinion." And, herewith, she sailed out of the room, by the door through which Kicksey had carried poor Mrs. Deuceace.

" Well, well," says my lord, as Lady Crabs swept by, " I was in hopes she had forgiven you; but I know the whole story, and I must confess, you used her cruelly ill. Two strings to your bow ! —that was your game, was it, you rogue ? "

" Do you mean, my lord, that you know all that past between me and Lady Grif—Lady Crabs, before our quarrel ? "

" Perfectly—you made love to her, and she was almost in love with you; you jilted her for money, she got a man to shoot your hand off in revenge; no more dice-boxes, now, Deuceace; no more *sauter la coupe.* I can't think how the deuce you will manage to live without them."

" Your lordship is very kind, but I have given up play altogether," says Deuceace, looking mighty black and uneasy.

"Oh, indeed! Benedick has turned a moral man, has he? This is better and better. Are you thinking of going into the church, Deuceace?"

"My lord, may I ask you to be a little more serious?"

"Serious! *à quoi bon?* I am serious—serious in my surprise that, when you might have had either of these women, you should have preferred that hideous wife of yours."

"May I ask you, in turn, how you came to be so little squeamish about a wife, as to choose a woman who had just been making love to your own son?" says Deuceace, growing fierce.

"How can you ask such a question? I owe forty thousand pounds—there is an execution at Size's Hall—every acre I have is in the hands of my creditors; and that's why I married her. Do you think there was any love? Lady Crabs is a dev'lish fine woman, but she's not a fool—she married me for my coronet, and I married her for her money."

"Well, my lord, you need not ask me, I think, why I married the daughter-in-law."

"Yes, but I *do*, my dear boy. How the deuce are you to live? Dawkins's five thousand pounds won't last for ever; and afterwards?"

"You don't mean, my lord,—you don't—I mean, you can't ——D—!" says he, starting up, and losing all patience, "you don't dare to say that Miss Griffin had not a fortune of ten thousand a-year?"

My lord was rolling up, and wetting betwigst his lips, another segar; he lookt up, after he had lighted it, and said, quietly,

"Certainly, Miss Griffin had a fortune of ten thousand a-year."

"Well, sir, and has she not got it now? Has she spent it in a week?"

"*She has not got a sixpence now: she married without her mother's consent!*"

Deuceace sunk down in a chair; and I never see such a dreadful picture of despair as there was in the face of that retchid man!—he writhed, and nasht his teeth, he tore open his coat, and wriggled madly the stump of his left hand, until, fairly beat, he threw it over his livid pale face, and, sinking backwards, fairly wept alowd.

Bah! it's a dreddfle thing to hear a man crying! his pashn torn up from the very roots of his heart, as it must be before it can git such a vent. My lord, meanwhile, rolled his segar, lighted it, and went on.

"My dear boy, the girl has not a shilling. I wished to have left you alone in peace, with your four thousand pounds; you might have lived decently upon it in Germany, where money is at 5 per cent., where your duns would not find you, and a couple of hundred a year would have kept you and your wife in comfort. But, you see, Lady Crabs would not listen to it. You had injured her, and, after she had tried to kill you, and failed, she determined .to ruin you, and succeeded. I must own to you that I directed the arresting business, and put her up to buying your protested bills; she got them for a trifle, and as you have paid them, has made a good two thousand pounds by her bargain. It was a painful thing to be sure, for a father to get his son arrested; but *que voulez-vous!* I did not appear in the transaction; she would have you ruined; and it was absolutely necessary that *you* should marry before I could, so I pleaded your cause with Miss Griffin, and made you the happy man you are. You rogue, you rogue! you thought to match your old father, did you? But, never mind; lunch will be ready soon. In the meantime, have a segar, and drink a glass of Sauterne."

Deuceace, who had been listening to this speech, sprung up wildly.

"I'll not believe it," he said; "it's a lie, an infernal lie! forged by you, you hoary villain, and by the murderess and strumpet you have married. I'll not believe it; show me the will. Matilda! Matilda!" shouted he, screaming hoarsely, and flinging open the door by which she had gone out.

"Keep your temper, my boy. You *are* vexed, and I feel for you: but don't use such bad language: it is quite needless, believe me."

"Matilda!" shouted out Deuceace again; and the poor crooked thing came trembling in, followed by Miss Kicksey.

"Is this true, woman?" says he clutching hold of her hand.

"What, dear Algernon?" says she.

"What?" screams out Deuceace,—"what? Why that you are

a beggar, for marrying without your mother's consent—that you basely lied to me, in order to bring about this match—that you are a swindler, in conspiracy with that old fiend yonder, and the she-devil, his wife ?"

" It is true," sobbed the poor woman, " that I have nothing, but——"

" Nothing but what? Why don't you speak, you drivelling fool ?"

" I have nothing!—but you, dearest, have two thousand a-year. Is that not enough for us? You love me for myself, don't you, Algernon ? You have told me so a thousand times—say so again, dear husband; and do not, do not be so unkind." And here she sank on her knees, and clung to him, and tried to catch his hand, and kiss it.

" How much did you say ?" says my lord.

" Two thousand a-year, sir; he has told us so a thousand times."

" *Two thousand!* Two thou—ho, ho, ho!—haw! haw! haw!" roars my lord. " That is, I vow, the best thing I ever heard in my life. My dear creature, he has not a shilling—not a single maravedi, by all the gods and goddesses." And this exlnt noblemin began laffin louder than ever; a very kind and feeling genlmn he was, as all must confess.

There was a paws: and Mrs. Deuceace didn begin cussing and swearing at her husband as he had done at her: she only said, " O Algernon! is this true ?" and got up, and went to a chair and wep in quiet.

My lord opened the great box. " If you or your lawyers would like to examine Sir George's will, it is quite at your service; you will see here the proviso which I mentioned, that gives the entire fortune to Lady Griffin—Lady Crabs that is; and here, my dear boy, you see the danger of hasty conclusions. Her ladyship only showed you the *first page of the will*, of course, she wanted to try you. You thought you made a great stroke in at once proposing to Miss Griffin—do not mind it, my love, he really loves you now very sincerely!—when, in fact, you would have done much better to have read the rest of the will. You were completely bitten, my boy—humbugged, bamboozled—ay, and by your old father, you dog. I told you I would, you know, when you refused to lend me a portion of your Dawkins money. I told you I would; and I *did*. I had you the very next day. Let this be a lesson to you, Percy my boy; don't try your luck again against such old hands; look deuced well before you leap; *audi alteram partem*, my lad, which means, read both sides of the will. I think lunch is ready; but I see you don't smoke. Shall we go in?"

"Stop, my lord," says Mr. Deuceace, very humble; "I shall not share your hospitality—but—but you know my condition; I am penniless—you know the manner in which my wife has been brought up——"

"The Honourable Mrs. Deuceace, sir, shall always find a home here, as if nothing had occurred to interrupt the friendship between her dear mother and herself."

"And for me, sir," says Deuceace, speaking faint, and very slow, "I hope—I trust—I think, my lord, you will not forget me?"

"Forget you, sir; certainly not."

"And that you will make some provision?"

"Algernon Deuceace," says my lord, getting up from the sophy, and looking at him with sich a jolly malignity, as *I* never see, "I declare, before Heaven, that I will not give you a penny!"

Hereupon my lord held out his hand to Mrs. Deuceace, and said, "My dear will you join your mother and me? We shall always, as I said, have a home for you."

"My lord," said the poar thing, dropping a curtsy, "my home is with *him!*"

*   *   *   *   *

*   *   *   *

*   *   *   *   *

About three months after, when the season was beginning at Paris, and the autumn leafs was on the ground, my lord, my lady, me and Mortimer, were taking a stroal in the Boddy Balong, the carridge driving on slowly a head, and us as happy as possbill, admiring the pleasant woods, and the goldn sunset.

My lord was expayshating to my lady upon the exquizit beauty of the sean, and pouring forth a host of butifle and virtuous sentament sootable to the hour. It was dalitefle to hear him. "Ah!" said he, "black must be the heart, my love, which does not feel the influence of a scene like this; gathering as it were, from those sunlit skies, a portion of their celestial gold, and gaining somewhat of heaven with each pure draught of this delicious air!"

Lady Crabs did not speak, but prest his arm and looked upwards. Mortimer and I, too, felt some of the infliwents of the sean, and lent on our goold sticks in silence. The carriage drew up close to us, and my lord and my lady sauntered slowly tords it.

Jest at the place was a bench, and on the bench sate a poorly drest woman, and by her, leaning against a tree, was a man whom I thought I'd sean befor. He was drest in a shabby blew coat, with white seems and copper buttons; a torn hat was on his head, and great quantaties of matted hair and whiskers disfiggared his countnints. He was not shaved, and as pale as stone.

My lord and lady didn tak the slightest notice of him, but past on to the carridge. Me and Mortimer lickwise took *our* places. As we past, the man had got a grip of the woman's shoulder, who was holding down her head sobbing bitterly.

No sooner were my lord and lady seated, than they both, with igstream dellixy and good natur, bust into a ror of lafter, peal upon peal, whooping and screaching, enough to frighten the evening silents.

DEUCEACE turned round. I see his face now—the face of a devvle of hell! Fust, he lookt towards the carridge, and pinted to it with his maimed arm; then he raised the other, *and struck the woman by his side.* She fell, screaming.

Poor thing! Poor thing!

MR. YELLOWPLUSH'S AJEW.

THE end of Mr. Deuceace's history is going to be the end of my corrispondince: I wish the public was as sory to part with me as I am with the public; becaws I fansy reely that we've become frends, and feal for my part a becoming greaf at saying ajew.

It's imposbill for me to continyow, however, a writin, as I have done—violetting the rules of authography, and trampling upon the fust princepills of English grammar. When I began, I knew no better : when I'd carrid on these papers a little further, and grew accustmd to writin, I began to smel out somethink quear in my style. Within the last sex weaks I have been learning to spell : and when all the world was rejoicing at the festivvaties of our youthful quean—when all i's were fixt upon her long sweet of ambasdors and princes, following the splendid carridge of Marshle the Duke of Damlatiar, and blinking at the pearls and dimince of Prince Oystereasy—Yellowplush was in his loanly pantry—*his* eyes were fixt upon the spelling-book—his heart was bent upon mastring the difficleties of the littery professhn. I have been, in fact, *convertid*.

You shall here how. Ours, you know, is a Wig house ; and ever sins his third son has got a place in the Treasury, his secknd a captingsy in the Guards, his fust, the secretary of embasy at Pekin, with a prospick of being appinted ambasdor at Loo Choo —ever sins master's sons have reseaved these attentions, and master himself has had the promis of a pearitch, he has been the most reglar, consistnt, honrabble Libbaral, in or out of the House of Cominins.

Well, being a Whig, it's the fashn, as you know, to reseave littery pipple ; and accordingly, at dinner, tother day, whose name do you think I had to hollar out on the fust landing-place about a wick ago ? After several dukes and markises had been enounced, a very gentell fly drives up to our doar, and out steps two gentle-men. One was pail, and wor spektickles, a wig, and a white neckcloth. The other was slim with a hoo'k nose, a pail fase, a small waist, a pare of falling shoulders, a tight coat, and a cata-rack of black satting tumbling out of his busm, and falling into a gilt velvet weskit. The little genlmn settled his wigg, and pulled out his ribbins ; the younger one fluffed the dust of his shoos, looked at his wiskers in a little pockit-glas, settled his crevatt ; and they both mounted up stairs.

" What name, sir ? " says I, to the old genlmn.

" Name !—a ! now, you thief o' the wurrld," says he, " do you pretind nat to know *me ?* Say it's the Cabinet Cyclopa—no, I mane the Litherary Chran—psha!—bluthanowns!—say it's Doothor Dioclesian Larner—I think he'll know me now— ay, Nid?" But the genlmn called Nid was at the botm of the stare, and pretended to be very busy with his shoo-string. So the little genlmn went up stares alone.

"Doctor Diolesius Larner!" says I.

"Doctor Athanasius Lardner!" says Greville Fitz-Roy, our secknd footman, on the fust landing-place.

"Doctor Ignatius Lopola!" says the groom of the chambers, who pretends to be a schollar; and in the little genlmn went. When safely housed, the other chap came; and when I asked him his name, said, in a thick, gobbling kind of voice:

"Sawedwadgeorgeearllittnbulwig."

"Sir what?" says I, quite agast at the name.

"Sawedwad—no, I mean *Mista*wedwad Lyttn Bulwig."

My neas trembled under me, my i's fild with tiers, my voice shook, as I past up the venrabble name to the other footman, and saw this fust of English writers go up to the drawing-room!

It's needless to mention the names of the rest of the compny, or to dixcribe the suckmstansies of the dinner. Suffiz to say that the two littery genlmn behaved very well, and seamed to have good appytights; igspecially the little Irishman in the Whig, who et, drunk, and talked as much as ½ a duzn. He told how he'd been presented at cort by his friend, Mr. Bulwig, and how the quean had received 'em both, a dignity undigscribable, and how her blessid majisty asked what was the bony fidy sale of the Cabinit Cyclopædy, and how he (Doctor Larner) told her that, on his honner, it was under ten thowsnd.

You may guess that the Doctor, when he made this speach, was pretty far gone. The fact is, that whether it was the coronation, or the goodness of the wine (cappitle it is in our house, *I* çan tell you), or the natral propensaties of the gests assembled, which made them so igspecially jolly, I don't know, but they had kep up the meating pretty late, and our poar butler was quite tired with the perpechual baskits of clarrit which he'd been called upon to bring up. So that about 11 o'clock, if I were to say they were merry, I should use a mild term; if I wer to say they were intawsicated, I should use an igspresshn more near to the truth, but less rispeckful in one of my situashn.

The cumpany reseaved this annountsmint with mute extonishment.

" Pray, Doctor Larnder," says a spiteful genlmn, willing to keep up the littery conversation, "what is the Cabinet Cyclopædia? "

" It's the littherary wontherr of the wurrld," says he; "and sure your lordship must have seen it; the latther numbers ispicially —cheap as durrt, bound in gleezed calico, six shillings a vollum. The illusthrious neems of Walther Scott, Thomas Moore, Docther Southey, Sir James Mackintosh, Docther Donovan, and meself, are to be found in the list of conthributors. It's the Phaynix of Cyclopajies—a litherary Bacon."

" A what? " says the genlmn nex to him.

" A Bacon, shiniug in the darkness of our age; fild wid the pure end lambent flame of science, burning with the gorrgeous scintillations of divine litherature—a *monumintum*, in fact, *are perinnius*, bound in pink calico, six shillings a vollum."'

" This wigmawole," said Mr. Bulwig (who seemed rather disgusted that his friend should take up so much of the convassation), " this wigmawole is all vewy well; but it's cuwious that you don't wemember, in chawactewising the litewawy mewits of the vawious magazines, cwonicles, weviews, and encyclopædias, the existence of a cwitical weview and litewawy chwonicle, which, though the æwa of its appeawance is dated only at a vewy few months pwevious to the pwesent pewiod is, nevertheless, so wemarkable for its intwinsic mewits as to be wead, not in the metwopolis alone, but in the countwy—not in Fwance merely, but in the west of Euwope—whewever our pure Wenglish is spoken, it stwetches its peaceful sceptre—pewused in Amewica, fwom New York to Niagawa—wepwinted in Canada, from Montweal to Towonto—and, as I am gwatified to hear fwom my fwend the governor of Cape Coast Castle, wegularly weceived in Afwica, and twanslated into the Mandingo language by the missionawies and the bushwangers. I need not say, gentlemen—sir—that is, Mr. Speaker—I mean, Sir John—that I allude to the Litewawy Chwonicle, of which I have the honour to be pwincipal contwibutor."

"Very true, my dear Mr. Bullwig," says my master; "you and
I being Whigs, must of course, stand by our own friends; and
I will agree, without a moment's hesitation, that the Literary
what-d'ye-callem is the prince of periodicals."

"The Pwince of pewiodicals?" says Bullwig; "my dear Sir
John, it's the empewow of the pwess."

"Soit,—let it be the emperor of the press, as you poetically
call it: but, between ourselves, confess it,—Do not the Tory
writers beat your Whigs hollow? You talk about magazines.
Look at ——"

"Look at hwat?" shouts out Larder. "There's none, Sir
Jan, compared to ourrs."

"Pardon me, I think that ——"

"It is Bentley's Mislany you mane?" says Ignatius, as sharp
as a niddle.

"Why no ; but ——"

"O thin, it's Co'burn, sure ; and that divvle Thayo dor—a pretty
paper, sir, but light—thrashy, milk-and-wathery—not sthrong, like
the Litherary Chran—good luck to it."

"Why, Doctor Lander, I was going to tell at once the name of
the periodical,—it is FRASER'S MAGAZINE."

"FRESER!" says the Doctor. "O thunder and turf!"

"FWASER!" says Bullwig. "O—ah—hum—haw—yes—no—
why,—that is weally—no, weally, upon my weputation, I never
before heard the name of the pewiodical. By the by, Sir John,
what wemarkable good clawet this is ; is it Lawose or Laff—— ?"

Laff, indeed! he cooden git beyond laff ; and I'm blest if I
could kip it neither,—for hearing him pretend ignurnts, and being
behind the skreend, settlin sumthink for the genlmn, I bust into
such a raw of laffing as never was igseeded.

"Hullo !" says Bullwig, turning red. "Have I said anything
impwobable, aw widiculous ? for, weally, I never befaw wecollect
to have heard in society such a twemendous peal of cachinnation,
—that which the twagic bard who fought at Mawathon has called
an *anëwithmon gelasma*."

"Why, be the holy piper," says Larder, "I think you are
dthrawing a little on your imagination. Not read *Fraser!* Don't
believe him, my lord duke ; he reads every word of it, the rogue !

The boys about that magazine baste him as if he was a sack of oatmale. My reason for crying out, Sir Jan, was because you mintioned *Fraser* at all. Bullwig has every syllable of it by heart —from the paillitix down to the ' Yellowplush Correspondence.' "

" Ha, ha! " says Bullwig, affecting to laff (you may be sure my years prickt up when I heard the name of the ' Yellowplush Correspondence'). " Ha, ha! why, to tell twuth, I *have* wead the cowespondence to which you allude; it's a gweat favowite at court. I was talking with Spwing Wice and John Wussell about it the other day."

" Well, and what do you think of it? " says Sir John, looking mity waggish,—for he knew it was me who roat it.

" Why, weally and twuly, there's considewable cleverness about the cweature; but it's low, disgustingly low: it violates pwobability, and the orthogwaphy is so carefully inaccuwate, that it requires a positive study to compwehend it."

" Yes, faith," says Larner, the " arthagraphy is detestible; it's as bad for a man to write bad spillin as it is for 'em to speak wid a brrouge. Iducation furst, and ganius afterwards. Your health, my lord, and good luck to you."

" Yaw wemark," says Bullwig, " is vewy appwopwiate. You will wecollect, Sir John, in Hewodotus (as for you, doctor, you know more about Iwish than about Gweek),—you will wecollect, without doubt, a stowy nawwated by that cwedulous though fascinating chwonicler, of a certain kind of sheep which is known only in a certain distwict of Awabia, and of which the tail is so enormous, that it either dwaggles on the gwound, or is bound up by the shepherds of the country into a small wheelbawwow, or cart, which makes the chwonicler sneewingly wemark, that thus ' the sheep of Awabia have their own chawiots.' I have often thought, sir (this clawet is weally nectaweous)—I have often, I say, thought that the wace of man may be compawed to these Awabian sheep—genius is our tail, education our wheelbawwow. Without art and education to pwop it, this genius dwops on the gwound, and is polluted by the mud, or injured by the wocks upon the way: with the wheelbawwow it is stwengthened, incweased, and supported—a pwide to the owner, a blessing to mankind."

" A very appropriate simile," says Sir John; " and I am afraid that the genius of our friend Yellowplush has need of some such support."

"*Apropos*," said Bullwig; "who *is* Yellowplush? I was given to understand that the name was only a fictitious one, and that the papers were written by the author of the *Diary of a Physician*; if so, the man has wonderfully improved in style, and there is some hope of him."

"Bah!" says the Duke of Doublejowl; "every body know's it's Barnard, the celebrated author of 'Sam Slick.'"

"Pardon, my dear duke," says Lord Bagwig; "it's the authoress of *High Life, Almacks,* and other fashionable novels."

"Fiddlestick's end!" says Doctor Larner; "don't be blushing, and pretinding to ask questions: don't we know you, Bullwig! It's you yourself, you thief of the world; we smoked you from the very beginning."

Bullwig was about indignantly to reply, when Sir John interrupted them, and said,—"I must correct you all, gentlemen; Mr. Yellowplush is no other than Mr. Yellowplush: he gave you, my dear Bullwig, your last glass of champagne at dinner, and is now an inmate of my house, and an ornament of my kitchen!"

"Gad!" says Doublejowl, "let's have him up."

"Hear, hear!" says Bagwig.

"Ah, now," says Larner, "your grace is not going to call up and talk to a footman, sure? Is it gintale?"

"To say the least of it," says Bullwig, "the pwactice is iwwegular, and indecowous; and I weally don't see how the inter-view can be in any way pwofitable."

But the vices of the company went against the two littery men, and every body excep them was for having up poor me. The bell was wrung; butler came. "Send up Charles," says master; and Charles, who was standing behind the skreand, was persnly abliged to come in.

"Charles," says master, "I have been telling these gentlemen who is the author of the 'Yellowplush Correspondence' in *Fraser's Magazine*."

"It's the best magazine in Europe," says the duke.

"And no mistake," says my lord.'

"Hwat!" says Larner; "and where's the Litherary Chran?"

I said myself nothink, but made a bough, and blusht like pickle cabbitch.

" Mr. Yellowplush," says his grace, " will you, in the first place, drink a glass of wine ? "

I boughed agin.

" And what wine do you prefer, sir ? humble port or imperial burgundy ? "

" Why, your grace," says I, " I know my place, and aint above kitchin wines. I will take a glass of port, and drink it to the health of this honrabble compny."

When I'd swigged off the bumper, which his grace himself did me the honour to pour out for me, there was a silints for a minnit ; when my master said:

" Charles Yellowplush, I have perused your memoirs in *Fraser's Magazine* with so much curiosity, and have so high an opinion of your talents as a writer, that I really cannot keep you as a footman any longer, or allow you to discharge duties for which you are now quite unfit. With all my admiration for your talents, Mr. Yellowplush, I still am confident that many of your friends in the servants' hall will clean my boots a great deal better than a gentleman of your genius can ever be expected to do—it is for this purpose that I employ footmen, and not that they may be writing articles in magazines. But—you need not look so red, my good fellow, and had better take another glass of port—I don't wish to throw you upon the wide world without means of a livelihood, and have made interest for a little place which you will have under government, and which will give you an income of eighty pounds per annum, which you can double, I presume, by your literary labours."

" Sir," says I, clasping my hands, and busting into tears, " do not—for Heaven's sake, do not!—think of any such think, or drive me from your suvvice, because I have been fool enough to write in magaseens. Glans but one moment at your honor's plate —every spoon is as bright as a mirror ; condysend to igsamine your shoes—your honour may see reflected in them the fases of every one in the company. *I* blacked them shoes, *I* cleaned that there plate. If occasionally I've forgot the footman in the litterary man, and committed to paper my remindicences of fashnabble life, it was from a sincere desire to do good, and promote nollitch: and I appeal to your honour,—I lay my hand on my busm, and in the fase of this noble company beg you to say, When you rung your bell, who came to you fust? When you stopt out at Brooke's till morning, who sate up for you? When you was ill, who forgot the natral dignities of his station, and answered the two-pair bell? O sir," says I, "I know what's what; don't send me away. I know them littery chaps, and, beleave me, I'd rather be a footman. The work's not so hard—the pay is better: the vittels incompyrably supearor. I have but to clean my things, and run my errints, and you put clothes on my back, and meat in my mouth: Sir! Mr. Bullwig! an't I right? shall I quit *my* station and sink —that is to say, rise—to *yours*."

Bullwig was violently affected; a tear stood in his glistening i. "Yellowplush," says he, seizing my hand, "you *are* right. Quit not your present occupation; black boots, clean knives, wear plush, all your life, but dou't turn literary man. Look at me. I am the first novelist in Europe. I have ranged with eagle wing over the wide regions of literature, and perched on every eminence in its turn. I have gazed with eagle eyes on the sun of philosophy, and fathomed the mysterious depths of the human mind. All languages are familiar to me, all thoughts are known to me, all men understood by me. I have gathered wisdom from the honeyed lips of Plato, as we wandered in the gardens of Acadames—wisdom, too, from the mouth of Job Johnson, as we smoked our 'backy in Seven Dials. Such must be the studies, and such is the mission, in this world, of the Poet-Philosopher. But the knowledge is only emptiness; the initiation is but misery; the initiated, a man shunned and bann'd by his fellows. O," said Bullwig, clasping his hands, and throwing his fine i's up to the chaudelier, "the curse of Pwometheus descends upon his wace. Wath and punishment pursue them from genewation to genewation! Wo to genius, the heaven-scaler, the fire-stealer! Wo and thrice bitter desolation! Earth is the wock on which Zeus, wemorseless, stwetches his withing victim—men, the vultures that feed and fatten on him. Ai, Ai! it is agony eternal—gwoaning and solitawy despair! And you, Yellowplush, would penewtate these mystewies: you would waise the awful veil, and stand in the twemendous

Pwesence. Beware; as you value your peace, beware! With-dwaw, wash Neophyte! For Heaven's sake—O, for Heaven's sake!—" here he looked round with agony—"give me a glass of bwandy and water, for this clawet is beginning to disagwee with me."

Bullwig having concluded this spitch, very much to his own sattasfackshn, looking round to the compny for aplaws, and then swigged off the glass of brandy and water, giving a sollum sigh as he took the last gulph; and then Doctor Ignatius, who longed for a chans, and, in order to show his independence, began flatty contradicting his friend, and addressed me, and the rest of the genlmn present, in the following manner :—

" Hark ye," says he, " my gossoon, doant be led asthray by the nonsinse of that divil of a Bullwig. He's jillous of ye, my bhoy; that's the rale, undoubted thruth; and it's only to keep you out of litherary life that he's palavering you in this way : I'll tell you what—Plush, ye blackguard,—my honourable frind, the mimber there, has told me a hunder times by the smallest computation of his intense admiration of your talents, and the wonderful sthir they were making in the worlld. He can't bear a rival. He's mad with envy, hatred, oncharatableness. Look at him, Plush, and look at me. My father was not a juke exactly, nor aven a markis, and see, nevertheliss, to what a pitch I am come. I spare no ixpinse; I'm the iditor of a cople of pariodicals; I dthrive about in me carridge; I dine wid the lords of the land; and why —in the name of the piper that pleed before Mosus, hwy? Be-cause I'm litherary man. Because I know how to play me cards. Because I'm Docther Larner, in fact, and mimber of every society in and out of Europe. I might have remained all my life in Thrinity Colledge, and never made such an incom as that offered you by Sir Jan; but I came to London—to London, my boy, and now, see! Look again at me friend Bullwig. He *is* a gentle-man, to be sure, and bad luck to 'im, say I; and what has been the result of his litherary labour? I'll tell you what, and I'll tell this gintale society, by the shade of Saint Patrick, they're going to make him A BARINET."

" A BARNET, Doctor! " says I; " you don't mean to say they're going to make him a barnet! "

K

"As sure as I've made meself a docthor," says Larner.

"What, a baronet, like Sir John?"

"The divle a bit else."

"And pray what for?"

"What faw?" says Bullwig. "Ask the histowy of litwatuwe what faw? Ask Colburn, ask Bentley, ask Saunders and Otley, ask the gweat Bwitish nation, what faw? The blood in my veins comes puwified thwough ten thousand years of chivalwous ancestwy; but that is neither here nor there: my political principles —the equal wights which I have advocated—the gweat cause of fweedom that I have celebwated, are known to all. But this, I confess, has nothing to do with the question. No, the question is this—on the thwone of litewature I stand unwivalled, pweeminent; and the Bwitish government, honowing genius in me, compliments the Bwitish nation by lifting into the bosom of the heweditawy nobility, the most gifted member of the democwacy." (The honrabble genlm here sunk down amidst repeated cheers.)

"Sir John," says I, "and my lord duke, the words of my rivrint frend, Ignatius, and the remarks of the honrabble genlmn who has just sate down, have made me change the detummination which I had the honor of igspressing just now.

"I igsept the eighty pound a-year; knowing that I shall have plenty of time for pursuing my littery career, and hoping some day to set on that same bentch of barranites, which is deckarated by the presnts of my honrabble friend.

"Why shooden I? It's trew I aint done anythink as *yet* to deserve such an honour; and it's very probable that I never shall But what then?—*quaw dong*, as our friends say. I'd much rayther have a coat of arms than a coat of livry. I'd much rayther have my blud-red hand spralink in the middle of a shield, than underneath a tea-tray. A barranit I will be, and, in consiquints, must cease to be a footmin.

"As to my politticle princepills, these, I confess, aint settled: they are, I know, necessary; but they aint necessary *until askt for;* besides, I reglar read the *Sattarist* newspaper, and so ignirince on this pint would be inigscusable.

"But if one man can git to be a doctor, and another a barranit, and another a capting in the navy, and another *a* countess, and another the wife of a governor of the Cape of Good Hope, I begin to perseave that the littery trade aint such a very bad un; igspecially if you're up to snough, and know what's o'clock. I'll learn to make myself usefle, in the fust place; then I'll larn to spell; and, I trust, by reading the novvles of the honrabble member, and the scieutafick treatiseses of the reverend doctor, I may find the secrit of suxess, and git a litell for my own share. I've sevral frends in the press, having paid for many of those chaps' drink, and given them other treets; and so I think I've got all the emilents of suxess; therefore, I am detummined, as I said, to igsept your kind offer, and beg to withdraw the wuds which I made yous of when I refyoused your hoxpatable offer. I must, however——"

"I wish you'd withdraw yourself," said Sir John, busting into a most igstrorinary rage, "and not interrupt the company with your infernal talk! Go down, and get us coffee; and, heark ye! hold your impertinent tongue, or I'll break every bone in your body. You shall have the place, as I said; and while you're in my service, you shall be my servant; but you don't stay in my service after to-morrow. Go down stairs, sir; and don't stand staring here!"

* * * * * *

In this abrupt way, my evening ended: it's with a melancholy regret that I think what came of it. I don't wear plush any more. I am an altered, a wiser, and, I trust, a better man.

I'm about a novvle (having made great progriss in spelling), in the style of my friend Bullwig; and preparing for publigation, in the Doctor's Cyclopedear, The Lives of Eminent Brittish and Foring Washerwomen

EPISTLES TO THE LITERATI.

———◆———

NOTUS.

THE suckmstansies of the following harticle are as follos :—
Me and my friend, the sellabrated Mr. Smith, reckonised each
other in the Haymarket Theatre, during the performints of the
new play. I was settn in the gallery, and sung out to him (he
was in the pit), to jine us after the play, over a glass of bear and
a cold hoyster, in my pantry, the family being out.

Smith came as appinted. We descorsed on the subjick of the
comady ; and, after sefral glases, we each of us agreed to write a
letter to the other, giving our notiums of the pease. Paper was
brought that momint; and Smith writing his harticle across the
knife-bord, I dasht off mine on the dresser.

Our agreement was, that I (being remarkabble for my style of
riting) should cretasize the languidge, whilst he should take up
with the plot of the play; and the candied reader will parding me
for having holtered the original address of my letter, and directed
it to Sir Edward himself; and for having incopperated Smith's
remarks in the midst of my own.

Mayfair, Nov. 30, 1839. Midnite.

Honrabble Barnet !—Retired from the littery world a year or
moar, I didn't think anythink would injuice me to come forrards
again; for I was content with my share of reputation, and pro-
poas'd to add nothink to those immortial wux which have rendered
this Magaseen so sallybrated.

Shall I tell you the reazn of my re-appearants ?—a desire for
the benefick of my fellow-creatures ? Fiddlestick! A mighty
truth with which my busm laboured, and which I must bring
forth or die ? Nonsince—stuff: money's the secret, my dear

Barnet,—money—*l'argong*, *gelt*, *spicunia*. Here's quarter-day coming, and I'm blest if I can pay my landlud, unless I can ad hartificially to my inkum.

This is, however, betwigst you and me. There's no need to blacard the streets with it, or to tell the British public that Fitzroy Y-ll-wpl-sh is short of money, or that the sallybrated hauthor of the Y—— Papers is in peskewniary difficklties, or is fiteagued by his superhuman littery labors, or by his famly suckmstansies, or by any other pusnal matter : my maxim, dear B, is on these pints to be as quiet as posbile. What the juice does the public care for you or me ? Why must we always, in prefizzes and what not, be a talking about ourselves and our igstrodnary merrats, woas, and injaries ? It is on this subjick that I porpies, my dear Barnet, to speak to you in a frendly way ; and praps you'll find my advise tolrabbly holesum.

Well, then,— if you care about the apinions, fur good or evil, of us poor suvvants, I tell you, in the most candied way, I like you, Barnet. I've had my fling at you in my day (for, *entry nou*, that last stoary I roat about you and Larnder was as big a bownsir as ever was)—I've had my fling at you ; but I like you. One may objeck to an immence deal of your writings, which, betwigst you and me, contain more sham scentiment, sham morallaty, sham poatry, than you'd like to own ; but, in spite of this, there's the *stuff* in you : you've a kind and loyal heart in you, Barnet—a trifle deboshed, perhaps ; a kean i, igspecially for what's comic (as for your tradgady, it's mighty flatchulent), and a ready plesnt pen. The man who says you are an As is an As himself. Don't believe him, Barnet ! not that I suppose you wil,—for, if I've formed a correck apinion of you from your wucks, you think your smallbeear as good as most men's : every man does,—and why not ? We brew, and we love our own tap—amen ; but the pint betwigst us, is this stewpid, absudd way of crying out, because the public don't like it too. Why shood they, my dear Barnet ? You may vow that they are fools ; or that the critix are your enemies ; or that the wuld should judge your poams by your critticle rules, and not their own : you may beat your breast, and vow you are a marter, and you won't meud the matter. Take heart, man ! you're not so misrabble after all ; your spirits need not be so *very* cast down; you are not so *very* badly paid. I'd lay a wager that you make, with one thing or another—plays, novvles, pamphlicks, and little odd jobbs here and there—your three thowsnd a-year. There's many a man, dear Bullwig, that works for less, and lives content. Why shouldn't you ? Three thowsnd a-year is no such bad thing,—let alone the barnetcy : it must be a great comfort to have that bloody hand in your skitching.

But don't you sea, that in a wuld naturally envius, wickid, and fond of a joak, this very barnetcy, these very cumplaints,—this ceaseless groning, and moning, and wining of yours, is igsackly the thing which makes people laff and snear more ? If you were ever at a great school, you must recklect who was the boy most bullid, and buffitid, and purshewd—he who minded it most. He who could take a basting got but few ; he who rord and wep because the knotty boys called him nicknames, was nicknamed wuss and wuss. I recklect there was at our school, in Smithfield, a chap of this milksop, spoony sort, who appeared among the romping, ragged fellers in a fine flanning dressing-gownd, that his mama had given him. That pore boy was beaten in a way that his dear ma and aunts didn't know him : his fine flanning dressing-gownd was torn all to ribbings, and he got no pease in the school ever after, but was abliged to be taken to some other saminary, where, I make no doubt, he was paid off igsactly in the same way.

Do you take the halligory, my dear Barnet ? *Mutayto nominy* —you know what I mean. You are the boy, and your barnetcy is the dressing-gownd. You dress yourself out finer than other chaps, and they all begin to sault and hustle you ; it's human nature, Barnet. You show weakness, think of your dear ma, mayhap, and begin to cry : it's all over with you ; the whole school is at you—upper boys and under, big and little ; the dirtiest little fag in the place will pipe out blaggerd names at you, and take his pewny tug at your tail.

The only way to avoid such consperracies is to put a pair of stowt shoalders forrards, and bust through the crowd of raggy-muffins. A good bold fellow dubls his fistt, and cries, " Wha dares meddle wi' me ? " When Scott got *his* barnetcy, for instans, did any one of us cry out ? No, by the laws, he was our master ;

and wo betide the chap that said neigh to him! But there's
barnets and barnets. Do you recklect that fine chapter in
Squintin Durward, about the too fellos and eups, at the siege of
the bishop's castle? One of them was a brave warrier, and kep
his cup; they strangled the other chap—strangled him, and laffed
at him too.

With respeck, then, to the barnetcy pint, this is my advice;
brazen it out. Us littery men I take to be like a pack of school-
boys—childish, greedy, envius, holding by our friends, and always
ready to fight. What must be a man's conduck among such?
He must either take no notis, and pass on myjastick, or else turn
round and pummle soundly—one, two, right and left, ding dong
over the face and eyes; above all, never acknowledge that he is
hurt. Years ago, for instans (we've no ill blood, but only mention
this by way of igsample), you began a sparring with this Magaseen. Law bless you, such a ridicklus gaym I never see: a man
so belaybord, beflustered, bewolloped, was never known; it was
the laff of the whole town. Your intelackshal natur, respected
Barnet, is not fizzickly adapted, so to speak, for encounters of
this sort. You must not indulge in combats with us course
bullies of the press; you have not the *staminy* for a reglar set-to.
What, then, is your plan? In the midst of the mob to pass as
quiet as you can; you won't be undistubbed. Who is? Some
stray kix and buffits will fall to you—mortial man is subjick to
such; but if you begin to wins and cry out, and set up for a
marter, wo betide you!

These remarks, pusnal as I confess them to be, are yet, I assure
you, written in perfick good-natur, and have been inspired by
your play of the *Sea Capting*, and prefiz to it; which latter is on
matters intirely pusnal, and will, therefore, I trust, igscuse this
kind of *ad hominam* (as they say) diskcushion. I propose, honrabble Barnit, to cumsider calmly this play and prephiz, and to
speak of both with that houisty which, in the pantry or studdy,
I've been always phamous for. Let us, in the first place, listen to
the opening of the " Preface of the Fourth Edition:"

"No one can be more sensible than I am of the many faults and deficiencies
to be found in this play; but, perhaps, when it is considered how very rarely
it has happened in the history of our dramatic literature that good acting

plays have been produced, except by those who have either been actors themselves, or formed their habits of literature, almost of life, behind the scenes, I might have looked for a criticism more generous, and less exacting and rigorous, than that by which the attempts of an author accustomed to another class of composition have been received by a large proportion of the periodical press.

"It is scarcely possible, indeed, that this play should not contain faults of two kinds : first, the faults of one who has necessarily much to learn in the mechanism of his art: and, secondly, of one who, having written largely in the narrative style of fiction, may not unfrequently mistake the effects of a novel for the effects of a drama. I may add to these, perhaps, the deficiencies that arise from uncertain health and broken spirits, which render the author more susceptible than he might have been some years since to that spirit of depreciation and hostility which it has been his misfortune to excite amongst the general contributors to the periodical press; for the consciousness that every endeavour will be made to cavil, to distort, to misrepresent, and, in fine, if possible, to *run down*, will occasionally haunt even the hours of composition, to check the inspiration, and damp the ardour.

"Having confessed thus much frankly and fairly, and with a hope that I may ultimately do better, should I continue to write for the stage (which nothing but an assurance that, with all my defects, I may yet bring some little aid to the drama, at a time when any aid, however humble, ought to be welcome to the lovers of the art, could induce me to do), may I be permitted to say a few words as to some of the objections which have been made against this play ?"

Now, my dear sir, look what a pretty number of please you put forrards here, why your play shouldn't be good.

First.   Good plays are almost always written by actors.

Secknd.   You are a novice to the style of composition.

Third.   You *may* be mistaken in your effects, being a novelist by trade, and not a play-writer.

Fourthly.   Your in such bad helth and sperrits.

Fifthly.   Your so afraid of the critix, that they damp your arder.

For shame, for shame, man!   What confeshus is these,—what painful pewling and piping!   Your not a babby.   I take you to be some seven or eight and thutty years old—"in the morning of youth," as the flosofer says.   Don't let any such nonsince take your reazn prisoner.   What you, an old hand amongst us,—an old soljer of our sovring quean the press,—you, who have had the best pay, have held the topmost rank (ay, and *deserved* them too! —I gif you leaf to quot me in sasiaty, and say, "I *am* a man of genius: Y-ll-wpl-sh says so"),—you to lose heart, and cry pick-

avy, and begin to howl, because little boys fling stones at you!
Fie, man! take courage; and, bearing the terrows of your blood-
red hand, as the poet says, punish us, if we've ofended you, punish
us like a man, or bear your own punishment like a man.   Don't
try to come off with such misrabble lodgic as that above.

What do you?   You give four satisfackary reazns that the play
is bad (the secknd is naught,—for your no such chicking at play-
writing, this being the forth).   You show that the play must be
bad, and *then* begin to deal with the critix for finding folt!

Was there ever wuss generalship?   The play *is* bad,—your
right,—a wuss I never see or read.   But why kneed *you* say so?
If it was so *very* bad, why publish it?   *Because you wish to serve
the drama!*   O fie! don't lay that flattering function to your sole,
as Milton observes.   Do you believe that this *Sea Capting* can
serve the drama?   Did you never inteud that it should serve any
thing, or any body *else?*   Of cors you did!   You wrote it for
money,—money from the maniger, money from the bookseller,—
for the same reason that I write this.   Sir, Shakspeare wrote for
the very same reasons, and I never heard that he bragged about
serving the drama.   Away with this canting about great motifs!
Let us not be too prowd, my dear Barnet, and fansy ourselves
marters of the truth, marters or apostels.   We are but tradesmen,
working for bread, and not for righteousness' sake.   Let's try and
work honestly; but don't let us be prayting pompisly about our
"sacred calling."   The taylor who makes your coats (and very
well they are made too, with the best of velvit collars)—I say
Stulze, or Nugee, might cry out that *their* motifs were but to
assert the eturnle truth of tayloring, with just as much reazn;
and who would believe them?

Well; after this acknollitchmint that the play is bad, come
sefral pages of attack on the critix, and the folt those gentry have
found with it.   With these I shan't middle for the presnt.   You
defend all the characters 1 by 1, and conclude your remarks as
follows:—

"I must be pardoned for this disquisition on my own designs.   When
every means is employed to misrepresent, it becomes, perhaps, allowable to
explain.   And if I do not think that my faults as a dramatic author are to be
found in the study and delineation of character, it is precisely because *that*

is the point on which all my previous pursuits in literature and actual life would be most likely to preserve me from the errors I own elsewhere, whether of misjudgment or inexperience.

" I have now only to add my thanks to the actors for the zeal and talent with which they have embodied the characters intrusted to them. The sweetness and grace with which Miss Faucit embellished the part of Violet, which, though only a sketch, is most necessary to the colouring and harmony of the play, were perhaps the more pleasing to the audience from the generosity, rare with actors, which induced her to take a part so far inferior to her powers. The applause which attends the performance of Mrs. Warner and Mr. Strickland attests their success in characters of unusual diffi- culty; while the singular beauty and nobleness, whether of conception or execution, with which the greatest of living actors has elevated the part of Norman (so totally different from his ordinary range of character), is a new proof of his versatility and accomplishment in all that belongs to his art. It would be scarcely gracious to conclude these remarks without expressing my acknowledgment of that generous and indulgent sense of justice which, forgetting all political differences in a literary arena, has enabled me to appeal to approving audiences—from hostile critics. And it is this which alone encou- rages me to hope that, sooner or later, I may add to the dramatic literature of my country something that may find, perhaps, almost as many friends in the next age as it has been the fate of the author to find enemies in this."

See, now, what a good comfrabble vanaty is! Pepple have quarld with the dramatic characters of your play. " No," says you; " if I *am* remarkabble for anythink, it's for my study and delineation of character; *that* is presizely the pint to which my littery purshuits have led me." Have you read Jil Blaw, my dear sir? Have you pirouzed that exlent tragady, the *Critic?* There's something so like this in Sir Fretful Plaguy, and the Archbishop of Granadiers, that I'm blest if I can't laff till my sides ake. Think of the critix fixing on the very pint for which you are famus!—the roags! And spose they had said the plot was absudd, or the langwitch absudder, still, don't you think you would have had a word in defens of them too—you who hope to find frends for your dramatic wux in the nex age? Poo! I tell thee, Barnet, that the nex age will be wiser and better than this; and do you think that it will imply itself a reading of your traja- dies? This is misantrofy, Barnet—reglar Byronism; and you ot to have a better apinian of human natur.

Your apinion about the actors I shan't here middle with. They all acted exlently as far as my humbile judgement goes, and your write in giving them all possbile prays. But let's consider the last sentence of the prefiz, my dear Barnet, and see what a pretty set of apiniuns you lay down.

1. The critix are your inymies in this age.

2. In the nex, however, you hope to find newmrous frends.

3. And it's a satisfackshn to think that, in spite of politticle diffrances, you have found frendly aujences here.

Now, my dear Barnet, for a man who begins so humbly with what my friend Father Prout calls au *argamantum ad misericorjam*, who ignoledges that his play is bad, that his pore dear helth is bad, and those cussid critix have played the jiuce with him—I say, for a man who begins in such a humbill toan, it's rayther *rich* to see how you end.

My dear Barnet, *do* you suppose that *politticle diffrances* prejudice pepple against *you?* What *are* your politix? Wig, I presume—so are mine, *ontry noo*. And what if they *are* Wig, or Raddiccle, or Cumsuvvative? Does any mortial man in England care a phig for your politix? Do you think yourself such a mity man in parlymint, that critix are to be angry with you, and aujences to be cumsidered magnanamous because they treat you fairly? There, now, was Sherridn, he who roat the *Rifles* and *School for Scandle* (I saw the *Rifles* after your play, and, O Barnet, if you *knew* what a relief it was!)—there, I say, was Sherridn— he *was* a politticle character, if you please—he *could* make a spitch or two—do you spose that Pitt, Purseyvall, Castlerag, old George the Third himself, wooden go to see the *Rivles*— ay, and clap hands too, and laff and ror, for all Sherry's Wiggery? Do you spose the critix wouldn't applaud too? For shame, Barnet! what ninnis, what hartless raskles, you must beleave them to be,—in the fust plase, to fancy that you are a politticle genius; in the secknd, to let your politix interfear with their notiums about littery merits!

"Put that nonsince out of your head," as Fox said to Bonypart. Wasn't it that great genus, Dennis, that wrote in Swiff and Poop's time, who fansid that the French king wooden make pease unless Dennis was delivered up to him? Upon my wud, I doant think he carrid his diddlusion much further than a serting honrabble barnet of my aquentance.

And, then, for the nex age. Respected sir, this is another

diddlusion ; a grose misteak on your part, or my name is not Y—sh. These plays immortial ?   Ah, *parrysampe*, as the French say, this is too strong—the small-beer of the *Sea Capting*, or of any sux-essor of the *Sea Capting*, to keep sweet for sentries and sentries! Barnet, Barnet ! do you know the natur of bear ?   Six weeks is not past, and here your last casque is sour—the public won't even now drink it ; and I lay a wager that, betwigst this day (the thuttieth November) and the end of the year, the barl will be off the stox altogether, never, never to return.

I've notted down a few frazes here and there, which you will do well do igsamin :—

NORMAN.

" The eternal Flora
Woos to her odorous haunts the western wind ;
While circling round and upwards from the boughs,
Golden with fruits that lure the joyous birds,
Melody, like a happy soul released,
Hangs in the air, and from invisible plumes
Shakes sweetness down ! "

NORMAN.

" And these the lips
Where, till this hour, the sad and holy kiss
Of parting linger'd, as the fragrance left
By *angels* when they touch the earth and vanish."

NORMAN.

" Hark ! she has blessed her son ! I bid ye witness,
Ye listening heavens—thou circumambient air :
The ocean sighs it back—and with the murmur
Rustle the happy leaves.   All nature breathes
Aloud—aloft—to the Great Parent's ear,
The blessing of the mother on her child."

NORMAN.

" I dream of love, enduring faith, a heart
Mingled with mine—a deathless heritage,
Which I can take unsullied to the *stars*,
When the Great Father calls his children home.

NORMAN.

" The blue air, breathless in the *starry* peace,
After long silence hushed as heaven, but filled
With happy thoughts as heaven with *angels*."

NORMAN.

" Till one calm night, when over earth and wave
Heaven looked its love from all its numberless *stars*."

NORMAN.

" Those eyes, the guiding *stars* by which I steered."

NORMAN.

" That great mother
(The only parent I have known), whose face
Is bright with gazing ever on the *stars*—
The mother-sea."

NORMAN.

" My bark shall be our home;
The *stars* that light the *angel* palaces
Of air, our lamps."

NORMAN.

" A name that glitters, like a *star*, amidst
The galaxy of England's loftiest born."

LADY ARUNDEL.

" And see him princeliest of the lion tribe,
Whose swords and coronals gleam around the throne,
The guardian *stars* of the imperial isle."

The fust spissymen has been going the round of all the papers,
as real, reglar poatry. Those wickid critix! they must have been
laffing in their sleafs when they quoted it. Malody, suckling
round and uppards from the bows, like a happy soul released,
hangs in the air, and from invizable plumes shakes ˈsweetness
down. Mighty fine, truly! but let mortial man tell the meanink
of the passidge. Is it *musickle* sweetniss that Malody shakes
down from its plumes—its wings, that is, or tail—or some
pekewliar scent that proceeds from happy souls released, and
which they shake down from the trees when they are suckling
round and uppards? *Is* this poatry, Barnet? Lay your hand on
your busm, and speak out boldly: Is it poatry, or sheer windy
humbugg, that sounds a little melojous, and won't bear the com-
manest test of comman sence?

In passidge number 2, the same bisniss is going on, though in a
more comprehensable way: the air, the leaves, the otion, are fild

with emocean at Capting Norman's happiness. Pore Nature is
dragged in to partisapate in his joys, just as she has been befor.
Once in a poem, this universle simfithy is very well; but once is
enuff, my dear Barnet: and that once should be in some great
suckmstans, surely,—such as the meeting of Adam and Eve, in
Paradice Lost, or Jewpeter and Jewno, in Hoàmer, where there
seems, as it were, a reasn for it.   But sea-captings should not be
eternly spowting and invoking gods, hevns, starrs, angels, and
other silestial influences.   We can all do it, Barnet; nothing in
life is esier.   I can compare my livry buttons to the stars, or the
clouds of my backopipe to the dark vollums that ishew from Mount
Hetna; or I can say that angels are looking down from them, and
the tobacco silf, like a happy sole released, is circling round and
upwards, and shaking sweetness down.   All this is as esy as drink;
but it's not poatry, Barnet, nor natural.   People, when their
mothers reckonise them, don't howl about the suckumambient air,
and paws to think of the happy leaves a rustling—at least, one
mistrusts them if they do.   Take another instans out of your
own play.   Capting Norman (with his eternll *slack-jaw!*) meets
the gal of his art:—

> " Look up, look up, my Violet—weeping? fie !
> And trembling too—yet leaning on my breast.
> In truth, thou art too soft for such rude shelter.
> Look up !   I come to woo thee to the seas,
> My sailor's bride !   Hast thou no voice but blushes?
> Nay—From those roses let me, like the bee,
> Drag forth the secret sweetness !"

> VIOLET.
>   " Oh what thoughts
> Were kept for *speech* when we once more should meet,
> Now blotted from the *page;* and all I feel
> Is—*thou* art with me !"

Very right, Miss Violet—the scentiment is natral, affeckshnit,
pleasing, simple (it might have been in more grammaticle languidge, and no harm done): but never mind, the feeling is pritty:
and I can fancy, my dear Barnet, a pritty, smiling, weeping lass,
looking up in a man's face and saying it.   But the capting !—O
this capting !—this windy, spouting captain, with his prittinesses,

and conseated apollogies for the hardness of his busm, and his old, stale, vapid simalies, and his wishes to be a bee! Pish! Men don't make love in this finniking way. It's the part of a sentymentle, poeticle taylor, not a galliant gentleman, in command of one of her madjisty's vessels of war.

Look at the remaining extrac, honored Barnet, and acknollidge that Capting Norman is eturnly repeating himself, with his endless jabber, about stars and angels. Look at the neat grammaticle twist of Lady Arundel's spitch, too, who, in the corse of three lines, has made her son a prince, a lion, with a sword and coronal, and a star. Why jumble and sheak up metafors in this way? Barnet, one simily is quite enuff in the best of sentenses (and, I preshume, I kneedn't tell you that it's as well to have it *like*, when you are about it). Take my advise, honrabble sir—listen to a humble footmin: it's genrally best in poatry to understand puffickly what you mean yourself, and to ingspress your meaning clearly afterwoods—in the simpler words the better, praps. You may, for instans, call a coronet a coronal (an "ancestral coronal," p. 74), if you like, as you might call a hat a "swart sombrero," "a glossy four-and-nine," "a silken helm, to storm impermeable, and lightsome as the breezy gossamer;" but, in the long run, it's as well to call it a hat. It *is* a hat; and that name is quite as poetticle as another. I think it's Playto, or els Harrystottle, who observes that what we call a rose by any other name would swell as sweet. Confess, now, dear Barnet, don't you long to call it a Polyanthus?

I never see a play more carelessly written. In such a hurry you seem to have bean, that you have actially in some sentences forgot to put in the sence. What is this, for instance?—

> "This thrice precious one
> Smiled to my eyes—drew being from my breast—
> Slept in my arms;—the very tears I shed
> Above my treasures were to men and angels
> Alike such holy sweetness!"

In the name of all the angels that ever you invoked—Raphael, Gabriel, Uriel, Zadkiel, Azrael—what does this "holy sweetness" mean? We're not spinxes to read such durk conandrums. If you knew my state sins I came upon this passidg—I've neither slep nor eton; I've neglected my pantry; I've been wandring from house to house with this riddl in my hand, and nobody can understand it. All Mr. Frazier's men are wild, looking gloomy at one another, and asking what this may be. All the cumtri-butors have been spoak to. The Doctor, who knows every lan-guitch, has tried and giv'n up; we've sent to Docter Pettigruel, who reads horyglifics a deal ezier than my way of spellin'—no anser. Quick! quick with a fifth edition, honored Barnet, and set us at rest! While your about it, please, too, to igsplain the two last lines:—

> " His merry bark with England's flag to crown her."

See what dellexy of igspreshn, " a flag to crown her!"

> "His merry bark with England's flag to crown her,
> Fame for my hopes, and woman in my cares."

Likewise the following :—

> " Girl, beware,
> THE LOVE THAT TRIFLES ROUND THE CHARMS IT GILDS
> OFT RUINS WHILE IT SHINES."

Igsplane this, men and angels! I've tried every way; backards, forards, and in all sorts of trancepositions, as thus :—

> The love that ruins round the charms it shines,
> Gilds while it trifles oft;

Or,

> The charm that gilds around the love it ruins,
> Oft trifles while it shines;

Or,

> The ruins that love gilds and shines around,
> Oft trifles where it charms;

Or,

> Love, while it charms, shines round, and ruins oft
> The trifles that it gilds ;

Or,

> The love that trifles, gilds and ruins oft,
> While round the charms it shines.

All which are as sensable as the fust passidge.

And with this I'll alow my friend Smith, who has been silent all this time, to say a few words. He has not written near so much as me (being an infearor genus, betwigst ourselves), but he says he never had such mortial difficklty with any thing as with the dixcripshn of the plott of your pease.   Here his letter.

To CH-RL-S F-TZR-Y PL-NT-G-N-T Y-LL-WPL-SH, ESQ., *&c. &c.*

30th Nov. 1839.

My dear and honoured Sir,—I have the pleasure of laying before you the following description of the plot, and a few remarks upon the style of the piece called *The Sea Captain*.

Five-and-twenty years back, a certain Lord Arundel had a daughter, heiress of his estates and property; a poor cousin, Sir Maurice Beevor (being next in succession); and a page, Arthur Le Mesnil by name.

The daughter took a fancy for the page, and the young persons were married unknown to his lordship.

Three days before her confinement (thinking, no doubt, that period favourable for travelling), the young couple had agreed to run away together, and had reached a chapel near on the sea-coast, from which they were to embark, when Lord Arundel abruptly put a stop to their proceedings by causing one Gaussen, a pirate, to murder the page.

His daughter was carried back to Arundel House, and, in three days, gave birth to a son.   Whether his lordship knew of this birth I cannot say; the infant, however, was never acknow-ledged, but carried by Sir Maurice Beevor to a priest, Onslow by name, who educated the lad and kept him for twelve years in profound ignorance of his birth.   The boy went by the name of Norman.

Lady Arundel meanwhile married again, again became a widow, but had a second son, who was the acknowledged heir, and called Lord Ashdale.   Old Lord Arundel died, and her ladyship became countess in her own right.

When Norman was about twelve years of age, his mother, who wished to " *waft* young Arthur to a distant land," had him sent on board ship.   Who should the captain of the ship be but Gaussen, who received a smart bribe from Sir Maurice Beevor to kill the lad. Accordingly, Gaussen tied him to a plank, and pitched him overboard.

    *   *   *   *   *   *

About thirteen years after these circumstances, Violet, an orphan niece of Lady Arundel's second husband, came to pass a few weeks with her ladyship. She had just come from a sea-voyage, and had been saved from a wicked Algerine by an English sea captain. This sea captain was no other than Norman, who had been picked up off his plank, and fell in love with, and was loved by, Miss Violet.

A short time after Violet's arrival at her aunt's the captain came to pay her a visit, his ship anchoring off the coast, near Lady Arundel's residence. By a singular coincidence, that rogue Gaussen's ship anchored in the harbour too. Gaussen at once knew his man, for he had "tracked" him, (after drowning him,) and he informed Sir Maurice Beevor that young Norman was alive.

Sir Maurice Beevor informed her ladyship. How should she get rid of him? In this wise. He was in love with Violet, let him marry her and be off; for Lord Ashdale was in love with his cousin too; and, of course, could not marry a young woman in her station of life. "You have a chaplain on board," says her ladyship to Captain Norman; "let him attend to-night in the ruined chapel, marry Violet, and away with you to sea." By this means she hoped to be quit of him for ever.

But unfortunately, the conversation had been overheard by Beevor, and reported to Ashdale. Ashdale determined to be at the chapel and carry off Violet; as for Beevor, he sent Gaussen to the chapel to kill both Ashdale and Norman, thus there would only be Lady Arundel between him and the title.

Norman, in the meanwhile, who had been walking near the chapel, had just seen his worthy old friend, the priest, most barbarously murdered there. Sir Maurice Beevor had set Gaussen upon him; his reverence was coming with the papers concerning Norman's birth, which Beevor wanted in order to extort money from the countess. Gaussen was, however, obliged to run before he got the papers; and the clergyman had time, before he died, to tell Norman the story, and give him the documents, with which Norman sped off to the castle to have an interview with his mother.

He lays his white cloak and hat on the table, and begs to be left alone with her ladyship. Lord Ashdale, who is in the room, surlily quits it; but, going out cunningly, puts on Norman's cloak. "It will be dark," says he, "down at the chapel; Violet won't know me; and, egad! I'll run off with her!"

Norman has his interview. Her ladyship acknowledges him, for she cannot help it; but will not embrace him, love him, or have anything to do with him.

Away he goes to the chapel. His chaplain was there waiting to marry him to Violet, his boat was there to carry him on board his ship, and Violet was there, too.

"Norman," says she, in the dark, "dear Norman, I knew you by your white cloak; here I am." And she and the man in a cloak go off to the inner chapel to be married.

There waits Master Gaussen; he has seized the chaplain and the boat's crew, and is just about to murder the man in the cloak, when—

Norman rushes in and cuts him down, much to the surprise of Miss, for she never suspected it was sly Ashdale who had come, as we have seen, disguised, and very nearly paid for his masquerading.

Ashdale is very grateful; but, when Norman persists in marrying Violet, he says—no, he shan't. He shall fight; he is a coward if he doesn't fight. Norman flings down his sword, and says he *won't* fight; and—

Lady Arundel, who has been at prayers all this time, rushing in, says, "Hold! this is your brother, Percy—your elder brother!" Here is some restiveness on Ashdale's part, but he finishes by embracing his brother.

Norman burns all the papers; vows he will never peach; reconciles himself with his mother; says he will go loser; but, having ordered his ship to "veer" round to the chapel, orders it to veer back again, for he will pass the honeymoon at Arundel Castle.

As you have been pleased to ask my opinion, it strikes me that there are one or two very good notions in this plot. But the author does not fail, as he would modestly have us believe, from ignorance of stage-business; he seems to know too much, rather than too little, about the stage, to be too anxious to cram in effects, incidents, perplexities. There is the perplexity concerning Ashdale's murder, and Norman's murder, and the priest's murder, and the page's murder, and Gaussen's murder. There is the perplexity about the papers, and that about the hat and cloak, (a silly, foolish obstacle,) which only tantalise the spectator, and retard the march of the drama's action; it is as if the author had said, "I must have a new incident in every act, I must keep tickling the spectator perpetually, and never let him off until the fall of the curtain."

The same disagreeable bustle and petty complication of intrigue you may remark in the author's drama of *Richelieu*. *The Lady of Lyons* was a much simpler and better-wrought plot. The incidents following each other either not too swiftly or startlingly. In *Richelieu*, it always seemed to me as if one heard doors perpetually clapping and banging; one was puzzled to follow the train of conversation, in the midst of the perpetual small noises that distracted one right and left.

Nor is the list of characters of *The Sea Captain* to be despised. The outlines of all of them are good. A mother, for whom one feels a proper tragic mixture of hatred and pity; a gallant single-hearted son, whom she disdains, and who conquers her at last by his noble conduct; a dashing haughty Tybalt of a brother; a wicked poor cousin, a pretty maid, and a fierce buccanier. These people might pass three hours very well on the stage, and interest the audience hugely; but the author fails in filling up the outlines. His language is absurdly stilted, frequently careless; the reader or spectator hears a number of loud speeches, but scarce a dozen lines that seem to belong of nature to the speakers.

Nothing can be more fulsome or loathsome to my mind than the continual sham-religious clap-traps which the author has put into the mouth of his hero; nothing more unsailor-like than his namby-pamby starlit descriptions, which my ingenious colleague has, I see, alluded to. "Thy faith my anchor, and thine eyes my haven," cries the gallant captain to his lady. See how loosely the sentence is constructed, like a thousand others in the book.

The captain is to cast anchor with the girl's faith in her own eyes; either image might pass by itself, but together, like the quadrupeds of Kilkenny, they devour each other. The captain tells his lieutenant *to bid his bark veer round* to a point in the harbour. Was ever such language? My lady gives Sir Maurice a thousand pounds to *waft* him (her son) to some distant shore. Nonsense, sheer nonsense; and what is worse, affected nonsense!

Look at the comedy of the poor cousin. "There is a great deal of game on the estate—partridges, hares, wild-geese, snipes, and plovers (*smacking his lips*)—besides a magnificent preserve of sparrows, which I can sell to the *little blackguards* in the streets at a penny a hundred. But I am very poor—a very poor old knight."

Is this wit, or nature? It is a kind of sham wit; it reads as if it were wit, but it is not. What poor, poor stuff, about the little blackguard boys! what flimsy ecstasies and silly "smacking of lips" about the plovers! Is this the man who writes for the next age? O fie! Here is another joke :—

> "*Sir Maurice.* Mice! zounds, how can I
> Keep mice! I can't afford it! They were starved
> To death an age ago. The last was found
> Come Christmas three years, stretched beside a bone
> In that same larder, so consumed and worn
> By pious fast, 'twas awful to behold it!
> I canonised its corpse in spirits of wine,
> And set it in the porch—a solemn warning
> To thieves and beggars!"

Is not this rare wit? "Zounds! how can I keep mice?" is well enough for a miser; not too new, or brilliant either; but this miserable dilution of a thin joke, this wretched hunting down of the poor mouse! It is humiliating to think of a man of *esprit* harping so long on such a mean, pitiful string. A man who aspires to immortality, too! I doubt whether it is to be gained thus; whether our author's words are not too loosely built to make "starry pointing pyramids of." Horace clipped and squared his blocks more carefully before he laid the monument which, *imber edax*, or *Aquila impotens*, or *fuga temporum*, might assail in vain. Even old Ovid, when he raised his stately, shining heathen temple, had placed some columns in it, and hewn out a statue or two which deserved the immortality that he prophesied (somewhat arrogantly) for himself.   But let not all be looking forward to a future, and fancying that, *"incerti spatium dum finiat avi,"* our books are to be immortal.   Alas! the way to immortality is not so easy, nor will our *Sea Captain* be permitted such an unconscionable cruise.   If all the immortalities were really to have their wish, what a work would our descendants have to study them all!

Not yet, in my humble opinion, has the honourable baronet achieved this deathless consummation.   There will come a day (may it be long distant!) when the very best of his novels will be forgotten; and it is reasonable to suppose that his dramas will pass out of existence, some time or other, in the lapse of the *secula seculorum.*   In the meantime, my dear Plush, if you ask me what the great obstacle is towards the dramatic fame and merit of our friend, I would say that it does not lie so much in hostile critics or feeble health, as in a careless habit of writing, and a peevish vanity which causes him to shut his eyes to his faults. The question of original capacity I will not moot; one may think very highly of the honourable baronet's talent, without rating it quite so high as he seems disposed to do.

And to conclude: as he has chosen to combat the critics in person, the critics are surely justified in being allowed to address him directly.

With best compliments to Mrs. Yellowplush,
I have the honour to be, dear Sir,
Your most faithful and obliged
humble servant,
JOHN THOMAS SMITH.

And now, Smith having finisht his letter, I think I can't do better than clothes mine lickwise; for though I should never be tired of talking, praps the public may of hearing, and therefore it's best to shut up shopp.

What I've said, respected Barnit, I hoap you woan't take unkind.   A play, you see, is public property for every one to say his say on; and I think, if you read your prefez over agin, you'll see that it ax as a direct incouridgemint to us critix to come forrard and notice you. But don't fansy, I besitch you, that we are actiated by hostillaty; fust write a good play, and you'll see we'll prays it fast enuff. Waiting which, *Agray, Munseer le Chevaleer, l' ashurance de ma hot cumsideratun.*

Voter distangy,

Y

THE DIARY

OF

C. JEAMES DE LA PLUCHE, ESQ.

THE DIARY

OF

C. JEAMES DE LA PLUCHE, ESQ.

A LUCKY SPECULATOR.

"CONSIDERABLE sensation has been excited in the upper and lower circles in the West End, by a startling piece of good fortune which has befallen James Plush, Esq., lately footman in a respected family in Berkeley Square.

" One day last week, Mr. James waited upon his master, who is a banker in the City; and after a little blushing and hesitation, said he had saved a little money in service, was anxious to retire, and to invest his savings to advantage.

" His master (we believe we may mention, without offending delicacy, the well-known name of Sir George Flimsy, of the house of Flimsy, Diddler, and Flash,) smilingly asked Mr. James what was the amount of his savings, wondering considerably how, out of an income of thirty guineas—the main part of which he spent in bouquets, silk stockings, and perfumery—Mr. Plush could have managed to lay by anything.

" Mr. Plush, with some hesitation, said he had been *speculating in railroads,* and stated his winnings to have been thirty thousand pounds. He had commenced his speculations with twenty, borrowed from a fellow-servant. He had dated his letters from the house in Berkeley Square, and humbly begged pardon of his master for not having instructed the Railway Secretaries who answered his applications to apply at the area-bell.

" Sir George, who was at breakfast, instantly rose, and shook Mr. P. by the hand; Lady Flimsy begged him to be seated, and partake of the breakfast which he had laid on the table; and has subsequently invited him to her grand *déjeuner* at Richmond, where it was observed that Miss Emily Flimsy, her beautiful and accomplished seventh daughter, paid the lucky gentleman *marked attention.*

" We hear it stated that Mr. P. is of a very ancient family, (Hugo de la Pluche came over with the Conqueror); and the new Brougham which he has started, bears the ancient coat of his race.

" He has taken apartments in the Albany, and is a director of thirty-three railroads. He proposes to stand for Parliament at the next general election on decidedly conservative principles, which have always been the politics of his family.

" Report says, that even in his humble capacity Miss Emily Flimsy had remarked his high demeanour.   Well, ' None but the brave,' say we, ' deserve the fair.' "—*Morning Paper.*

This announcement will explain the following lines, which have been put into our box * with a West-End post-mark.   If, as we believe, they are written by the young woman from whom the Millionaire borrowed the sum on which he raised his fortune, what heart will not melt with sympathy at her tale, and pity the sorrows which she expresses in such artless language?

If it be not too late ; if wealth have not rendered its possessor callous ; if poor Maryanne *be still alive ;* we trust, we trust, Mr. Plush will do her justice.

JEAMES OF BUCKLEY SQUARE.

A HELIGY.

Come all ye gents vot cleans the plate,
  Come all ye ladies maids so fair—
Vile I a story vill relate
  Of cruel Jeames of Buckley Square.
A tighter lad, it is confest,
  Neer valked with powder in his air,
Or vore a nosegay in his breast,
  Than andsum Jeames of Buckley Square.

O Evns ! it vas the best of sights,
  Behind his Master's coach and pair,
To see our Jeames in red plush tights,
  A driving hoff from Buckley Square.
He vel became his hagwilletts,
  He cocked his at with *such* a hair ;
His calves and viskers *vas* such pets,
  That hall loved Jeames of Buckley Square.

He pleased the hup-stairs folks as vell,
  And o ! I vithered vith despair,
Missis *vould* ring the parler bell,
  And call up Jeames in Buckley Square.

* The letter-box of *Mr. Punch,* in whose columns these papers were first published.

Both heer and sperrits he abhord,
  (Sperrits and beer I can't a bear,)
You would have thought he vas a lord
  Down in our All in Buckley Square.

Last year he visper'd, " Mary Ann,
  Ven I've an under'd pound to spare,
To take a public is my plan,
  And leave this hojous Buckley Square."
O how my gentle heart did bound,
  To think that I his name should bear.
" Dear Jeames," says I, " I've twenty pound,"
  And gev them him in Buckley Square.

Our master vas a City gent,
  His name's in railroads everywhere,
And lord, vot lots of letters vent
  Betwigst his brokers and Buckley Squaro !
My Jeames it was the letters took,
  And read them all, (I think it's fair,)
And took a loaf from Master's book,
  As *hothers* do in Buckley Square.

Encouraged with my twenty pound,
  Of which poor *I* was unavare,
He wrote the Companies all round,
  And signed hisself from Buckley Square,
And how John Porter used to grin,
  As day by day, share after share,
Came railvay letters pouring in,
  " J. Plush, Esquire, in Buckley Square."

Our servants' All was in a rage—
  Scrip, stock, curves, gradients, bull and bear,
Vith butler, coachman, groom and page,
  Vas all the talk in Buckley Square.
But O ! imagine vot I felt
  Last Vensday veek as ever were ;
I gits a letter, which I spelt
  " Miss M. A. Hoggins, Buckley Square."

He sent me back my money true—
  He sent me back my lock of air,
And said, " My dear, I bid ajew
  To Mary Hann and Buckley Square.
Think not to marry, foolish Hann,
  With people who your betters are;
James Plush is now a gentleman,
  And you—a cook in Buckley Square.

"I've thirty thousand guineas won,
   In six short months, by genus rare ;
You little thought what Jeames was on,
   Poor Mary Hann, in Buckley Squarc.
I've thirty thousand guineas net,
   Powder and plush I scorn to vear;
And so, Miss Mary Hann, forget
   For hever Jeames, of Buckley Square."

*   *   *   *   *   *

The rest of the MS. is illegible, being literally washed away in
a flood of tears.

A LETTER FROM "JEAMES, OF BUCKLEY SQUARE."

Albany, Letter X. August 10, 1845.

" Sir,—Has a reglar suscriber to your emusing paper, I beg
leaf to state that I should never have done so, had I supposed
that it was your abbit to igspose the mistaries of privit life, and
to hinjer the delligit feelings of umble individyouals like myself,
who have *no ideer* of being made the subject of newspaper criticism.

" I elude, Sir, to the unjustafiable use which has been made of
my name in your Journal, where both my muccantile speclations
and the *hinmost pashsn of my art* have been brot forrards in a
ridicklus way for the public emusemint.

" What call, Sir, has the public to inquire into the suckmstansies of my engagements with Miss Mary Hann Oggins, or to
meddle with their rupsher ?   Why am I to be maid the hobjick of
your *redicule in a doggril ballit* impewted to her ? I say *impewted*,
because, in *my* time at least, Mary Hann could only sign her +
mark (has I've hoften witnist it for her when she paid hin at the
Savings Bank) and has for *sacrificing to the Mewses* and making
poatry, she was as *hincapible* as Mr. Wakley himself.

" With respect to the ballit, my baleaf is, that it is wrote by a
footman in a low famly, a pore retch who attempted to rivle me
in my affections to Mary Hann—a feller not five foot six, and
with no more calves to his legs than a donkey—who was always a
ritin (having been a doctor's boy) and who I nockt down with a
pint of porter (as he well recklex) at the 3 Tuns Jerming Street,
for daring to try to make a but of me. He has signed Miss

H's name to his *nonsince and lies :* and you lay yourself hopen to a haction for lible for insutting them in your paper.

"It is false that I have treated Miss H. hill in *hany* way. That I borrowed 20lb of her is *trew*. But she confesses I paid it back. Can hall people say as much of the money *they've* lent or borrowed? No. And I not only paid it back: but giv her the andsomest pres'nts *which I never should have eluded to*, but for this attack. Fust, a silver thimble (which I found in Missus's work-box); secknd, a vollom of Byrom's poems: third, I halways brought her a glas of Curasore, when we ad a party, of which she was remarkable fond. I treated her to Hashley's twice, (and halways a srimp or a hoyster by the way,) ·and a *thowsnd deligit attentions*, which I sapose count for *nothink*.

"Has for marridge. Haltered suckmstancies rendered it himpossable. I was gone into a new spear of life—mingling with my native aristoxy. I breathe no sallible of blame aginst Miss H. but his a hilliterit cookmaid fit to set at a fashnable table. Do young fellers of rank genrally marry out of the Kitching? If we cast our i's upon a low-born gal, I needn say its only a tempory distraction, *pore passy le tong*. So much for *her* claims upon me. Has for *that beest of a Doctor's boy* he's unwuthy the notas of a Gentleman.

"That I've one thirty thousand lb, *and praps more*, I dont deny. Ow much has the Kilossus of Railroads one, I should like to know, and what was his cappitle? I hentered the market with 20lb, specklated Jewdicious, and ham what I ham. So may you be (if you have 20lb, and praps you haven't)—So may you be: if you choose to go in & win.

"I for my part am jusly *prowd* of my suxess, and could give you a hundred instances of my gratatude. For igsample, the fust pair of hosses I bought (and a better pare of steppers I dafy you to see in hany curracle,) I crisn'd Hull and Selby, in grateful elusion to my transackshns in that railroad. My riding Cob I called very unhaptly my Dublin and Galway. He came down with me the other day, and I've jest sold him at ¼ discount.

"At fust with prudence and modration I only kep two grooms for my stables, one of whom lickwise waited on me at table. I have now a confidenshle servant, a vally de shamber—He curls

my air; inspex my accounts, and hansers my hinvitations to
dinner. I call this Vally my *Trent Vally*, for it was the prophit
I got from that exlent line, which injuiced me to ingage him.

"Besides my North British Plate and Breakfast equipidge—I
have two handsom suvvices for dinner—the goold plate for Sun-
days, and the silver for common use. When I ave a great party,
'Trent,' I say to my man, 'we will have the London and Bum-
mingham plate to-day (the goold), or else the Manchester and
Leeds (the silver.)' I bought them after realising on the abuf
lines, and if people suppose that the companys made me a presnt
of the plate, how can I help it?

"In the sam way I say, 'Trent, bring us a bottle of Bristol
and Hexeter!' or, 'Put some Heastern Counties in hice!' *He*
knows what I mean: it's the wines I bought upon the hospicious tummination of my connexshn with those two railroads.

"So strong, indeed, as this abbit become, that being asked to
stand Godfather to the youngest Miss Diddle last weak, I had her
christened (provisionally) Rosamell—from the French line of
which I am Director; and only the other day, finding myself
rayther unwell, 'Doctor,' says I to Sir Jeames Clark, ''Ive sent
to consult you because my Midlands are out of horder; and I want
you to send them up to a premium.' The Doctor lafd, and I
beleave told the story subsquintly at Buckinum P—ll—s.

"But I will trouble you no father. My sole objict in writing
has been to *clear my carrater*—to show that I came by my money
in a honrable way: that I'm not ashaymd of the manner in
which I gayned it, and ham indeed grateful for my good fortune.

"To conclude, I have ad my podigree maid out at the Erald
Hoffis (I don't mean the *Morning Erald*), and have took for my
arms a Stagg. You are corrict in statiug that I am of hancient
Normin famly. This is more than Peal can say, to whomb I
applied for a barnetcy; but the primmier being of low igstraction,
natrally stickles for his horder. Consurvative though I be, *I may
change my opinions* before the next Election, when I intend to
hoffer myself as a Candydick for Parlymint.

"Meanwhile, I have the honor to be, Sir,

"Your most obeajnt Survnt,

"Fitz-James de la Pluche."

•

THE DIARY.
—•—

One day in the panic week, our friend Jeames called at our Office, evidently in great perturbation of mind and disorder of dress. He had no flower in his button-hole; his yellow kid gloves were certainly two days old. He had not above three of the ten chains he usually sports, and his great coarse knotty-knuckled old hands were deprived of some dozen of the rubies, emeralds, and other cameos with which, since his elevation to fortune, the poor fellow has thought fit to adorn himself.

"How's scrip? Mr. Jeames," said we pleasantly, greeting our esteemed contributor.

"Scrip be ——," replied he, with an expression we cannot repeat, and a look of agony it is impossible to describe in print, and walked about the parlour whistling, humming, rattling his keys and coppers, and showing other signs of agitation. At last, "Mr. Punch," says he, after a moment's hesitation, "I wish to speak to you on a pint of businiss. I wish to be paid for my contribewtions to your paper. Suckmstances is altered with me. I—I—in a word, can you lend me —£ for the account."

He named the sum. It was one so great that we don't care to mention it here; but on receiving a cheque for the amount (on Messrs. Pump and Aldgate, our bankers), tears came into the honest fellow's eyes. He squeezed our hand until he nearly wrung it off, and shouting to a cab, he plunged into it at our office-door, and was off to the City.

Returning to our study, we found he had left on our table an open pocket-book; of the contents of which (for the sake of safety) we took an inventory. It contained:—three tavern-bills, paid; a tailor's ditto, unsettled; forty-nine allotments in different companies, twenty-six thousand seven hundred shares in all, of which the market value we take, on an average, to be ¼ discount; and in an old bit of paper tied with pink riband a lock of chesnut hair, with the initials M. A. H.

In the diary of the pocket-book was a Journal, jotted down by

M

the proprietor from time to time. At first the entries are insig-
nificant; as, for instance:—"*3rd January*—Our beer in the
Suvnts' Hall so *precious* small at this Christmas time that I reely
muss give warning, & wood, but for my dear Mary Hann."
"*February 7*—That broot Screw, the Butler, wanted to kis her,
but my dear Mary Hann boxt his hold hears, & served him right.
I datest Screw."—and so forth. Then the diary relates to Stock
Exchange operations, until we come to the time when, having
achieved his successes, Mr. James quitted Berkeley Square and
his livery, and began his life as a speculator and a gentleman upon
town. It is from the latter part of his diary that we make the
following

EXTRAX :—

" Wen I anounced in the Servnts All my axeshn of forting, and
that by the exasize of my own talince and ingianiuty I had
reerlized a summ of 20,000 lb. (it was only 5, but what's the use
of a mann depreshiating the qualaty of his own mackyrel?).
Wen I enounced my abrup intention to cut—you should have
sean the sensation among hall the people! Cook wanted to
know whether I woodn like a sweatbred, or the slise of the breast
of a Cold Tucky. Screw, the butler, (womb I always detested
as a hinsalant hoverbaring beest) begged me to walk into the
Hupper Servnts All, and try a glass of Shuperior Shatto Margo.
Heven Visp, the coachmin, eld out his and, & said, 'Jeames, I
hopes theres no quarraling betwigst you & me, & I'll stand a pot
of beer with pleasure.'

" The sickofnts !—that wery Cook had split on me to the House-
keeper ony last.week (catchin me priggin some cold tuttle soop,
of which I'm remarkable fond). Has for the butler, I always
ebomminated him for his precious snears and imperence to all us
Gents who woar livry, (he never would sit in our parlour, fasooth,
nor drink out of our mugs) ; and in regard of Visp—why, it was
ony the day before the wulgar beest hoffered to fite me, and
thretnd to give me a good iding if I refused. ' Gentlemen and
ladies,' says I, as haughty as may be, 'there's nothink that I
want for that I can't go for to buy with my hown money, and
take at my lodgins in Halbany, letter Hex; if I'm ungry I've
no need to refresh myself in the *kitching*.' And, so saying, I took

a dignified ajew of these minnial domestics; and ascending to my
epartment in the 4 pair back, brushed the powder out of my air,
and taking off those hojous livries for hever, put on a new soot,
made for me by Cullin of St. Jeames Street, and which fitted my
manly figger as tight as whacks.

"There was *one* pusson in the house with womb I was rayther
anxious to evoid a persnal leave-taking—Mary Hann Oggins, I
mean—for my art is natural tender, and I can't abide seeing a
pore gal in pane. I'd given her previous the infamation of my
departure—doing the ansom thing by her at the same time—
paying her back 20lb., which she'd lent me 6 months before: and
paying her back not only the interest, but I gave her an andsome
pair of scissars and a silver thimbil, by way of boanus. 'Mary
Hann,' says I, 'suckimstancies has haltered our rellatif positions
in life. I quit the Servnts Hall for ever, (for has for your
marrying a person in my rank, that my dear is hall gammin,) aud
so I wish you a good by my good gal, and if you want to better
yourself, halways refer to me.'

"Mary Hann didn't hanser my speech (which I think was
remarkable kind), but looked at me in the face quite wild
like, and bust into somethink betwigst a laugh & a cry, and fell
down with her ed on the kitching dresser, where she lay until her
young Missis rang the dressing-room bell. Would you bleave it?
she left the thimbil & things, & my check for 20lb. 10s. on the
tabil when she went to hanser the bell? And now I heard her
sobbing and vimpering in her own room nex but one to mine,
vith the dore open, peraps expecting I should come in and say good
by. But, as soon as I was dressed, I cut down stairs, hony desiring
Frederick my fellow-servnt, to fetch me a cabb, and requesting
permission to take leaf of my lady & the famly before my departure."

＊   ＊   ＊   ＊   ＊

"How Miss Hemly did hogle me to be sure! Her ladyship
told me what a sweet gal she was—hamiable, fond of poetry, plays
the gitter. Then she hasked me if I liked blond bewties and
haubin hair. Haubin, indeed! I don't like carrits! as it must
be confest Miss Hemly's his—and has for a *blond buty* she has pink
I's like a Halbino, and her face looks as if it were dipt in a brann
mash. How she squeeged my & as she went away!

"Mary Hann now *has* haubin air, and a cumplexion like roses and hivory, and I's as blew as Evin.

"I gev Frederick two and six for fetchin the cabb—been resolved to hact the gentleman in hall things. How he stared!"

"25th.—I am now director of forty-seven hadvantageous lines, and have past hall day in the Citty. Although I've hate or nine new soots of close, and Mr. Cullin fits me heligant, yet I fansy they hall reckonise me. Conshns whispers to me—'Jeams, you'r hony a footman in disguise hafter all.'"

"28th.—Been to the Hopra. Music tol lol. That Lablash is a wopper at singing. I coodn make out why some people called out 'Bravo,' some 'Bravar,' and some 'Bravee.' 'Bravee, Lablash,' says I, at which hevery body laft.

"I'm in my new stall. I've had new cushings put in, and my harms in goold on the back. I'm dressed hall in black, excep a gold waistcoat and dimind studds in the embriderd busom of my shameese. I wear a Camallia Jiponiky in my button ole, and have a double-barreld opera glas, so big, that I make Timmins, my secnd man, bring it in the other cabb.

"What an igstronry exabishn that Pawdy Carter is! If those four gals are faries, Tellioni is sutnly the fairy Queend. She can do all that they can do, and somethink they can't. There's an indiscrible grace about her, and Carlotty, my sweet Carlotty, she sets my art in flams.

"Ow that Miss Hemly was noddin and winkin at me out of their box on the fourth tear?

"What linx i's she must av. As if I could mount up there!

"P.S. Talking of *mounting hup!* the St. Helena's walked up 4 per cent. this very day."

"*2nd July.* Rode my bay oss Desperation in the park. There was me, Lord George Ringwood (Lord Cinqbar's son), Lord Ballybunnion, Honorable Capting Trap, & sevral hother young swells. Sir John's carridge there in coarse. Miss Hemly lets fall her booky as I pass, and I'm obleged to get hoff and pick it hup, & get splashed up to the his. The gettin on hoss back agin

is halways the juice & hall. Just as I was hon, Desperation begins a
porring the hair with his 4 feet, and sinks down so on his anches,
that I'm blest if I didn't slip hoff agin over his tail; at which
Ballybunnion & the hother chaps rord with lafter.

"As Bally has istates in Queen's County, I've put him on the
St. Helena direotion.   We call it the 'Great St. Helena Napoleon
Junction,' from Jamestown to Longwood.   The French are taking
it hup heagerly."

"*6th July*.   Dined to-day at the London Tavin with one of the
Welsh bords of Direction I'm hon.   The Cwrwmwrw & Plmwyd-
dlywm, with tunnils through Snowding and Plinlimming.

"Great nashnallity of coarse.   Ap Shinkin in the chair, Ap
Llwydd in the vice; Welsh mutton for dinner; Welsh iron knives
& forks; Welsh rabbit after dinner; and a Welsh harper, be
hanged to him : he went strummint on his hojous hinstrument, and
played a toon piguliarly disagreeble to me.

"It was *Pore Mary Hann*. The clarrit holmost choaked me as
I tried it, and I very nearly wep myself as I thought of her
bewtifle blue i's.   Why *ham* I always thinkin about that gal ?
Sasiety is saciety, it's lors is irresistabl.   Has a man of rank
I can't marry a serving-made.   What would Cinqbar and Bally-
bunnion say ?

"P.S.—I don't like the way that Cinqbars has of borroing
money, & halways making me pay the bill.   Seven pound six at the
Shipp, Grinnidge, which I don't grudge it, for Derbyshire's brown
Ock is the best in Urup; nine pound three at the Trafflygar, and
seventeen pound sixteen & nine at the Star & Garter, Richmond,
with the Couutess St. Emilion & the Baroness Frontignac.   Not
one word of French could I speak, and in consquince had nothink
to do but to make myself halmost sick with heating hices and
desert, while the hothers were chattering & parlyvooing.

"Ha ! I remember going to Grinnidge once with Mary Hann,
when we were more happy (after a walk in the park, where we ad
one gingy-beer betwigst us), more appy with tea and a simple
srimp than with hall this splender ! "——

"*July* 24. My first floor apartmince in the Halbiny is now kimpletely and chasely furnished—the droring-room with yellow satting and silver for the chairs and sophies—hemrall green tabbinet curtings with pink velvet & goold borders & fringes ; a light blue Haxminster Carpit, embroydered with tulips; tables, secritaires, cunsoles, &c., as handsome as goold can make them, and candlesticks and shandalers of the purest Hormolew.

" The Dining-room funniture is all *hoak*, British Hoak ; round igspanding table, like a trick in a Pantimime, iccommadating any number from 8 to 24—to which it is my wish to restrict my parties—Curtings Crimsing damask, Chairs crimsing myrocky. Portricks of my favorite great men decorats the wall—namely, the Duke of Wellington. There's four of his Grace. For I've remarked that if you wish to pass for a man of weight and considdration you should holways praise and quote him—I have a valluble one lickwise of my Queend, and 2 of Prince Halbert—has a Field Martial and halso as a privat Gent. I despise the vulgar *snears* that are daily hullered aginst that Igsolted Pottentat. Betwigxt the Prins & the Duke hangs me, in the Uniform of the Cinqbar Malitia, of which Cinqbars has made me Capting.

" The Libery is not yet done.

" But the Bedd-roomb is the Jem of the whole—if you could but see it! such a Bedworr ! Ive a Shyval Dressing Glass festooned with Walanseens Lace, and lighted up of evenings with rose coloured tapers. Goold dressing case and twilet of Dresding Cheny—My bed white and gold with curtings of pink and silver brocayd held up a top by a goold Qpid who seems always a smilin angillicly hon me, has I lay with my Ed on my piller hall sarounded with the finist Mechlin. I have a own man, a yuth under him, 2 groombs, and a fimmale for the House—I've 7 osses : in cors if I hunt this winter I must increase my ixtablishment.

" N.B. Heverythink looking well in the City. Saint Helenas, 12 pm., Madagascars, 9⅝, Saffron Hill and Rookery Junction, 24, and the new lines in prospick equily incouraging.

———

" People phansy its hall gaiety and pleasure the life of us fashnabble gents about townd—But I can tell 'em its not hall goold that glitters. They don't know our momints of hagony, hour ours of studdy and reflecshun. They little think when they see Jeames de la Pluche, Exquire, worling round in walce at Halmax with Lady Hann, or lazaly stepping a kidrill with Lady Jane, poring helegant nothinx into the Countess's hear at dinner, or gallopin his hoss Desperation hover the exorcisin grouud in the Park,—they little think that leader of the tong, seaminkly so reckliss, is a careworn mann! and yet so it is.

"Imprymus. I've been ableged to get up all the ecomplishments at double quick, & to apply myself with treemenjuous energy.

" First,—in horder to give myself a hideer of what a gentleman reely is—I've read the novvle of Pelham six times, aud am to go through it 4 times mor.

"I practis ridin and the acquirement of 'a steady and & a sure seat across Country' assijuously 4 times a week, at the Hippydrum Riding Grounds. Many's the tumbil I've ad, and the aking boans I've suffered from, though I was grinnin in the Park or laffin at the Opra.

" Every morning from 6 till 9, the innabitance of Halbany may have been surprised to hear the sounds of music ishuing from the apartmince of Jeames de la Pluche, Exquire, Letter Hex. It's my dancing-master. From six to nine we have walces and polkies —at nine 'mangtiang & depotment,' as he calls it; & the manner of hentering a room, complimenting the ost & ostess & compotting yourself at table. At nine I henter from my dressing-room (has to a party), I make my bow—my master (he's a Marquis in France, and ad misfortins, being connected with young Lewy Nepoleum) reseaves me—I hadwance—speak abowt the weather & the toppix of the day in an elegant & cussory manner. Brekfst is enounced by Fitzwarren, my mann—we precede to the festive bord—complimence is igschanged with the manner of drinking wind, adressing your neighbour, employing your napking & finger-glas, &c. And then we fall to brekfst, when I prommiss you the Marquis don't eat like a commoner. He says I'm gettn on very well—soon I shall be able to inwite people to brekfst, like Mr. Mills, my rivle in Halbany; Mr. Macauly, (who wrote that sweet book of ballets, 'The Lays of Hancient Rum ;') & the great Mr. Rodgers himself.

" The above was wrote some weeks back. I *have* given brekfsts sins then, reglar *Deshunys*. I have ad Earls and Ycounts—Barnits as many as I chose : and the pick of the Railway world, of which I form a member. Last Sunday was a grand *Fate*. I had the *Eleet* of my friends : the display was sumptious ; the compauy *reshershy*. Everything that Dellixy could suggest was by Gunter provided. I had a Countiss on my right & (the Countess of Wigglesbury, that loveliest and most dashing of Staggs, who may be called the Railway Queend, as my friend George H—— is the Railway King)—on my left the Lady Blanche Bluenose—Prince Towrowski—the great Sir Huddlestone Fuddlestone, from the North, and a skoar of the fust of the fashn. I was in my *gloary*. The dear Countess and Lady Blanche was dying with laffing at my joax and fun. I was keeping the whole table in a roar—when there came a ring at my door-bell, and sudnly Fitzwarreu, my man, henters with an air of constanation ; ' Theres somebody at the door,' says he, in a visper.

" ' O, it's that dear Lady Hemily,' says I, ' and that lazy raskle of a husband of her's. Trot them in, Fitzwarren,' (for you see, by this time I had adopted quite the manners and hease of the arristoxy.)—And so, going out, with a look of wonder he returned presently, enouncing Mr. & Mrs. Blodder.

" I turned gashly pail. The table—the guests—the Counties— Towrouski, and the rest, weald round & round before my hagitated I's. *It was my Grandmother and* Huncle Bill. She is a washer-woman at Healing Common, and he—he keeps a wegetable donkey-cart.

" Y, Y hadn't John, the tiger, igscluded them ? He had tried. But the unconscious, though worthy creeters, advanced in spite of him, Huncle Bill bringiug in the old lady grinning on his harm !

" Phansy my feelinx."

" Immagin when these unfortnat members of my famly hen-tered the room : you may phansy the ixtonnishment of the nobil company presnt. Old Grann looked round the room quite es-tounded by its horientle splender, and huncle Bill (pulling off his phantail, & seluting the company as respeckfly as his wulgar natur would alow) says—' Crikey, Jeames, you've got a better birth here than you ad where you were in the plush and powder line.' 'Try a few of them plovers hegs, sir,' I says, whishing, I'm asheamed to say, that somethink would choke huncle B——; 'and I hope, mam, now you've ad the kindniss to wisit me, a little refreshment wont be out of your way.'

" This I said, detummind to put a good fase on the matter; and because, in herly times I'd reseaved a great deal of kindniss from the hold lady, which I should be a roag to forgit. She paid for my schooling; she got up my fine linning gratis; shes given me many & many a lb; and manys the time in appy appy days when me and Maryhann has taken tea. But never mind *that*. 'Mam,' says I, 'you must be tired hafter your walk.'

" 'Walk ? Nonsince, Jeames,' says she; 'its Saturday, & I came in, in *the cart*.' 'Black or green tea, maam ? ' says Fitzwarren, intarupting her. And I will say the feller showed his nouce & good breeding in this difficklt momink; for he'd halready silenced huncle Bill, whose mouth was now full of muffinx, am, Blowny sausag, Perrigole pie, and other dellixies.

" 'Wouldn't you like a little *somethink* in your tea, Mam,' says that sly wagg Cinqbars. ' *He* knows what I likes,' replies the hawfle hold Lady, pinting to me, (which I knew it very well, having often seen her take a glass of hojous gin along with her Bohee), and so I was ableeged to horder Fitzwarren to bring round the licures, and to help my unfortnit rellatif to a bumper of Ollands. She tost it hoff to the elth of the company, giving a smack with her lipps after she'd emtied the glas, which very nearly caused me to phaint with hagny. But, luckaly for me, she didn't igspose herself much farther: for when Cinqbars was pressing her to take another glas, I cried out, 'Don't my lord,' on which old Grann hearing him edressed by his title, cried out, 'A Lord! o law ! ' and got up and made him a cutsy, and coodnt be peswaded to speak another word. The presents of the noble gent. heavidently made her uneezy.

" The Countiss on my right and had shownt symtms of ixtream disgust at the beayviour of my relations, and having called for her carridge, got up to leave the room, with the most dignified hair. I, of coarse, rose to conduct her to her weakle. Ah, what a contrast it was ! There it stood, with stars and garters hall hover the pannels; the footmin in peach-coloured tites; the hosses worth 3 hundred a-peace;—and there stood the horrid *linnen-cart*, with 'Mary Blodder, Laundress, Ealing, Middlesex,' wrote on the bord, and waiting till my abaudind old parint should come out.

" Cinqbars insisted upon helping her in. Sir Huddlestone Fud-dlestone, the great barnet from the North, who, great as he is, is as stewpid as a howl, looked on, hardly trusting his goggle I's as they witnessed the sean.   But little lively good naterd Lady Kitty Quickset, who was going away with the Countiss, held her little & out of the carridge to me and said, ' Mr. De la Pluche, you are a much better man than I took you to be.   Though her Ladyship *is* horrified, & though your Grandmother *did* take gin for breakfast, don't give her up.   No one ever came to harm yet for honoring their father & mother.'

" And this was a sort of consolation to me, and I observed that all the good fellers thought none the wuss of me.   Cinqbars said I was a trump for sticking up for the old washerwoman; Lord George Gills said she should have his linning; and so they cut their joax, and I let them.   But it was a great releaf to my mind when the cart drove hoff.

" There was one pint which my Grandmother observed, and which, I muss say, I thought lickwise; ' Ho, Jeames,' says she, ' hall those fine ladies in sattns and velvets is very well, but there's not one of em can hold a candle to Mary Hann.' "

———————

" Railway Spec is going on phamusly.   You should see how polite they har at my bankers now !   Sir Paul Pump Aldgate, & Company.   They bow me out of the back parlor as if I was a Nybobb.   Every body says I'm worth half a millium.   The number of lines they're putting me upon, is inkumseavable. I've put Fitzwarren, my man, upon several.   Reginald Fitzwarren, Esquire, looks splended in a perspectus ; and the raskle owns that he has made two thowsnd.

" How the ladies & men too, foller and flatter me !   If I go into Lady Binsis hopra box, she makes room for me, who ever is there, and cries out, ' O do make room for that dear creature !'   And she complyments me on my taste in musick, or my new Broom-

oss, or the phansy of my weskit, and always ends by asking me
for some shares. Old Lord Bareacres, as stiff as a poaker, as
prowd as Loosyfer, as poor as Joab—even he condysends to be
sivvle to the great De la Pluche, and begged me at Harthur's,
lately, in his sollom, pompus way, 'to faver him with five minutes'
conversation.' I knew what was coming—application for shares
—put him down on my private list. Wouldn't mind the Scrag
End Junction passing through Bareacres—hoped I'd come down
and shoot there.

"I gave the old humbugg a few shares out of my own pocket.
'There, old Pride,' says I, 'I like to see you down on your
knees to a footman. There, old Pompossaty! Take fifty pound;
I like to see you come cringing and begging for it.' Whenever
I see him in a *very* public place, I take my change for my money.
I digg him in the ribbs, or slap his padded old shoulders. I call
him, 'Bareacres, my old buck!' and I see him wince. It does
my art good.

"I'm in low sperits. A disagreeable insadent has just occurred.
Lady Pump, the banker's wife, asked me to dinner. I sat on her
right, of coarse, with an uncommon gal ner me, with whom I was
getting on in my fassanating way—full of lacy ally (as the Marquis says) and easy plesntry. Old Pump, from the end of the
table, asked me to drink shampane; and on turning to tak the
glass I saw Charles Wackles (with womb I'd been imployed at
Colonel Spurriers' house) grinning over his shoulder at the
butler.

"The beest reckonised me. Has I was putting on my palto in
the hall, he came up again : '*How dy doo* Jeames,' says he, in a
findish visper. 'Just come out here, Chawles,' says I, 'I've a
word for you, my old boy.' So I beckoned him into Portland
Place, with my pus in my hand, as if I was going to give him a
sovaring.

"'I think you said "Jeames," Chawles,' says I, 'and grind at
me at dinner?'

"'Why, sir,' says he, 'we're old friends, you know.'

"'Take that for old friendship then,' says I, and I gave him
just one on the noas, which sent him down on the pavemint as
if he'd been shot. And mounting myjesticly into my cabb, I

left the rest of the grinning scoundrills to pick him up, & droav to the Clubb."

"Have this day kimpleated a little efair with my friend George, Earl Bareacres, which I trust will be to the advantidge both of self & that noble gent. Adjining the Bareacre proppaty is a small piece of land of about 100 acres, called Squallop Hill, igseeding advantageous for the cultivation of sheep, which have been found to have a pickewlear fine flaviour from the natur of the grass, tyme, heather, and other hodarefarus plants which grows on that mounting in the places where the rox and stones dont prevent them. Thistles here is also remarkable fine, and the land is also devided hoff by luxurient Stone Hedges—much more usefle and ickonomicle than your quickset or any of that rubbishing sort of timber ; indeed the sile is of that fine natur, that timber refuses to grow there altogether. I gave Bareacres 50l. an acre for this land (the igsact premium of my St. Helena Shares)—a very handsom price for land which never yielded two shillings an acre ; and very convenient to his Lordship I know, who had a bill coming due at his Bankers which he had given them. James de la Pluche, Esquire, is thus for the fust time a landed propriator— or rayther, I should say, is about to reshume the rank & dignity in the country which his Hancestors so long occupied."

"I have caused one of our inginears to make me a plann of the Squallop Estate, Diddlesexshire, the property of &c., &c., bordered on the North by Lord Bareacres' Country ; on the West by Sir Granby Growler ; on the South by the Hotion. An Arkytect & Survare, a young feller of great emagination, womb we have employed to make a survey of the Great Caffrarian line, has built me a beautiful Villar (on paper), Plushton Hall, Diddlesex, the seat of I de la P., Esquire. The house is reprasented a handsome Itallian Structer, imbusmd in woods, and circumwented by beautiful gardings. Theres a lake in front with boatsful of nobillaty and musitions floting on its placid sufface—and a curricle is a driving up to the grand hentrance, and me in it, with Mrs., or perhaps Lady Hangelana de la Pluche. I speak advisedly. *I may* be going to form a noble kinexion. I may be (by marridge) going to unight my family once more with Harrystoxy, from which misfortu has for some sentries separated us. I have dreams of that sort.

" I've sean sevral times in a dalitifle vishn *a serting Erl*, standing in a hattitude of bennydiction, and rattafying my union with a serting butifle young lady, his daughter. Phansy Mr. or Sir Jeames and lady Hangelina de la Pluche! Ho! what will the old washywoman, my grandmother, say? She may sell her mangle then, and shall too by my honour as a Gent."

" As for Squallop Hill, its not to be emadgind that I was going to give 5000 lb. for a bleak mounting like that, unless I had some ideer in vew. Ham I not a Director of the Grand Diddlesex? Don't Squallop lie amediately betwigst Old Bone House, Single Gloster, and Scrag End, through which cities our liue passes? I will have 400,000 lb. for that mounting, or my name is not Jeames. I have arranged a little barging too for my friend the Erl. The line will pass through a hangle of Bareacre Park. He shall have a good compensation I promis you; and then I shall get back the 3000 I lent him. His banker's acount, I fear, is in a horrid state."

> [The Diary now for several days contains particulars of no interest to the public:—Memoranda of City dinners— meetings of Directors—fashionable parties in which Mr. Jeames figures, and nearly always by the side of his new friend, Lord Bareacres, whose " pompossaty," as previously described, seems to have almost entirely subsided.]

We then come to the following:—

" With a prowd and thankfle Art, I copy off this morning's *Gyzett* the folloing news :—

> " ' Commission signed by the Lord Lieutenant of the County of Diddlesex.

> " ' JAMES AUGUSTUS DE LA PLUCHE, Esquire, to be Deputy Lieutenant.' "

> " ' North Diddlesex Regiment of Yeomanry Cavalry.

> " ' James Augustus de la Pluche, Esquire, to be Captain, *vice* Blowhard, promoted.' "

" And his it so ? Ham I indeed a landed propriator—a Deppaty
Leftnant—a Capting ?   May I hatend the Cort of my Sovring ?
and dror a sayber in my country's defens ?   I wish the French
wood land, and me at the head of my squadring on my hoss
Desparation.   How I'd extonish 'em !   How the gals will stare
when they see me in youniform !   How Mary Hann would—but
nonsince !   I'm halways thinking of that pore gal.   She's left Sir
John's.   She couldn't abear to stay after I went, I've heerd say.
I hope she's got a good place.   Any summ of money that would
sett her up in bisniss, or make her comfarable, I'd come down
with like a mann.   I told my granmother so, who sees her, and
rode down to Healing on porpose on Desparation to leave a five lb
noat in an anvylope.   But she's sent it back, sealed with a thimbill."

" *Tuesday*. Reseavd the folloing letter from Lord B——, rellatiff
to my presntation at Cort and the Youniform I shall wear on that
hospicious seramony :—

" ' MY DEAR DE LA PLUCHE,

" ' I think you had better be presented as a Deputy Lieutenant.
As for the Diddlesex Yeomanry, I hardly know what the uniform
is now.   The last time we were out, was in 1803, when the Prince
of Wales reviewed us, and when we wore French grey jackets,
leathers, red morocco boots, crimson pelisses, brass helmets with
leopard-skin and a white plume, and the regulation pig-tail of
eighteen inches.   That dress will hardly answer at present, and
must be modified, of course.   We were called the White Feathers,
in those days.   For my part, I decidedly recommend the Deputy
Lieutenant.

" ' I shall be happy to present you at the Levee and at the
Drawing-room.   Lady Bareacres will be in town for the 13th,
with Angelina, who will be presented on that day.   My wife has
heard much of you, and is anxious to make your acquaintance.

" ' All my people are backward with their rents : for Heaven's
sake, my dear fellow, lend me five hundred and oblige

" ' Yours, very gratefully,

" ' BAREACRES.'

" Note.   Bareacres may press me about the Depity Leftnant—
but *I'm* for the cavvlery."

"Jewly will always be a sacrid anniwussary with me. It was in that month that I became persnally ecquaintid with my Prins and my gracious Sovarink.

"Long before the hospitious event acurd, you may imadgin that my busm was in no triffling flutter. Sleaplis of nights, I past them thinking of the great ewent—or if igsosted natur *did* clothes my highlids—the eyedear of my waking thoughts pevaded my slummers. Corts, Erls, presntations, Goldstix, gracious Sovarinx mengling in my dreembs unceasnly. I blush to say it (for humin prisumpshn never surely igseeded that of my wicked wickid vishn). One night I actially dremt that Her R. H. the Princess Hallis was grown up, and that there was a Cabinit Counsel to detummin whether her & was to be bestoad on me or the Prins of Sax-Muffinhausen-Pumpenstein, a young Prooshn or Germing zion of nobillaty. I ask umly parding for this hordacious ideer.

"I said, in my fommer remarx, that I had detummined to be presented to the notus of my reveared Sovaring in a melintary coschewm. The Court-shoots in which Sivillians attend a Levy are so uncomming like the—the—livries (ojous wud! I 8 to put it down) I used to wear before entering sosiaty, that I couldn't abide the notium of wearing one. My detummination was fumly fixt to apeer as a Yominry Cavilry Hoffiser, in the galleant youniform of the North Diddlesex Huzzas.

"Has that redgmint had not been out sins 1803, I thought myself quite hotherized to make such halterations in the youniform as shuited the presnt time and my metured and elygint taste. Pigtales was out of the question. Tites I was detummind to mintain. My legg is praps the finist pint about me, and I was risolved not to hide it under a booshle.

"I phixt on scarlit tites, then, imbridered with goold as I have seen Widdicomb wear them at Hashleys when me and Mary Hann used to go there. Ninety-six guineas worth of rich goold lace and cord did I have myhandering hall hover those shoperb inagspressables.

"Yellow marocky Heshn boots, red eels, goold spurs and goold tassles as bigg as belpulls.

"Jackit—French gray and silver oringe fasings & cupbs,

according to the old patn; belt, green and goold, tight round my pusn, & settin hoff the cemetry of my figgar *not disadvintajusly*.

"A huzza paleese of pupple velvit & sable fir. A sayber of Demaskus steal, and a sabertash (in which I kep my Odiclone and imbridered pocket ankercher), kimpleat my acooterments, which without vannaty, was, I flatter myself, *uneak*.

"But the crownding triumph was my hat. I couldnt wear a cock At. The huzzahs dont use 'em. I wouldnt wear the hojous old brass Elmet & Leppardskin. I choas a hat which is dear to the memry of hevery Brittn; an at which was inwented by my Feeld Marshle and adord Prins; an At which *vulgar prejidis & Joaking* has in vane etempted to run down. I chose the HALBERT AT. I didnt tell Bareacres of this egsabishn of loilty, intending to *surprise* him. The white ploom of the West Diddlesex Yomingry I fixt on the topp of this Shacko, where it spread hout like a shaving-brush.

"You may be sure that befor the fatle day arrived, I didnt niglect to practus my part well; and had sevral *rehustles*, as they say.

"This was the way. I used to dress myself in my full togs. I made Fitzwarren, my boddy servnt, stand at the dor, and figger as the Lord in Waiting. I put Mrs. Bloker, my laundress, in my grand harm chair to reprasent the horgust pusn of my Sovring— Frederick, my secknd man, standing on her left, in the hattatude of an illustrus Prins Consort. Hall the Candles were lighted. ‘ *Captain de la Pluche, presented by Herl Bareacres,*’ Fitzwarren, my man, igsclaimed, as adwancing I made obasins to the Thrown. Nealin on one nee, I cast a glans of unhuttarable loilty towards The British Crownd, then stepping gracefully hup, (my Dimascus Simiter *would* git betwigst my ligs, in so doink, which at fust was wery disagreeble)—rising hup grasefly, I say, I flung a look of manly but respeckfl hommitch tords my Prins, and then ellygntly ritreated backards out of the Roil Presents. I kep my 4 suvnts hup for 4 hours at this gaym the night before my presntation, and yet I was the fust to be hup with the sunrice. I *coodnt* sleep that night. By abowt six o'clock in the morning I was drest in my full uniform—and I didnt know how to pass the interveaning hours.

"‘My Granmother hasnt seen me in full phigg,' says I. ‘It

will rejoice that pore old sole to behold one of her race so suxesfle in life.' Has I ave read in the novle of 'Kennleworth,' that the Herl goes down in Cort dress and extoneshes *Hamy Robsart*, I will go down in all my splender and astownd my old washywoman of a Granmother. To make this detumminatiou; to horder my Broom; to knock down Frederick the groomb for delaying to bring it; was with me the wuck of a momint. The next sor as galliant a cavyleer as hever rode in a cabb, skowering the road to Healing.

"I arrived at the well-known cottitch. My huncle was habsent with the cart; but the dor of the humble eboad stood hopen, and I passed through the little garding where the close was hanging out to dry. My snowy ploom was ableeged to bend under the lowly porch, as I hentered the apartmint.

"There was a smell of tea there—there's always a smell of tea there—the old lady was at her Bohee as usual. I advanced tords her; but ha! phansy my extonishment when I sor Mary Hann!

"I halmost faintid with himotion. 'Ho, Jeames!' (she has said to me subsquintly) 'mortial mann never looked so bewtifle as you did when you arrived on the day of the Levy. You were no longer mortial, you were diwine!'

"R! what little Justas the Hartist has done to my mannly etractions in the groce carriketure he's made of me."

*   *   *   *   *   *

"Nothing, perhaps, ever created so great a sensashun as my hentrance to St. Jeames's, on the day of the Levy. The Tuckish Hambasdor himself was not so much remarked as my shuperb turn out.

"As a Millentary man, and a North Diddlesex Huzza, I was resolved to come to the ground on *hossback*. I had Desparation phigd out as a charger, and got 4 Melentery dresses from Ollywell Street, in which I drest my 2 men (Fitzwarren, hout of livry, woodnt stand it), and 2 fellers from Rimles, where my hosses stand at livry. I rode up St. Jeames's Street, with my 4 Hadycongs—the people huzzaying—the gals waving their hankerchers, as if I were a Foring Prins—hall the winders crowdid to see me pass.

"The guard must have taken me for a Hempror at least, when I came, for the drums beat, and the guard turned out and seluted me with presented harms.

"What a momink of triumth it was! I sprung myjestickly from Desperation. I gav the rains to one of my borderlies, and, salewting the crowd, I past into the presnts of my Most Gracious Mrs.

"You, peraps, may igspect that I should narrait at lenth the suckmstanzas of my hawjince with the British Crown. But I am not one who would gratafy *imputtnint curaiosaty.* Rispect for our reckonized instatewtions is my fust quallaty. I, for one, will dye rallying round my Thrown.

"Suffise it to say, when I stood in the Horgust Presnts,—when I sor on the right & of my Himperial Sovring that Most Gracious Prins, to admire womb has been the chief Objick of my life, my busum was seased with an imotium which my Penn rifewses to dixcribe—my trembling knees halmost rifused their hoffis—I reckleck nothing mor until I was found phainting in the harms of the Lord Chamberling. Sir Robert Peal apnd to be standing by (I knew our wuthy Primmier by *Punch's* picturs of him, igspecially his ligs), and he was conwussiug with a man of womb I shall say nothink, but that he is a Hero of 100 fites, *and hevery fite he fit he one.* Nead I say that I elude to Harthur of Wellingting? I introjuiced myself to these Jents, and intend to improve the equaintance, and peraps ast Guvmint for a Barnetcy.

"But there was *another* pusn womb on this droring-room I fust had the inagspressable dalite to beold. This was that Star of fashing, that Sinecure of neighbouring i's, as Milting observes, the ecomplisht Lady Hangelina Thistlewood, daughter of my exlent frend, John George Godfrey de Bullion Thistlewood, Earl of Bareacres, Baron Southdown, in the Peeridge of the United Kingdom, Baron Haggismore, in Scotland, K.T., Lord Leftnant of the County of Diddlesex, &c. &c. This young lady was with her Noble Ma, when I was kinducted tords her. And surely never lighted on this hearth a more delightfle vishn. In that gallixy of Bewty the Lady Hangelina was the fairest Star—in that reath of Loveliness the sweetest Rosebud! Pore Mary Hann, my Art's young affeckshns had been senterd on thee; but like water through a sivv, her immidge disapeared in a momink, and left me intransd in the presnts of Hangelina!

"Lady Bareacres made me a myjestick bow—a grand and hawfle

pusnage her Ladyship is, with a Roming Nose, and an enawmus ploom of Hostridge phethers; the fare Hangelina smiled with a sweetness perfickly bewhildring, and said, ' O, Mr. De la Pluche, I'm so delighted to make your acquaiutance, I have often heard of you.'

"' Who,' says I, ' has mentioned my insiggnificknt igsistance to the fair Lady Hangeliua, *kel bonure igstrame poor mwaw;* ' (for you see I've not studdied *Pelham* for nothink, and have lunt a few French phraces, without which no Gent of fashn speaks now.)

"' O,' replies my lady, ' it'was Papa first; and then a very, *very* old friend of yours.'

"' Whose name is,' says I, pusht on by my stoopid curaw-saty——

"' Hoggins—Mary Ann Hoggins '—ansurred my lady (laffing phit to splitt her little sides.) ' She is my maid, Mr. De la Pluche, and I'm afraid you are a very sad, sad person.'

"' A mere baggytell,' says I. ' In fommer days I *was* equainted with that young woman; but haltered suckmstancies have seppar-ated us for hever, and *mong cure* is irratreevably *perdew* elsewhere.'

"' Do tell me all about it. Who is it? When was it? We are all dying to know.'

"' Since about two minnits, and the Ladys name begins with a *Ha,*' says I, looking her tendarly in the face, and conjring up hall the fassanations of my smile.

"' Mr. De la Pluche,' here said a gentleman in whiskers and mistashes standing by, ' hadn't you better take your spurs out of the Couutess of Bareacres' train?'—' Never mind Mamma's train' (said Lady Hangelina): ' this is the great Mr. De la Pluche, who is to make all our fortuues—yours too. Mr. De la Pluche, let me present you to Captain George Silvertop.'—The Capting bent just one jint of his back very slitely; I retund his stare with equill hottiness. ' Go and see for Lady Bareacres' carridge, Charles,' says his Lordship; aud vispers to me, ' a cousin of ours—a poor relation.' So I took no notis of the feller when he came back, nor in my subsquint visits to Hill Street, where it seems a knife and fork was laid reglar for this shabby Capting."

" *Thusday Night.*—O Hangelina, Hangelina, my pashn for you hogments daily ! I've bean with her two the Hopra. I sent her a bewtifle Camellia Jyponiky from Covn Garding, with a request she would wear it in her raving Air. I woar another in my butn-ole. Evns, what was my sattusfackshn as I leant hover her chair, and igsammined the house with my glas !

"She was as sulky and silent as pawsble, however—would scarcely speek ; although I kijoled her with a thowsnd little plesntries. I spose it was because that wulgar raskle Silvertop, *wood* stay in the box. As if he didn' know (Lady B.'s as deaf as a poast and counts for nothink) that people *sometimes* like a *tatytaty.*"

" *Friday.*—I was sleeples all night. I gave went to my feelings in the folloring lines—there's a hair out of Balfe's Hopera that she's fond of. I edapted them to that mellady.

" She was in the droring-room alone with Lady B. She was wobbling at the pyanna as I hentered. I flung the convasation upon mewsick ; said I sung myself, (I've ad lesns lately of Signor Twankydillo) ; and, on her rekwesting me to faver her with somethink, I bust out with my pom :

" 'WHEN MOONLIKE OER THE HAZURE SEAS.

" ' When moonlike ore the hazure seas
　　In soft effulgence swells,
When silver jews and balmy breaze
　　Bend down the Lily's bells ;
When calm and deap, the rosy sleap
　　Has lapt your soal in dreems,
R Hangeline ! R lady mine !
　　Dost thou remember Jeames ?

" ' I mark thee in the Marhle All,
　　Where Englands loveliest shine—
I say the fairest of them hall
　　Is Lady Hangeline.
My soul, in desolate eclipse,
　　With recollection teems—
And then I hask, with weeping lips,
　　Dost thou remember Jeames ?

> " ' Away ! I may not tell thee hall
> This soughring heart endures—
> There is a lonely sperrit-call
> That Sorrow never curss ;
> There is a little, little Star,
> That still above me beams ;
> It is the Star of Hope—but ar !
> Dost thou remember Jeames ?'

" When I came to the last words, ' Dost thou remember Je-e-e-ams,' I threw such an igspresshn of unuttrable tenderniss into the shake at the hend, that Hangelina could bare it no more. A bust of uncumtrollable emotium seized her. She put her ankercher to her face and left the room. I heard her laffing and sobbing histerickly in the bedwor.

" O Hangelina—My adord one, My Arts joy ! "   *   *   *

" BAREACRES, me, the ladies of the famly, with their sweet, Southdown, B's eldest son, and George Silvertop, the shabby Capting (who seames to git leaf from his ridgmint whenhever he likes), have beene down into Diddlesex for a few days, enjying the spawts of the feald there.

" Never having done much in the gunning line (since when a hinnasent boy, me and Jim Cox used to go out at Healing, and shoot sparrers in the Edges with a pistle)—I was reyther dowtfle as to my suxes as a shot, and practusd for some days at a stoughd bird in a shooting gallery, which a chap histed up and down with a string. I sugseaded in itting the hannimle pretty well. I bought Awker's ' Shooting-Guide,' two double-guns at Mantings, and salected from the French prints of fashn the most gawjus and ellygant sportting ebillyment. A lite blue velvet and goold cap, woar very much on one hear, a cravatt of yaller & green imbroidered satting, a weskit of the McGrigger plaid, & a jacket of the McWhirter tartn, (with large motherapurl butns, engraved with coaches & osses, and sporting subjix), high leather gayters, and marocky shooting shoes, was the simple hellymence of my costewm, and I flatter myself set hoff my figger in rayther a fayverable way. I took down none of my own pusnal istablish-mint except Fitzwarren, my hone mann, and my grooms, with

Desparation and my curricle osses, and the Fourgong containing my dressing-case and close.

" I was heverywhere introjuiced in the county as the great Railroad Cappitlist, who was to make Diddlesex the most prawsperous districk of the hempire. The squires prest forrards to welcome the new comer amongst 'em; and we had a Hagricultural Meating of the Bareacres tenantry, where I made a speech droring tears from heavery i. It was in compliment to a layborer who had brought up sixteen children, and lived sixty years on the istate on seven bobb a week. I am not prowd, though I know my station. I shook hands with that mann in lavinder kidd gloves. I told him that the purshuit of hagriculture was the noblist hockupations of humaunaty : I spoke of the yoming of Hengland, who (under the command of my hancisters) had conquered at Hadjincourt & Cressy ; and I gave him a pair of new velveteen inagspressables, with two and six in each pocket, as a reward for three score years of labor. Fitzwarren, my man, brought them forrards on a satting cushing. Has I sat down, defning chears selewted the horator ; the band struck up ' The Good Old English Gentleman.' I looked to the ladies galry ; my Hangelina waived her ankasher and kissd her & ; and I sor in the distans that pore Mary Hann efected evidently to tears by my ellaquints."

———

" What an adwance that gal has made since she's been in Lady Hangelina's company ! Sins she wears her young lady's igsploded gownds and retired caps and ribbings, there's an ellygance abowt her which is puffickly admarable ; and which, haddid to her own natral bewty & sweetniss, creates in my boozum serting sensatiums * * * Shor ! I *mustn't* give way to fealinx unwuthy of a member of the aristoxy. What can she be to me but a mear recklection—a vishn of former ears ?

" I'm blest if I didn mistake her for Hangelina herself yesterday. I met her in the grand Collydore of Bareacres Castle. I sor a lady in a melumcolly hattatude gacing outawinder at the setting sun, which was eluminating the fair parx and gardings of the hancient demean.

" ' Bewchus Lady Hangelina,' says I—' A penny for your Ladyship's thought,' says I.

"'Ho Jeames! Ho, Mr. De la Pluche!' hansered a well-known vice, with a haxnt of sadnis which went to my art. ' *You* know what my thoughts are, well enough. I was thinking of happy, happy old times, when both of us were poo—poo—oor,' says Mary Hann, busting out in a phit of crying, a thing I can't ebide. I took her and tried to cumft her: I pinted out the diffrents of our sitawashns; igsplained to her that proppaty has its jewties as well as its previletches, and that *my* juty clearly was to marry into a noble famly. I kep on talking to her (she sobbing and going hon hall the time) till Lady Hangelina herself came up—'The real Siming Pewer,' as they say in the play.

" There they stood together—them two young women. I don't know which is the ansamest. I coodn help comparing them; and I coodnt help comparing myself to a certing Hannimle I've read of, that found it difficklt to make a choice betwigst 2 Bundles of A."

" That ungrateful beest Fitzwarren—my oan man—a feller I've maid a fortune for—a feller I give 100 lb. per hannum to!—a low bred Wallydyshamber! *He* must be thinking of falling in love too! and treating me to his imperence.

" He's a great big athlatic feller—six foot i, with a pair of black whiskers like air-brushes—with a look of a Colonel in the harmy—a dangerous pawmpus-spoken raskle I warrunt you. I was comiug ome from shuiting this hafternoon—and passing through Lady Hangelina's flour-garding, who should I see in the summerouse, but Mary Hann pretending to em an ankyshr and Mr. Fitzwarren paying his cort to her.

"'You may as well have me, Mary Hann,' says he. 'I've saved money. We'll take a public-house and I'll make a lady of you. I'm not a purse-proud ungrateful fellow like Jeames—who's such a snob ('such a snobb' was his very words!) that I'm ashamed to wait on him—who's the laughing stock of all the gentry and the housekeeper's room too—try a *man*,' says he —'don't be taking on about such a humbug as Jeames.'

" Here young Joe the keaper's sun, who was carrying my bagg, bust out a laffing—thereby causing Mr. Fitzwarren to turn round and intarupt this polite convasation.

"I was in such a rayge. 'Quit the building, Mary Hann,' says I to the young woman—'and you, Mr. Fitzwarren, have the goodness to remain.'

"'I give you warning,' roars he, looking black, blue, yaller— all the colours of the ranebo.

"'Take hoff your coat, you imperent, hungrateful scoundrl,' says I.

"'It's not your livery,' says he.

"'Peraps you'll understand me, when I take off my own,' says I, unbuttoning the motherapurls of the MacWhirter tartn. 'Take my jackit, Joe,' says I to the boy,—and put myself in a hattitude about which there was *no mistayk*.

*   *   *   *   *   *

"He's 2 stone heavier than me—and knows the use of his ands as well as most men; but in a fite, *blood's everythink;* the Snobb can't stand before the gentleman; and I should have killed him, I've little doubt, but they came and stopt the fite betwigst us before we'd had more than 2 rounds.

"I punisht the raskle tremenjusly in that time, though ; and I'm writing this in my own sittn-room, not being able to come down to dinner on account of a black-eye I've got, which is sweld up and disfiggrs me dreadfl."

————

"On account of the boffle black i which I reseaved in my rang-counter with the hinfimus Fitzwarren, I kep my roomb for sevral days, with the rose-coloured curtings of the apartmint closed, so as to form an agreeable twilike; and a light-bloo sattin shayd over the injard pheacher. My woons was thus made to become me as much as pawsable; and (has the Poick well observes 'Nun but the Brayv desuvs the Fare') I cumsoled myself in the sasiaty of the ladies for my tempory disfiggarment.

"It was Mary Hann who summind the House and put an end to my phistycoughs with Fitzwarren. I licked him and bare him no mallis: but of corse I dismist the imperent scoundrill from my suvvis, apinting Adolphus, my page, to his post of confidenshle Valley.

"Mary Hann and her young and lovely Mrs. kep paying me contiuyoul visits during my retiremint. Lady Hangelina was

halways sending me messidges by her: while my exlent friend,
Lady Bareacres (on the contry) was always sending me toakns
of affeckshn by Hangelina. Now it was a coolin hi-lotium,
inwented by herself, that her Ladyship would perscribe—then,
agin, it would be a booky of flowers (my favrit polly hanthuses,
pellagoniums, and jyponikys), which none but the fair &s of
Hangelina could dispose about the chamber of the hinvyleed.
Ho! those dear mothers! when they wish to find a chans for a
galliant young feller, or to ixtablish their dear gals in life, what
awpertunities they *will* give a man! You'd have phansied I was
so hill (on account of my black hi), that I couldut live exsep upon
chicking and spoon-meat, and jellies, and blemonges, and that I
couldnt eat the latter dellixies (which I ebomminate onternoo,
prefurring a cut of beaf or muttn to hall the kickpshaws of France),
unless Hangelina brought them. I et 'em, and sacrafised myself
for her dear sayk.

"I may stayt here that in privit convasations with old Lord B.
and his son, I had mayd my propoasls for Hangelina, and was
axepted, and hoped soon to be made the appiest gent in Hengland.

"'You must break the matter gently to her,' said her hexlent
father. 'You have my warmest wishes, my dear Mr. De la
Pluche, and those of my Lady Bareacres; but I am not—not
quite certain about Lady Angelina's feelings. Girls are wild and
romantic. They do not see the necessity of prudent establish-
ments, and I have never yet been able to make Angelina understand the embarrassments of her family. These silly creatures
prate about love and a cottage, and despise advantages which
wiser heads than theirs know how to estimate.'

"'Do you mean that she aint fassanated by me?' says I, busting
out at this outrayjus ideer.

"'She *will* be, my dear sir. You have already pleased her,—
your admirable manners must succeed in captivating her, and a
fond father's wishes will be crowned on the day in which you
enter our family.'

"'Recklect, gents,' says I to the 2 lords,—'a barging's a
barging—I'll pay hoff Southdown's Jews, whem I'm his brother
—as a *straynger*—(this I said in a sarcastickle toan)—I wouldnt

take such *a libbaty.* When I'm your suninlor I'll treble the valyou of your estayt. I'll make your incumbrinces as right as a trivit, and restor the ouse of Bareacres to its herly splender. But a pig in a poak is not the way of transacting bisniss imployed by Jeames De la Pluche, Esquire.'

" And I had a right to speak in this way. I was one of the greatest scrip-holders in Hengland; and calclated on a kilossle fortune. All my shares was rising immence. Every poast brot me noose that I was sevral thowsnds richer than the day befor I was detummind not to reerlize till the proper time, and then to buy istates; to found a new family of Delapluches, and to alie myself with the aristoxy of my country.

" These pints I reprasented to pore Mary Hann hover and hover agin. ' If you'd been Lady Hangelina, my dear gal,' says I, ' I would have married you : and why don't I ? Because my dooty prewents me. I'm a marter to dooty; and you, my pore gal, must cumsole yorself with that ideer.'

" There seamd to be a consperracy, too, between that Silvertop and Lady Hangelina to drive me to the same pint. ' What a plucky fellow you were, Pluche,' says he (he was rayther more familliar than I liked), ' in your fight with Fitzwarren !—to engage a man of twice your strength and science, though you were sure to be beaten (this is an etroashous folsood : I should have finnisht Fitz in 10 minnits), for the sake of poor Mary Hann! That's a generous fellow. I like to see a man risen to eminence like you, having his heart in the right place. When is to be the marriage, my boy ? '

" ' Capting S.,' says I, ' my marridge consunns your most umble servnt a precious sight more than you ; '—and I gev him to understand I didn't want him to put in *his* ore—I wasn't afrayd of his whiskers, I prommis you, Capting as he was. I'm a British Lion, I am : as brayv as Bonypert, Hannible, or Holiver Crummle, and would face bagnits as well as any Evy drigoon of 'em all.

" Lady Hangelina, too, igspawstulated in her hartfl way. ' Mr. De la Pluche (seshee), why, why press this point ? You can't suppose that you will be happy with a person like me ? '

" ' I adoar you, charming gal ! ' says I, ' Never, never go to say any such thing.'

" ' You adored Mary Ann first;' answers her Ladyship; 'you can't keep your eyos off her now. If any man courts her you grow so jealous that you bogin beating him. You will break the girl's heart if you don't marry her, and perhaps some one else's—but you don't mind *that*.'

" ' Break yours, you adoarible creature! I'd die first! And as for Mary Hann, she will git over it; people's arts aint broakn so easy. Once for all, suckmstances is changed betwigst me and er. It's a pang to part with her, (says I, my fine hi's filling with tears), but part from her I must.'

" It was curius to remark abowt that singlar gal, Lady Hangelina, that melumcolly as she was when she was talking to me, and ever so disml—yet she kep on laffing every minute like the juice and all.

" ' What a sacrifice!' says she, 'it's like Napoleon giving up Josephine. What anguish it must cause to your susceptible heart!'

" ' It does,' says I—'Hagnies!' (Another laff.)

" ' And if—if I don't accept you—you will invade the States of the Emperor, my Papa, and I am to be made the sacrifice and the occasion of peace between you!'

" ' I don't know what you're eluding to about Joseyfeen and Hemperors your Pas; but I know that your Pa's estate is over hedaneers morgidged; that if some one don't elp him, he's no better than an old pawper; that he owes me a lot of money; and that I'm the man that can sell him up hoss & foot; or set him up agen—*that's* what I know, Lady Hangelina,' says I, with a hair as much as to say, " Put *that* in your ladyship's pipe and smoke it.'

" And so I left her, and nex day a serting fashnable paper enounced—   •

" ' MARRIAGE IN HIGH LIFE.—We hear that a matrimonial union is on the *tapis* between a gentleman who has made a colossal fortune in the Railway World, and the only daughter of a noble earl, whose estates are situated in D—ddles—x. An early day is fixed for this interesting event.' "

_____

"Contry to my expigtations (but when or ow can we reckn upon

the fealinx of wimming?) Mary Han didn't seem to be much
efected by the hideer of my marridge with Hangelinar. I was
rayther disapinted peraps that the fickle young gal reckumsiled
herself so easy to giving me hup, for we Gents are creechers of
vannaty after all, as well as those of the hopsit secks: and
betwigst you and me there *was* mominx, when I almost whisht
that I'd been borne a Myommidn or Turk, when the Lor would
have permitted me to marry both these sweet beinx, wherehas I
was now condemd to be appy with ony one.

"Meanwild every-think went on very agreeble betwigst me and
my defianced bride. When we came back to town I kemishnd
Mr. Showery the great Hoctionear to look out for a town
manshing sootable for a gent of my quallaty. I got from the
Erald Hoffis (not the *Mawning* Erald—no no, I'm not such a
Mough as to go *there* for ackrit infamation) an account of my
famly, my harms and pedigry.

"I horderd in Long Hacre, three splendid equipidges, on which
my arms and my adord wife's was drawn & quartered; and I got
portricks of me and her paynted by the sellabrated Mr. Shalloon,
being resolved to be the gentleman in all things, and knowing
that my character as a man of fashn wasn't compleat unless I sat
to that dixtinguished Hartist. My likenis I presented to
Hangelina. It's not considered flattring—and though *she* parted
with it, as you will hear, mighty willingly, there's *one* young lady
(a thousand times handsomer) that values it as the happle of
her hi.

"Would any man beleave that this picture was soald at my sale
for about a twenty-fifth part of what it cost me? It was bought
in by Maryhann, though :—'O dear Jeames,' says she, often
(kissing of it & pressing it to her art) 'it isn't ½ ansum enough
for you, and hasn't got your angellick smile and the igspreshn of
your dear dear i's.'

"Hangelina's pictur was kindly presented to me by Countess B.,
her mamma, though of coarse, I paid for it. It was engraved
for the *Book of Bewty* the same year.

"With such a perfusion of ringlits I should scarcely have known
her—but the ands, feat, and i's, was very like. She was painted in
a gitar supposed to be singing one of my little melladies; and

her brother Southdown, who is one of the New England poits,
wrote the follering stanzys about her:—

"LINES UPON MY SISTER'S PORTRAIT.

BY THE LORD SOUTHDOWN.

" The castle towers of Bareacres are fair upon the lea,
Where the cliffs of bonny'Diddlesex rise up from out the sea:
I stood upon the donjon keep and view'd the country o'er,
I saw the lands of Bareacres for fifty miles or more.
I stood upon the donjon keep—it is a sacred place,—
Where floated for eight hundred years the banner of my race;
Argent, a dexter sinople, and gules an azure field,
There ne'er was nobler cognizance on knightly warrior's shield.

" The first time England saw the shield 'twas round a Norman neck,
On board a ship from Valery, King William was on deck.
A Norman lance the colours wore, in Hastings' fatal fray —
St. Willibald for Bareacres ! 'twas double gules that day !
O Heaven and sweet St. Willibald ! in many a battle since
A loyal-hearted Bareacres has ridden by his Prince !
At Acre with Plantagenet, with Edward at Poitiers,
The pennon of the Bareacres was foremost on the spears !

" 'Twas pleasant in the battle-shock to hear our war-cry ringing:
O grant me, sweet St. Willibald, to listen to such singing !
Three hundred steel-clad gentlemen, we drove the foe before us,
And thirty score of British bows kept twanging to the chorus !
O knights, my noble ancestors ! and shall I never hear
Saint Willibald for Bareacres through battle ringing clear?
I'd cut me off this strong right hand a single hour to ride,
And strike a blow for Bareacres, my fathers, at your side !

"Dash down, dash down, yon Mandolin, beloved sister mine !
Those blushing lips may never sing the glories of our line :
Our ancient castles echo to the clumsy feet of churls,
The spinning Jenny houses in the mansion of our Earls.
Sing not, sing not, my Angeline ! in days so base and vile,
'Twere sinful to be happy, 'twere sacrilege to smile.
I'll hie me to my lonely hall, and by its cheerless hob
I'll muse on other days, and wish—and wish I were—A SNOB.

" All young Hengland, I'm told, considers the poim bewtifle.
They're always writing about battleaxis and shivvlery, these young
chaps ; but the ideer of Southdown in a shoot of armer, and his
cuttin hoff his ' strong right hand,' is rayther too good ; the
feller is about 5 fit hi,—as ricketty as a babby, with a vaist like a

gal,—and, though he may have the art and curridge of a Bengal
tyger, I'd back my smallest cab-boy to lick him,—that is, if I *ad*
a cab-boy.   But io ! *my* cab-days is over.'

"Be still my hagnizing Art ! I now am about to hunfoald the
dark payges of the Istry of my life ! "

———

"My friends! you've seen me ither2 in the full kerear of Fortn,
prawsprus but not hover prowd of my prawsperraty ; not dizzy
though mounted on the haypix of Good Luck—feasting hall the
great (like the Good Old Henglish Gent in the song, which he
has been my moddle and igsample through life) but not forgitting
the small—No, my beayviour to my granmother at Healing shows
that.   I bot her a new donkey cart (what the French call a cart-
blansh) and a handsome set of peggs for anging up her linning,
and treated Huncle Jim to a new shoot of close, which he ordered
in St. Jeames's Street, much to the estonishment of my Snyder
there, namely an olliff-green velvyteen jackit and smalclose, and a
crimsn plush weskoat with glas-buttns. These pints of genarawsaty
in my disposishn I never should have eluded to, but to show that
I am naturally of a noble sort; and have that kind of galliant
carridge which is equel to either good or bad forting.

"What was the substns of my last chapter ? In that everythink
was prepayred for my marridge—the consent of the parents of my
Hangelina was gaynd, the lovely gal herself was ready (as I
thought) to be led to Himing's halter—the trooso was hordered
—the wedding dressis were being phitted hon—a weddinkake
weighing half a tunn was a gettn reddy by Mesurs Gunter, of
Buckley Square ; there was such an account for Shantilly and
Honiton laces as would have staggerd hennyboddy (I know they
did the Commissioner when I came hup for my Stiffikit) and has
for Injar-shawls I bawt a dozen sich fine ones as never was given
away—no not by Hiss Iness the Injan Prins Juggernaut Tygore.
The juils (a pearl and dimind shoot) were from the establishmint
of Mysurs Storr and Mortimer.   The honey-moon I intended to
pass in a continentle excussion, and was in treaty for the ouse at
Halberd-gate (hopsit Mr. Hudson's) as my town-house.   I waited
to cumclude the putchis untle the Share-Markit which was rayther

deprest (oing I think not so much to the atax of the misrabble *Times*, as to the prodidjus flams of the *Morning Erald*) was restored to its elthy toan. I wasn't goin to part with scrip which was 20 primmium at 2 or 3; and bein confidnt that the Markit would rally, had bought very largely for the two or three new accounts.

"This will explane to those unfortnight traydsmen to womb I gayv orders for a large igstent ow it was that I couldn't pay their accounts. *I* am the soal of onour—but no gent can pay when he has no money :—it's not *my* fault if that old screw Lady Bareacres cabbidged three hundred yards of lace, and kep back 4 of the biggest diminds and seven of the largist Injar Shawls—it's not *my* fault if the tradespeople didn git their goods back, and that Lady B. declared they were *lost*. I bogan the world afresh with the close on my back, and thirteen and six in money, concealing nothink, giving up heverythink, Onist and undismayed, and though beat, with pluck in me still, and ready to begin agin.

"Well—it was the day before that apinted for my Unium. The *Ringdove* steamer was lying at Dover ready to carry us hoff. The Bridle apartmince had been hordered at Salt Hill, and subsquintly at Balong sur Mare—the very table cloth was laid for the weddn brexfst in Ill Street, and the Bride's Right Reverend Huncle, the Lord Bishop of Bullocksmithy, had arrived to sellabrayt our unium. All the papers were full of it. Crowds of the fashnable world went to see the trooso : and admire the Carridges in Long Hacre. Our travleng charrat (light bloo lined with pink satting, and vermillium and goold weals) was the hadmaration of all for quiet ellygns. We were to travel only 4, viz., me, my lady, my vally, and Mary Hann as famdyshamber to my Hangelina. Far from oposing our match, this worthy gal had quite givn into it of late, and laught and joakt, and enjoyd our plans for the fewter igseedinkly.

"I'd left my lovely Bride very gay the night before—aving a multachewd of bisniss on, and Stockbrokers and bankers' accounts to settle : atsettrey atsettrey. It was layt before I got these in horder : my sleap was feavrish, as most mens is when they are going to be marrid or to be hanged. I took my chocklit in bed about one : tride on my wedding close, and found as ushle that they became me exeedingly.

" One thing distubbed my mind—two weskts had been sent home. A blush-white sattiug and gold, and a kinary coloured tabbinet imbridered in silver;—which should I wear on the hospicious day? This hadgitated and perplext me a good deal. I detummined to go down to Hill Street and cumsult the Lady whose wishis were henceforth to be my *hallinall;* and wear whichever *she* phixt on.

" There was a great bussel and distubbans in the Hall in Ill Street: which I etribyouted to the eproaching event. The old porter stared most uncommon when I kem in—the footman who, was to enounce me laft I thought—I was going up stairs—

" ' Her ladyship's not—not at *home,*' says the man; ' and my lady's hill in bed.'

" ' Git lunch,' says I, ' I'll wait till Lady Hangelina returns.

" At this the feller loox at me for a momint with his cheex blown out like a bladder, and then busts out in a reglar guffau! the porter jined in it, the impident old raskle : and Thomas says, slapping his and on his thy, without the least respect—'*I say, Huffy, old boy! isn't this a good un ?* '

" ' Wadyermean, you infunnle scoundrel,' says I, ' hollaring and laffing at me ? '

" ' O here's Miss Mary Hann coming up,' says Thomas, ' ask *her* '—and indeed there came my little Mary Hann tripping down the stairs—her &s in her pockits ; and when she saw me *she* began to blush and look hod & then to grin too.

" ' In the name of Imperence,' says I, rushing on Thomas, and collaring him fit to throttle him—'no raskle of a flunky shall insult *me,*' and I sent him staggerin up aginst the porter, and both of 'em into the hall-chair with a flopp—when Mary Hann, jumping down, says, ' O James! O Mr. Plush! read this '—and she pulled out a billy doo.

" I reckanized the and-writing of Hangelina.

" Deseatful Hangelina's billy ran as follows :—

" ' I had all along hoped that you would have relinquished pretensions which you must have seen were so disagreeable to me ; and have spared me the painful necessity of the step which I am compelled to take. For a long time I could not believe my parents were serious in wishing to sacrifice me, but have in vain entreated them to spare me. I cannot undergo the shame and misery of a union with you. To the very last hour I remonstrated in vain, and only now anticipate, by a few hours, my departure from a home from which they themselves were about to expel me.

" ' When you receive this, I shall be united to the person to whom, as you are aware, my heart was given long ago. My parents are already informed of the step I have taken. And I have my own honour to consult, even before their benefit : they will forgive me, I hope and feel, before long.

" ' As for yourself, may I not hope that time will calm your exquisite feelings too ? I leave Mary Ann behind me to console you. She admires you as you deserve to be admired, and with a constancy which I entreat you to try and imitate. Do, my dear Mr. Plush, try—for the sake of your sincere friend and admirer,

" ' A.

" ' P.S. I leave the wedding-dresses behind for her : the diamonds are beautiful, and will become Mrs. Plush admirably.' "

" This was hall!—Confewshn ! And there stood the footmen sniggerin, and that hojus Mary Hann half a cryin, half a laffing at me ! ' Who has she gone hoff with ? ' rors I ; and Mary Hann (smiling with one hi) just touched the top of one of the Johns' canes who was goin out with the noats to put hoff the brekfst. It was Silvertop then !

" I bust out of the house in a stayt of diamoniacal igsitement !

" The stoary of that ilorpmint I have no art to tell. Here it is from the ' Morning Tatler ' newspaper.

"ELOPEMENT IN HIGH LIFE.

"THE ONLY AUTHENTIC ACCOUNT.

" The neighbourhood of Berkeley Square, and the whole fashionable world, has been thrown into a state of the mos painful excitement by an event which has just placed a nobl family in great perplexity and affliction.

" It has long been known among the select nobility and gentry

o

that a marriage was on the tapis between the only daughter of a
Noble Earl, and a Gentleman whose rapid fortunes in the railway
world have been the theme of general remark.   Yesterday's paper,
it was supposed, in all human probability would have contained an
account of the marriage of James De la Pl—che, Esq., and the
Lady Angelina,——, daughter of the Right Honourable the Earl
of B—re—cres.   The preparations for this ceremony were complete: we had the pleasure of inspecting the rich *trousseau*
(prepared by Miss Twiddler, of Pall Mall); the magnificent
jewels from the establishment of Messrs. Storr and Mortimer;
the elegant marriage cake, which, already cut up and portioned,
is, alas! not destined to be eaten by the friends of Mr. De la
Pl—che; the superb carriages, and magnificent liveries, which had
been provided in a style of the most lavish yet tasteful sumptuo-
sity.   The Right Reverend the Lord Bishop of Bullocksmithy
had arrived in town to celebrate the nuptials, and is staying at
Mivart's.   What most have been the feelings of that venerable
prelate, what those of the agonised and noble parents of the Lady
Angelina—when it was discovered, on the day previous to the
wedding, that her Ladyship had fled the paternal mansion!   To
the venerable Bishop the news of his noble niece's departure
might have been fatal: we have it from the waiters of Mivart's
that his Lordship was about to indulge in the refreshment of
turtle soup when the news was brought to him; immediate apoplexy was apprehended; but Mr. Macaun, the celebrated surgeon
of Westminster, was luckily passing through Bond Street at the
time, and being promptly called in, bled and relieved the exemplary patient.   His Lordship will return to the Palace, Bullocksmithy, to-morrow.

"The frantic agonies of the Right Honourable the Earl of
Bareacres can be imagined by every paternal heart.   Far be it
from us to disturb—impossible is it for us to describe their noble
sorrow.   Our reporters have made inquiries every ten minutes at
the Earl's mansion in Hill Street, regarding the health of the
Noble Peer and his incomparable Countess.   They have been
received with a rudeness which we deplore but pardon.—One was
threatened with a cane; another, in the pursuit of his official inquiries, was saluted with a pail of water   a third gentleman was

menaced iu a pugilistic manner by his Lordship's porter; but being of an Irish nation, a man of spirit and sinew, and Master of Arts of Trinity College, Dublin, the gentleman of our establishment confronted the menial, and haviug severely beaten him, retired to a neighbouring hotel much frequented by the domestics of the surrounding nobility, and there obtained what we believe to be the most accurate particulars of this extraordinary occurrence.

" George Frederick Jennings, third footman in the establishment of Lord Bareacres, stated to our *employé* as follows :—Lady Angelina had been promised to Mr. De la Pluche for near six weeks. She never could abide that gentleman. He was the laughter of all the servants' hall. Previous to his elevation he had himself been engaged in a domestic capacity. At that period he had offered marriage to Mary Ann Hoggins, who was living in the quality of ladies' maid in the family where Mr. De la P. was employed. Miss Hoggins became subsequently ladies' maid to Lady Angelina—the elopement was arranged between those two. —It was Miss Hoggins who delivered the note which informed the bereaved Mr. Plush of his loss.

" Samuel Buttons, page to the Right Honourable the Earl of Bareacres, was ordered on Friday afternoon at eleven o'clock to fetch a cabriolet from the stand in Davies Street. He selected the cab, No. 19,796, driven by George Gregory Macarty, a one-eyed man from Clonakilty, in the neighbourhood of Cork, Ireland (*of whom more anon*), and waited, according to his instructions, at the corner of Berkeley Square with his vehicle. His young lady, accompanied by her maid, Miss Mary Ann Hoggins, carrving a band-box, presently arrived, and entered the cab with the box : what were the contents of that box we have never been able to ascertain. On asking her Ladyship whether he should order the cab to drive in any particular direction, he was told to drive to Madame Crinoline's, the eminent milliner in Cavendish Square. On requesting to know whether he should accompany her ladyship, Buttons was peremptorily ordered by Miss Hoggins to go about his business.

" Having now his clue, our reporter instantly went in search of cab 19,796, or rather the driver of that vehicle, who was discovered with no small difficulty at his residence, Whetstone Park,

Lincoln's Inn Fields, where he lives with his family of nine children. Having received two sovereigns, instead doubtless of two shillings (his regular fare, by the way, would have been only one and eightpence), Macarty had not gone out with the cab for the two last days, passing them in a state of almost ceaseless intoxication. His replies were very incoherent in answer to the queries of our reporter; and, had not that gentleman himself been a compatriot, it is probable he would have refused altogether to satisfy the curiosity of the public.

" At Madame Crinoline's, Miss Hoggins quitted the carriage, and *a gentleman* entered it. Macarty describes him as a very *clever* gentleman (meaning tall) with black moustaches, Oxford-grey trowsers, and black hat and a pea-coat. He drove the couple *to the Euston Square Station*, and there left them. How he employed his time subsequently we have stated.

" At the Euston Square Station, the gentleman of our establishment learned from Frederick Corduroy, a porter there, that a gentleman answering the above description had taken places to Derby. We have despatched a confidential gentleman thither, by a special train, and shall give his report in a second edition.

"SECOND EDITION.

" (*From our Reporter.*)

" ' *Newcastle, Monday.*

" ' I am just arrived at this ancient town, at the Elephant and Cucumber Hotel. A party travelling under the name of *Mr. and Mrs. Jones*, the gentleman wearing moustaches, and having with them a blue band-box, arrived by the train two hours before me, and have posted onwards to *Scotland*. I have ordered four horses, and write this on the hind boot, as they are putting to.'

"THIRD EDITION.

" ' *Gretna Green, Monday Evening.*

" ' The mystery is at length solved. This afternoon, at four o'clock, the Hymeneal Blacksmith, of Gretna Green, celebrated the marriage between George Granby Silvertop, Esq., a Lieutenant in the 150th Hussars, third son of General John Silvertop, of

Silvertop Hall, Yorkshire, and Lady Emily Silvertop, daughter of the late sister of the present Earl of Bareacres, and the Lady Angelina Amelia Arethusa Anaconda Alexandrina Alicompania Annemaria Antoinetta, daughter of the last-named Earl Bareacres.'

(*Here follows a long extract from the Marriage Service in the Book of Common Prayer, which was not read on the occasion, and need not be repeated here.*)

" ' After the ceremony, the young couple partook of a slight refreshment of sherry and water—the former, the Captain pronounced to be execrable ; and, having myself tasted some glasses from the *very same bottle* with which the young and noble pair were served, I must say I think the Captain was rather hard upon mine host of the Bagpipes Hotel and Posting House, whence they instantly proceeded. I follow them as soon as the horses have fed.

"FOURTH EDITION.

" ' SHAMEFUL TREATMENT OF OUR REPORTER.

" ' *Whistlebinkie, N.B. Monday, midnight.*

" ' I arrived at this romantic little villa about two hours after the newly-married couple, whose progress I have the honour to trace, reached Whistlebinkie. They have taken up their residence at the Cairngorm Arms—mine are at the other hostelry, the Clachan of Whistlebinkie.

" ' On driving up to the Cairngorm Arms, I found a gentleman of military appearance standing at the door, and occupied seemingly in smoking a cigar. It was very dark as I descended from my carriage, and the gentleman in question exclaimed, ' Is it you, Southdown, my boy ? You have come too late ; unless you are come to have some supper ; ' or words to that effect. I explained that I was not the Lord Viscount Southdown, and politely apprised, Captain Silvertop (for I justly concluded the individual before me could be no other) of his mistake.

" ' Who the deuce (the captain used a stronger term) are you, then ? ' said Mr. Silvertop. ' Are you Baggs and Tapewell, my uncle's attorneys ? If you are, you have come too late for the fair.'

" ' I briefly explained that I was not Baggs and Tapewell, but that my name was J——ns, and that I was a gentleman connected with the establishment of the *Morning Tatler* newspaper.

" ' And what has brought you here, Mr. Morning Tatler ? ' asked my interlocutor, rather roughly. My answer was frank —that the disappearance of a noble lady from the house of her friends had caused the greatest excitement in the metropolis, and that my employers were anxious to give the public every particular regarding an event so singular.

" ' And do you mean to say, sir, that you have dogged me all the way from London, and that my family affairs are to be published for the readers of the *Morning Tatler* newspaper? The *Morning Tatler* be —— (the Captain here gave utterance to an oath which I shall not repeat) and you too, sir; you impudent meddling scoundrel.'

" ' Scoundrel, sir ! ' said I. ' Yes,' replied the irate gentleman, seizing me rudely by the collar—and he would have choked me, but that my blue satin stock and false collar gave way, and were left in the hands of this *gentleman*. ' Help, landlord ! ' I loudly exclaimed, adding, I believe, ' murder,' and other exclamations of alarm. In vain I appealed to the crowd, which by this time was pretty considerable; they and the unfeeling post-boys only burst into laughter, and called out, ' Give it him, Captain.' A struggle ensued, in which, I have no doubt, I should have had the better, but that the Captain, joining suddenly in the general and indecent hilarity, which was doubled when I fell down, stopped, and said, ' Well, Jims, I won't fight on my marriage-day. Go into the tap, Jims, and order a glass of brandy-and-water at my expense—and mind I don't see your face tomorrow morning, or I'll make it more ugly than it is.'

" ' With these gross expressions and a cheer from the crowd, Mr. Silvertop entered the inn. I need not say that I did not partake of his hospitality, and that personally I despise his insults. I make them known that they may call down the indignation of the body of which I am a member, and throw myself on the sympathy of the public, as a gentleman shamefully assaulted and insulted in the discharge of a public duty.' "

" Thus you've sean how the flower of my affcckshns was tawn
out of my busm, and my art was left bleading. Hangelina! I
forgive thee. Mace thou be appy! If ever artfelt prayer for others
wheel awailed on i, the beink on womb you trampled addresses
those subblygations to Evn in your be½!

" I went home like a maniack, after hearing the anouncement
of Hangelina's departer. She'd been gone twenty hours when I
heard the fatle noose. Purshoot was vain. Suppose I *did* kitch
her up, they were married, and what could we do ? This sensable
remark I made to Earl Bareacres, when that distragted nobleman
igspawstulated with me. Er who was to have been my mother-in-
lor, the Countiss, I never from that momink sor agin. My presnts,
troosoes, juels, &c., were sent back—with the igsepshn of the
diminds and Cashmear shawl, which her Ladyship *coodn't find*.
Ony it was wispered that at the nex buthday she was seen with a
shawl *igsackly of the same pattn*. Let er keep it.

" Southdown was phurius. He came to me hafter the ewent,
and wanted me to adwance 50 lb, so that he might purshew his
fewgitif sister—but I wasn't to be ad with that sort of chaugh—
there was no more money for *that* famly. So he went away, and
gave huttrance to his feelinx in a poem, which appeared (price 2
guineas) in the *Bel Asombly.*

" All the juilers, manchumakers, lacemen, coch bilders, apolstrers,
hors dealers, and weddencake makers came pawring in with their
bills, haggravating feelings already woondid beyond enjurants.
That madniss didn't seaze me that night was a mussy. Fever,
fewry, and rayge rack'd my hagnized braind, and drove sleap from
my throbbink ilids. Hall night I follered Hangelinar in imadgana-
tion along the North Road. I wented cusses & mallydickshuns
on the hinfamus Silvertop. I kickd and rord in my unhuttarable
whoe! I seazd my pillar: I pitcht into it: pummld it, strangled
it, ha har! I thought it was Silvertop writhing in my Jint grasp ;
and taw the hordayshis villing lim from lim in the terrible strenth
of my despare! . . . . . Let me drop a cutting over the
memries of that night. When my boddy-suvnt came with my ot
water in the mawning, the livid copse in the charnill was not
payler than the gashly De la Pluche!

" ' Give me the Share-list, Mandeville,' I micanickly igsclaimed.

I had not perused it for the past 3 days, my etention being engayged elseware. Hevns & huth!—what was it I red there? What was it that made me spring outabed as if sumbady had given me cold pig?—I red Rewin in that Share list—the Pannick was in full hoparation!

* * * * *

" Shall I describe that kitastrafy with which hall Hengland is fimilliar? My & rifewses to cronnicle the misfortns which lassarated my bleeding art in Hoctober last. On the fust of Hawgust where was I? Director of twenty-three Companies; older of scrip hall at a primmium, and worth at least a quarter of a millium. On Lord Mare's day, my Saint Helena's quotid at 14 pm, were down at ⅛ discount; my Central Ichaboes at ⅜ discount; my Table Mounting & Hottentot Grand Trunk, no where; my Bathershins and Derrynane Beg, of which I'd bought 2000 for the account at 17 primmium down to nix; my Juan Fernandez, & my Great Central Oregons prostrit. There was a momint when I thought I shouldn't be alive to write my own tail!"

(Here follow in Mr. Plush's MS. about twenty-four pages of railroad calculations, which we pretermit.)

" Those beests, Pump & Aldgate, once so cringing and umble, wrote me a threatnen letter because I overdrew my account three-and-sixpence: woodn't advance me five thousand on 25000 worth of scrip; kep me waiting 2 hours when I asked to see the house; and then sent out Spout, the jewnior partner, saying they wouldn't discount my paper, and implawed me to clothes my accouut. I did: I paid the three-and-six balliance, and never sor 'em mor.

" The market fell daily. The Rewin grew wusser and wusser. Hagnies, Hagnies! It wasn't in the city aloan my misfortns came upon me. They beerded me in my own ome. The biddle who kips watch at the Halbany wodn keep misfortn out of my chambers; and Mrs. Twiddler, of Pall Mall, and Mr. Hunx, of Long Acre, put egsicution into my apartmince, and swep off every stick of my furniture. 'Wardrobe & furniture of a man of fashion.' What an adwertisement George Robins did make of it; and what a crowd was collected to laff at the prospick of my ruing! My chice plait; my seller of wine; my picturs—that of myself included (it was Maryhann, bless her! that bought it, unbeknown to me); all—all went to the ammer. That brootle Fitzwarren, my ex-vally, womb I met, fimilliarly slapt me on the sholder, and said, 'Jeames, my boy, you'd best go into suvvis aginn.'

"I *did* go into suvvis—the wust of all suvvices—I went into the Queen's Bench Prison, and lay there a misrabble captif for 6 mortial weeks. Misrabble shall I say? no, not misrabble altogether; there was sunlike in the dunjing of the pore prisner. I had visitors. A cart used to drive hup to the prizn gates of Saturdays; a washywoman's cart, with a fat old lady in it, and a young one. Who was that young one? Every one who has an art can gess, it was my blue-eyed blushing hangel of a Mary Hann! 'Shall we take him out in the linnen-basket, grandmamma?' Mary Hann said. Bless her, she'd already learned to say grandmamma quite natral; but I didn't go out that way; I went out by the door a white-washed man. Ho, what a feast there was at Healing the day I came out! I'd thirteen shillings left when I'd bought the gold ring. I wasn't prowd. I turned the mangle for three weeks; and then Uncle Bill said, 'Well, there *is* some good in the feller;' and it was agreed that we should marry."

The Plush manuscript finishes here: it is many weeks since we saw the accomplished writer, and we have only just learned his fate. We are happy to state that it is a comfortable and almost a prosperous one.

The Honorable and Right Reverend Lionel Thistlewood, Lord Bishop of Bullocksmithy, was mentioned as the uncle of Lady Angelina Silvertop. Her elopement with her cousin caused deep emotion to the venerable prelate: he returned to the palace at Bullocksmithy, of which he had been for thirty years the episcopal ornament, and where he married three wives, who lie buried in his Cathedral Church of St. Boniface, Bullocksmithy.

The admirable man has rejoined those whom he loved. As he was preparing a charge to his clergy in his study after dinner, the Lord Bishop fell suddenly down in a fit of apoplexy; his butler, bringing in his accustomed dish of devilled-kidneys for supper, discovered the venerable form extended on the Turkey carpet with a glass of Madeira in his hand; but life was extinct: and surgical aid was therefore not particularly useful.

All the late prelate's wives had fortunes, which the admirable man increased by thrift, the judicious sale of leases which fell in during his episcopacy, &c. He left three hundred thousand pounds—divided between his nephew and niece—not a greater sum than has been left by several deceased Irish prelates.

What Lord Southdown has done with his share we are not called upon to state. He has composed an epitaph to the Martyr of Bullocksmithy, which does him infinite credit. But we are happy to state that Lady Angelina Silvertop presented five hundred pounds to her faithful and affectionate servant, Mary Ann Hoggins, on her marriage with Mr. James Plush, to whom her Ladyship also made a handsome present—namely, the lease, good-will, and fixtures of the " Wheel of Fortune " public house, near Sheppherd's Market, May Fair ; a house greatly frequented by all the nobility's footmen, doing a genteel stroke of business in the neighbourhood, and where, as we have heard, the " Butlers' Club " is held.

Here Mr. Plush lives happy in a blooming and interesting wife : reconciled to a middle sphere of life, as he was to a humbler and a higher one before. He has shaved off his whiskers, and accommodates himself to an apron with perfect good humour. A gentleman connected with this establishment dined at the Wheel of Fortune, the other day, and collected the above particulars. Mr. Plush blushed rather, as he brought in the first dish, and told his story very modestly over a pint of excellent port. He had only one thing in life to complain of, he said—that a witless version of his adventures had been produced at the Princess's theatre, " without with your leaf or by your leaf," as he expressed it. " Has for the rest," the worthy fellow said, " I'm appy—praps betwixt you and me I'm in my proper spear. I enjy my glass of beer or port (with your elth & my suvvice to you, sir), quite as much as my clarrit in my prawsprus days. I've a good busniss, which is likely to be better. If a man can't be appy with such a wife as my Mary Hann, he's a beest : and when a christening takes place in our famly, will you give my complments to *Mr. Punch*, and ask him to be godfather."

London: Printed by SMITH, ELDER AND Co., Old Bailey, E.C.